Christmas 2020

JESUS' SILENT YEARS

Dear Janice & Jerry

VOLUME 1

*Thank you two for all you do to
live out God's calling*

For Jesus' sake

Foundations

VANCE SHEPPERSON

Vance & Bethyl

Published by Carpenter's Son, Nashville, TN

Publisher's Note

This is a work of fiction. Names, characters, places, and incidents either are the product of the author's imagination or are used fictitiously, and any resemblance to actual persons, living or dead, events, or locales is entirely coincidental.

Printed in the United States of America.
Cover and interior illustrations by Dorine Deen

LIST OF MAJOR CHARACTERS

In Alphabetical Order

Abby, Claudia's Jewish friend, daughter of rich Sepphoris merchant

Abishag, ex-whore friend of Jesus, lives between Nazareth and Sepphoris

Achan, Ach, Moabite father of Leah, married to mother of Gomaria and Leah, descendent of the Amalekites.

Alexander, Simon the Cyrene's younger son

Augustus, also known as Tavius to family, Roman emperor, and sometimes called First Citizen or Caesar Augustus

Caligula, third emperor of Rome after Tiberius, son of Germanicus, grandson of Drusus, Tiberius' brother

Claudia, daughter to Tribune Gaius and Livena, granddaughter of Caesar Augustus

Claudius, twin brother to Claudia

Cleopas, Jesus' uncle, Mary's brother who lived in Sepphoris

Deborah, Jesus' baby sister, the youngest sibling

El Abba, Father, God the Father in Hebrew Scriptures

Eliazar, Jesus' uncle, married to Abigail, Joe's younger brother, also a carpenter

Esther, Rav Moshe's wife

Firenza, friend to Claudia, daughter of another tribune in Sepphoris

Gaius, Roman tribune, father of the twins, Claudius and Claudia, husband to Livena

Giorgos, Greek physician, father of Luke and Sophia

Gomaria, Go, sister to Leah, wife of Laz, name changed to Slow by Jesus

Ioanna, Greek wife to Giorgos, mother of Luke and Sophia

Jabez, neighbor of Jesus' family, executed; father of Amos

James, Jesus' next youngest brother, three years younger

John, also called John, John the Baptist, Jesus' second cousin

Jesus, also called: Jesus bar Joseph, Messiah, Jesus of Nazareth, Jeez (by close friends)

Joseph, Jesus' adoptive father, sometimes called Joe or Abba

Jude, Jesus' middle brother, after James, before Justus

Julia, Antonio the tutor's wife, governess of Claudius and Claudia

Justus, Jesus' youngest brother

Laz, called Lazarus, Jesus' close friend, husband to Gomaria

Leah, daughter of Achan, sister to Gomaria; wife to Rabbus

Livena, wife to Tribune Gaius, illegitimate daughter of Caesar Augustus

Livia, wife to Caesar Augustus, also known as Augusta

Maltesa, Maltie, husband to Rastus, rich merchant in Jericho

Mary, wife to Ehud, daughter of Hez and Beta, sister to Martha and Laz

Mary, Jesus' mother, daughter of Eli, a scribe

Martha, wife to Mordi, daughter of Hez and Beta, sister to Mary and Laz

Menachim, an elder in Nazareth's synagogue

Miriam, Jesus' younger sister

Mordi, Martha's husband; Laz's brother-in-law

Moshe, called Rav, Jesus' teacher from age eight to twenty-eight

Penelope, Simon the Cyrene's wife

Rastus, murderer-thief-leper who Jesus healed and who married Maltesa, half-brother to Zacchaeus

Rufus, Simon and Penelope's older son

Simon, Mary's husband, Laz's brother-in-law

Simon the Cyrene, traveling Jew, husband of Penelope

Sophia, daughter of Greek physician Giorgos and sister to Luke

Tiberius, adopted son of Augustus, birth son of Augusta (or Livia), Roman emperor after Augustus' death, brother to Drusus, uncle to Germanicus, great-uncle to Caligula

Zacchaeus, tax collector in Jericho, husband to Esmeralda, half-brother to Rastus

Zachariah, John's father

Stretch your imagination.
Most of the folks, in part or whole, live within you.

AUTHOR'S NOTE

Sacred writings tell us very little of Jesus' life. This series of four books, entitled *Jesus' Silent Years*, is a work of historical fiction viewed through the eyes of an American psychologist.

All of us go through the same tasks: leaving home, managing puberty, hormones, shaping identity, forming friends, finding a vocation, and acquiring a life partner—or lack of one. Jesus was no exception.

Each of the four volumes in *Jesus' Silent Years* tells stories of Jesus' life—how he grows up, shaped by family, friends, enemies—and those other Two, Father and Spirit. *Foundations* tells stories about Jesus' life from age thirteen to seventeen years old; *Parables*, eighteen to twenty-two years old; *Journey*, twenty-three to twenty-six years old; and *Homecoming*, twenty-eight to thirty years old. This book series ends with his baptism at age thirty. So, think two thousand years ago, Middle Eastern culture, an enemy-occupied country, and a growing Son of Man.

Embedded in these stories is a training manual for how to live a wise life, regardless of your faith or lack of it. And what's a wise life? Knowing what to do when the rules don't apply.

Strap yourself in. Get ready for a wild ride.

CONTENTS

LIST OF MAJOR CHARACTERS...3
AUTHOR'S NOTE 5

1   JESUS...9
2   MARY 14
3   JESUS...18
4   WINDY...21
5   JESUS...22
6   WINDY...26
7   CLAUDIA...28
8   WINDY...32
9   CLAUDIA...34
10 JESUS...37
11 CLAUDIA...43
12 JESUS...45
13 WINDY...48
14 CLAUDIA...49
15 JESUS...56
16 WINDY...59
17 MARY 62
18 JESUS...66
19 WINDY...69
20 GO 73
21 JESUS...76
22 CLAUDIA...80
23 JESUS...83
24 GO 87
25 JESUS...90
26 LEAH..93
27 JESUS...97

28 WINDY..100
29 JESUS..103
30 JESUS..107
31 WINDY..111
32 GO..114
33 WINDY..119
34 CLAUDIA..123
35 JESUS..127
36 GO..130
37 WINDY..134
38 CLAUDIA..139
39 GO..145
40 LEAH..150
41 JESUS..155
42 WINDY..159
43 MARY..163
44 LEAH..166
45 JESUS..171
46 WINDY..176
47 JESUS..178
48 MARY..184
49 WINDY..186
50 JESUS..190
51 WINDY..194
52 JESUS..198
53 WINDY..203
54 JESUS..206
55 CLAUDIA..211
56 WINDY..215
57 GO..218
58 WINDY..220
59 JESUS..222
60 WINDY..226
61 LEAH..229
62 JESUS..233

63   WINDY...239
64   JESUS..243
65   WINDY...250
66   JESUS..252

ACKNOWLEDGMENTS 259
DISCUSSION QUESTIONS 260
ABOUT THE AUTHOR....................................262

1

JESUS

It was an ordinary Wednesday morning when the ground began to shake. Our family had finished breakfast. We'd also finished talking about our dreams, and now we were reading the Torah. When the shaking began, Ma's face stiffened, and Abba's eyes widened with alarm. The smaller children were preoccupied with toy soldiers, playing on the floor—all except James.

He scrambled to the window. "Look, Ma! Real soldiers are outside!"

Ma snatched him up, put her forefinger to his mouth.

Ma's fear rattled me. I breathed, tuned my ears to Father's voice.

Get your abba below. Do it now!

"Abba, quick! Could you take the scroll down to its niche?"

Abba opened the trap door and dropped into the rock foundations of our house—a level below where we kept the animals. I dragged the rug back over our trapdoor.

Two platoons of special force troops were here, here in tiny Nazareth!

The voice again, *Father's voice. Stay inside. Sit on the floor beside your mother's knee. Keep Deborah on your lap.* I obeyed.

Rough men crashed through the door, saw only a woman with her children, and kept moving.

Jabez's Shoe Repair shop, across the street, had just opened for business. Two soldiers pulled Jabez from behind his counter and added him to a short string of village men. Soldiers surrounded them. Amos, Jabez's son, was taken hostage. If there was trouble of any kind, his child would join him on another cross.

Other neighbors, other sons, were taken. I quietly closed the shutters.

I sneaked out the back door, watched from the olive grove at the back of our home, and up the slope. I was confused. Why did they pick these men to die?

Out in the village square, soldiers strapped Jabez and the other neighbor men to the hitching post. Two burly executioners, stripped to the waist, lashed the men. Each soldier wielded a cat-o'-nine-tails embedded with bits of metal that flashed in the sun. The whips ripped through skin and muscle, down to bone.

I felt each wet splat of leather and metal on skin. I took it all personally.

My neighbors, now with raw meat for backs, were marched close to where I sat hidden from view in the branches of an ancient olive tree. Each prisoner hacked down his own tree, cut off the top, and hammered that top piece sideways into the main trunk with a seven-inch spike. The same hammer, similar spikes would soon be used on him, fastening him to a rough bed of his own making.

Father's voice—*Get down from your hiding place. Walk beside your friend.*

I left my safe place and walked next to Amos, behind his father. I looked at my friend's face, felt his terror. His wound, his *vulnus*, as the Romans say, opened up within me. I became vulnerable to all Amos refused to feel. I started bawling, afflicted with this dark gift from Father.

Amos sniffled. Together, we trudged behind his father.

Once, Jabez fell under the weight of his cross. I knelt, reached for him. "Let me carry your cross, Jabez bar Jonah."

The Roman sergeant whirled around and, with a casual swipe of his arm, sent me sprawling. "Get away, kid. This Zealot carries his own cross! Kill one of ours, we'll crucify five of yours!"

Then, I understood—we were being punished. Rogue bandits had killed a Roman soldier in our district.

Jabez carried his cross past the garbage dump south of our village, where we burned our trash. Yesterday's fires still smoldered. The wind blew smoke all around. The rising sun looked like a bleeding egg yolk, peppered with ash.

Jabez dug his grave dump-side, along with the other men. He worked harder at it than others, squaring off the corners, going deeper. He wanted to keep the dogs from getting at him once he was freed from this life. He dug his grave the same way he'd made my shoes—precisely. He'd always paid attention to detail.

Once the graves were dug, soldiers marched the prisoners single file back to the marketplace. I was so absorbed in this death-row scene that I almost missed a gold-colored chariot as it flashed by me heading toward Sepphoris. A tall man, a Roman officer, lashed the two horses. Two smaller people, teenagers, held on behind him.

My focus came back to this place of judgment. The executioners kicked Jabez's legs from under him, dropping him onto his cross. Then the hammer of a higher god, Caesar, ripped into his hands and feet. The soldier nailing Jabez missed the spike's head once, and his hammer crushed a toe. He didn't even say sorry. Instead, he tipped the cross up and dropped that cross in its hole. The jolt ripped hands and feet. Those spikes were the only things holding him on the execution stake, holding him at eye level with his killer and all passersby.

Amos was tied to the foot of his father's cross. Jabez's blood, sweat, and the stink of his terror fell on his son, and me. Other family and friends stood by, far or near, and wept. Some were quiet leakers. Others howled. Curious passersby, ones who loved a good killing, gawked. One of my neighbors looked at Jabez and muttered, "Glad I'm not you." The good citizens of Nazareth bought and sold sundries, bread, and vegetables in the market square. They seemed to carry the false hope that suffering like this wouldn't soon visit their own home.

I couldn't stop crying, looking at my own hands and feeling a strange, deep ache in each palm. I hated this gift of feeling with and for others. Everyone's horns fit my holes.

Two days later, Abba came to get me, but I would not be moved. I stayed with Amos and his abba, who still lived. Jabez's life dripped out of him in snivels, drool, and stool. His drippings landed on our heads, our backs. Present hope for future happiness was already a thing of the past for this naked man.

Death by suffocation requires absolute attention. Look how much effort it took to raise his chest a notch, sip one more shallow breath of air, then release.

Empty, be quiet, repeat.

A murder of crows wheeled overhead, impatient for dinner, waiting to land on his nose, peck out an eye. Jabez watched the crows watch him. He then gathered energy, raised his chest once again, kept the scavengers at bay for another second, another minute, with a wrench of his head and a whimper, or a howl.

Each breath became a tiny bit shallower than the one before, hovering this living soul between the dead and almost dead. The law took on flesh. *Cursed is everyone who hangs on a tree.*

Soldiers played cards, joking, in the shade of a nearby café. A stranger stood halfway between the soldiers and their victims, lounging in the shadows of the village gates. His gray prayer shawl shadowed his face. Who was he? I'd never seen him before.

Jabez whimpered. I did as well—our agony, exquisite.

My inner voice, Father's voice, whispered, *Now.*

I nudged Amos, leaned against his shoulder. Together we looked up. I'd never noticed that Jabez had such a long, crooked, hooked nose. He was so skinny I could count the ladder of his ribs. His eyes were luminous, black holes of need. Desperation spilled off his face, dripped off his nose and chin.

Both Jabez and his son turned to me, their eyes pleading with me, as they would have with anyone, *Help. Do something, anything.*

I asked for help.

Father hovered just beyond the cross, arms reaching toward me, compelling me to act.

Windy, Father's Spirit, breathed His intent like a strong wind through Her voice into my will[1].

I linked hands with Father and sighed out his permission. He pulled a trigger of mercy.

Jabez's life on earth winked out. Windy lifted the man's spirit out, up, and away.

I shivered, my mind's eye focused unbidden on an image, a coming mystery. Goosebumps rose on my arms. My palms, the back of my hands, turned bright red. Each hand leaked sweaty red ooze from the palm center. I stared at my bleeding, trembling hands, horrified. *Oh, calm me, Windy.*

She held me within her breath. *Breathe, sweetheart. Tell yourself, "This is not my time, not my day, not yet."*

I did as I was told. Breathed. Quivered all over—a pile of jelly.

The Roman sergeant glared at me with slitted eyes. He'd noted Jabez's death. The others on their trees still lived. He walked to where I sat with Amos and barked, "What'd you do to that man?"

"It was his time."

The giant snorted, hacked up a yellow wad of phlegm that landed on my right foot. He had a practiced grip on scorn. I could see in his eyes that I was one despised Jew of many, a no-name nobody. I felt his contempt slithering into me.

Windy said, *don't take in his spite, Son. It's a lie. Don't agree with it. Agree with Father and Me. You are Our precious child, put here, on this planet, for this moment in time.*

2

MARY

A few weeks had passed since the horrible executions. We'd buried our fellow villagers and sat Shiva. Mourning steeped inside us like bitter tea.

I stood inside the kitchen. The door framed my oldest son, who worked in the courtyard. The bright rising sun backlit him. His head looked as if light were coming out of it.

I ran his prayer shawl through my hands, the one the Jerusalem elders had given him at his rite of passage. Since then, the seasons had rushed by, turning like tumbleweed.

Jesus bent over the wood, biting his lower lip in that single-minded focus that so became him. He worked the wood. The wood worked him. Beads of sweat rolled down his face and shoulders. He learned his craft through mistakes, as do we all. He accepted Joe's frequent instruction and correction without complaint.

Even as a little child in Egypt, Jesus' focus could be pinned in place by husband. His love for Joe had focused into love for his true Father. Windy blew them into a knot: the young, the old, and the life everlasting. Each merged with the other, and love for any increased Jesus' love for all.

Jesus' youth ripened faster than my heart could fathom. His voice deepened and cracked. My handsome boy was morphing into a sturdy man. I didn't want to see this man. All I could see was the bareness of his side, his hands, his feet. They looked obscene, a hundred soft places where his life might be ended. But why howl now, after what Simeon had told me when my son was a babe in arms? The eagle had flown.

Later that day, Jesus and I walked the five miles to Sepphoris. My mother still lived there. Halfway between the villages, we passed the caves where our local down-and-outers lived.

I said, "Jesus, run these eggs and fresh figs over to the lepers, will you?"

"Sure, Ma. At least those people don't look down on us like lots of our neighbors." Then he trotted over to drop off the food.

I kept walking. When he caught up, I said, "You've not brought up neighbors' shunning in a long time. What happened?"

He looked away, heaved a sigh. "Some kids at school were calling me a *mamzer* again. I know the story you've told me, Gabriel telling you stuff. Like God making you pregnant with me. No one but Abba, you, and I believe that story. The kids at the synagogue school say, 'Sure, God made your gorgeous mother pregnant. Right.' And they run off and snicker."

Living with village gossip sometimes did me in. Whispers crept under windowsills, slipped past door hinges. Other mothers shunned me at the market, even after all this time.

He kept talking. "And I think sometimes even Abba doesn't believe anymore, even though the angel came to him too. I feel so alone most of the time."

I stopped and hugged him. "Sometimes we are called to be silent witnesses of the miraculous. This alone is a profound form of love for your true Father, El Abba."

Jesus hugged me back.

"Your Abba has you in training to be a carpenter. El Abba has you in training to be the Messiah."

He looked up at me, eyes wet, soft, and clear.

"Demons, moods, and normal restlessness will confuse you, make you feel crazy, and tempt you to think that I'm a loose woman."

Jesus mimed a sassy, soprano voice. "Everybody's out of step but Jesus."

I laughed with him, knowing we would either laugh or cry. "Son, your time is not yet. When kids bully you, laugh with them or say, 'Believe what you want.' Don't reveal your true identity. Not yet."

We passed a weeping willow tree. The wind was blowing, the tree bent in the breeze.

Jesus said, "The eucalyptus tree next to that weeper cracked off a branch in the last storm. The weeper stayed in one piece."

"Exactly, Son. Bend without breaking."

Jesus met James at the front door when we got home. He'd just gotten out of synagogue school. I warmed milk from our cow with some raisin cakes, and all three of us sat on the front steps along the Via Maris and watched people walk by while we had our snack. The smaller children were down for their afternoon nap.

James said, "Lots of travelers today, all headed north toward Damascus. I wonder if Herod's causing trouble again and people are leaving town. Maybe we'll have to go too. Leave again."

Looking upward, Jesus focused on the forested ridge at the back of our house. I think he'd had enough of people for the day. Busy places overwhelmed him. That's when he went wool-gathering in his thoughts.

I looked at my younger son. "We're safe for now. God would tell Abba, and Abba would tell us if we needed to leave. These wandering pilgrims are gifts, El Abba's hints about how big his kingdom really is."

Jesus said, "I pick out Greek, Latin, Hebrew, our own Aramaic, and more. Camels braying, old men praying, and us staying in place."

"Does anyone ever stay in place, content?" James asked.

It was a wise question from my second born. "Life regularly falls apart and then comes back together again, but differently. Much trouble comes from not being able to sit still in a room with God." I fingered Jesus' prayer shawl, the one he'd received at his coming-of-age ceremony in Jerusalem.

He said, "Can you tell me again about that day I became a man?"

"You both remember the journey south a couple of years ago, don't you?"

Jesus and James leaned in.

"We'd all traveled south four days' journey to the temple in Jerusalem. We had fun, heading down the King's Highway. But what I remember most was that one stunning act of separation."

My oldest son's smiling eyes locked on mine.

"You both remember making a shelter from wood and straw in the outer temple courtyard? You remember Abba's comment?"

Jesus said, "How one chapter of life moves to another, and the sukkot represents that?"

I nodded. "Exactly."

"And what happened next, James?"

"Jesus spent the night alone."

"Right. The ceremony happened the next morning. It was the sixth hour. I laid down directly in front of the sukkot on the sandy gravel. A temple priest blew the shofar, and you"—I bumped my shoulder against Jesus—"you walked alone out of that straw womb. Ever so carefully, you put your bare foot on my womb."

James said excitedly, "I remember him stomping on you, Ma. He gave you a good one."

"James, he didn't stomp on me. He pushed away into the world, across the hard pack of this good earth. He moved toward the place where only men can go."

3
JESUS

I sat in the temple sukkot, waiting for my coming-of-age ceremony. My heart was racing, and my face was a mess. I could almost feel pimples popping out on my forehead. My joints all ached. Abba called it growing pains.

I had trouble recognizing myself in a looking glass—all gaunt, knobby-kneed and stork-legged, acne-faced, wispy-whiskered. Who was this guy? And girls, well, they'd become interesting in an embarrassing way.

The shofar blew. It was time.

I stepped out of the symbolic womb, gently stepped on Ma's womb, and kept walking forward, from boy to man.

I'd never been so well surrounded as I was in this rite of passage. Spirit and physical worlds were packed full. Earth womb behind me, mother womb below me, Abba before me, El Abba over me, and Windy within me, whistling air in and out of my lungs.

Satan was also in attendance. His face floated a foot in front of mine. His mouth was a leering dark cavity with spiderwebs of spit glistening between sharp teeth. He was an ancient cannibal waiting to feast on me, if I gave in to fear.

I chose to focus on Father, not the Old Enemy.

Windy whispered, "Grow your courage muscles, Son. Move toward what you fear."

I strode through Satan and he vanished.

I moved toward the room where the temple elders awaited me. These men listened and questioned me as I recited my chosen portion of scripture. I felt relaxed, alert. Father was with me.

After the questioning was done, Abba and I joined Ma and the others for a party at Grandpa's house in Bethlehem. I helped family and friends to their seats, then gave them food and drink that I'd prepared. I fed each person their first bite. I dipped a piece of unleavened matzo bread into the sauce bowl. Together, the other person and I, hand in hand, moved food from the common bowl to that person's mouth. My deeds said, *I'm a man now, responsible for feeding myself and others.*

After my rite of passage, the whole family partied. I couldn't handle all the chatter. I found my moment after breakfast on the second day and walked to the Tower of the Flock, on the edge of Bethlehem. Unblemished temple sheep were examined in the tower and pastured behind it.

The open-air travelers' quadrangle next door shared a common wall with the tower. This was the spot where I'd been born. Animals still roamed on the ground floor, under the overhangs. A variety of stone mangers lined the walls. Priests used these mangers to mix the sacrificial lambs' special diet. I've never seen mangers like this anywhere else.

Cooking fires blazed in the middle of the courtyard, and travelers' bed-rolls bunched side by side on the second floor. People came and went all the time, then and now. I trembled at El Abba's choices—my birth, my separation from my mother, and my coming death. They all wound together in this place.

I kept walking the few miles from the Tower of the Flock back into Jerusalem. I came to the steep hill leading up the temple. Herod's temple crowded out the sun. Repair work on the walls was in progress. I felt a presence. Saw nothing but shadows, but smelled something like rotten eggs or sulfur. I pressed against the cool shade of the wall, sensing, feeling a quiver inside.

Something wasn't right. A creaking groan, the rumble of rocks. At the very top of the wall, backlit by the sun's glare, a stonemason's scaffolding collapsed. Men, bricks, platforms, and stones cascaded toward me. I pressed into the wall as two wild-eyed workmen careened past me to the rocks below.

I scrambled down to where they lay, all tangled and bloody. A few others picked their way over the rocks with me. These fallen men were past help in this world. Their fellow workers carried their bodies away. I stumbled back to the city wall's footings and sat, shocked into silence.

Satan's gleeful face flickered into view. Then, quick-quick, a vision of death smacked into me —my two-year-old sister, Deborah, facing away from me, shattered on the rocks at the base of a cliff, ocean waves pounding. Satan loitered, drifting next to me, feet barely scraping the ground, his stench filling my nostrils.

I shouted, "No!"

He disappeared, but his smell lingered, mixing with dread.

Windy said, Welcome to manhood, Jesus, to the battle that will be your life. Now, let the dead bury the dead. Be about Father's business. Go back to the temple elders. Let iron sharpen iron. Let them feel the power of Presence.

My family lost track of me and I lost track of them. Three days and nights flew by. Later, Ma told me they'd already begun their journey back to Nazareth when she realized I wasn't with all of our family and neighbors. Abba and Ma left the other children with neighbors. They returned to Jerusalem and found me at the temple, arguing Torah.

A day or two later, along the King's Highway, Ma told me, "Your stepping on me in the ceremony wasn't so bad. But when you stepped out into the world of words, you left me no word at all." Her face was tight as a kettle drum. "I'm frightened for us, Jesus. Untold dangers await. Don't leave me so much alone. Don't go."

A ragged spear splintered in our sides—in her, in me.

4
WINDY

Joe was snoozing in the shade. I woke him up and his adoptive son came into focus. Jesus sang softly while he sanded a table and finished a memory project. He leaned over the scroll, checked the Word, and then returned to sanding the table. His voice sang the Scriptures. Back and forth he went, memorizing, singing, sanding. I blazed words off that scroll, making dusty laws into loves within him. He chewed them like a dog gnaws a bone.

Joe walked outside and stretched his back. A warm wedge of sunshine splashed his face through a light morning shower.

Joe's brother, Eliazar, ran around a corner and called, "Hey, Joe. An old customer of yours, Tribune Gaius, sent a message. A string of new villas is going up in Sepphoris next to the fortress. He's commissioning you to do his villa!"

Joe slapped his knee. "Yes! I'd been praying for work, and El Abba has answered. This will meet all our needs for the rest of this year and the next. You remember the Tribune, don't you? He's boss over there at the Roman fortress. And remember this—his wife's father is the Roman emperor, Caesar Augustus!"

The two brothers and Hez, their cousin, stood just outside their shared shop where slanting sun met shade. Jesus joined them. These men—like bees making honey in a hive—all of them laughing and listening and interrupting at the same time. My peculiar people—I was so proud of them.

5

JESUS

The next morning our work crew walked the five miles to Sepphoris. We had our mules strapped with tools and supplies for the week.

We were the last work crew to arrive. A dozen other builders for a dozen other villas had already dug trenches for their foundations and were mixing concrete. Abba walked the site we were assigned. He grabbed a handful of dirt and let it slip through his fingers. "Huh! Shale, limestone, and scree. Let's dig for bedrock."

He put us to work. I started digging with my friend, Amos. Other men dug in other places. All of us sang from the Psalms as we worked. Pretty soon, we were all in over our heads. Other builders sauntered by, amused by what they saw. One man said to Abba, "There you go again, Joe. Digging for trouble that ain't there."

Abba smiled at his friend and told us to keep digging. When we hit rock, Abba lowered a rope, pulled us over ten feet up and out, and gave us water. Then he handed out work orders, "Judah, dig on the north perimeter. Amos, along the south boundary. Hez and Lazarus, the east. I'll work the west side with Jesus. Dig till you hit rock."

He continued, "Remember, Tribune's brought tons of supplies from Herod's underwater jetties at Caesarea. Lime slake, pozzolana ash, kurkar rubble, concrete powder. We'll use the same mix Herod did for his underwater work. That foundation will hold when the rains come."

I sat on a pile of rubble, rubbing my patchy stubble, scratching my zits. How long would this take? Sounded like the work of a lifetime.

Abba chewed his droopy mustache and spoke softly. "Other builders think I'm too picky, but I'm going with my sense of right. We'll dig to rock, build trenching forms, fill 'em with concrete."

Abba had no sooner finished speaking when Tribune Gaius approached. His two teenage children followed. I'd seen them before. This was the man, with his children, who'd flashed by in a chariot that day of the executions.

A brusque sergeant clomped along behind Tribune Gaius, thumping the butt of his spear on the ground with every step. I knew him too! He was the one who knocked me over when Jabez fell and I tried to help him.

Tribune Gaius said to Abba, "You met my sergeant, Cynico, yesterday. He is your contact about building matters. It's his pleasure to work with you."

Cynico's face was not precisely aligned with pleasure.

Another thin man, dressed in an ivory toga, followed. His broad forehead was covered with carefully styled silver ringlets.

Gaius said, "This is Antonio, the children's tutor. Finally, my son, Claudius, and, oh yes, his twin sister, Claudia."

The teens were good-looking, the girl taller and more developed than her brother.

Claudia watched me. I watched her. I was covered with dirt and sweat, dressed only in my filthy loincloth and sandals. She was gorgeous in her silk toga. I lowered my eyes. Laborers like me didn't look directly at nobles. The tribune ordered his children back to class.

Claudia glanced over her shoulder at me as she left, flashing her blue eyes. She struck me as the kind of girl who might deploy her beauty like a general would send out a raiding party. My body responded to her flirting. *Father, help. Help me with this body that has a mind of its own.*

Two days passed. Abba and I kept digging together. "Abba, did you see the tribune's daughter smiling at me the other day?"

Abba smiled. "Yes, she was using her power, all right. Makes sense— rich girl, poor boy. You seemed to be having a good flirt."

I was quiet for a while, digging for feelings. "Weird mix of excitement and danger. She's gorgeous. About Ma's age when she got pregnant with me, right?"

Abba nodded.

"A Gentile has never flirted with me," I said. "Torah commands light not to schmooze with darkness. And Cynico could have me killed if he noticed any flirting."

Abba kept working. "Good thinking."

I relaxed into his praise. "And, my body, my body was so embarrassing, exciting and scary all at once. Obvious to me, maybe her. These dangerous thoughts and feelings came at me sideways."

Abba grinned. "You have a battle between the two heads. The little head wants to rule the big one, and the big head fights back."

"How did you handle your two heads, Abba, when you were my age?"

Abba threw a shovelful of dirt out of his trench. "The fight between my two heads couldn't be avoided. Sometimes one head won, sometimes the other. But those fights at your age were getting me ready for a much bigger one, later." He paused. "The fight I had with God. Sometime after my first wife died, I fell in love with Mary. I thought she loved me. But then, she chose another and claimed he was God. Somehow, I'd lost her affection.

"She said, 'Joe, it's not another *man*. *God* impregnated me! So, she said. Well, Son, even if I believed her, I didn't like being second to anybody … even Him."

Abba sighed. "This all took a long time, but in the night, God grew up my faith."

"What do you mean?"

He grinned sadly. "Dreams. If God hadn't spoken to me in my dreams, I'd have done something stupid—like having her put away, or even stoned."

He paused. "Your friends still tease you about being a *mamzer*, huh? I know how that feels. When your ma got pregnant, my friends were merciless. They'd say, with a wink, 'Mary's a gorgeous woman, Joe. 'Everybody has slip-ups, even you as an older, righteous man.' My face must have turned red because they changed the subject. 'Perhaps she had a one-night stand. Or maybe a Roman raped her and ran.'

"No one talked about the only other option—your ma had gone stark raving mad. Angels, dreams, God having sex with her. That's the stuff of people wandering on the street and muttering to themselves." He shook his head. "I walked away from all that kind of talk. The first time that happened, you were less than a year old—before Egypt. Your ma and I comforted each other in bed that night."

Wow. Abba had never spoken about sex, never talked about how he felt being jilted by God. Never talked about his friends feeling sorry for him or jeering at him. Never talked about his wall of silence.

Ah-ya! I had sex on my brain. God and Ma. Abba and Ma. Me and this Roman girl. All these sexy feelings were *way* more than anything I'd felt before. I felt like *both* my heads were about to explode.

Windy said, *All this is normal. Every teenager goes through this.*

But Windy, what's causing this? My body going through the changes, Claudia flirting, her being forbidden fruit, or Father choosing me to be celibate?

All of those, Son. Why don't you go for a run in the hills?

I did as she said, and pounded my frustrations into the ground. Next morning, I woke up with another wet dream.

Foundations went slow. Solid soil alternated with loose basalt and sandy scree. Once we hit rock, the rest of the job went faster. Framing, roofing, plastering, tile, plumbing, finish work.

We did it all in the months that followed, carefully, down to the last detail.

All up and down the cliff 's edge, new villas for Roman officers and their families sprang up. I'd sit on top of the roof, setting tiles, and daydream of Claudia, particularly when I could see her. She, her twin, and their friends were noisy, full of laughter. They'd walk back and forth across the fortress courtyard between classes. I'd watch them from the rooftop.

What was that life of silk and privilege like? How must it feel to study cool stuff all day and not get their hands dirty?

Abba yelled. I went back to work.

Some of the dozen villas went up quickly, others slowly. Tribune Gaius' villa was the last one finished.

6

WINDY

Friends and family called him Tavius. Everyone else called him First Citizen or Caesar Augustus. Julius Caesar had called him son. I'd protected this man from assassination attempts more times than he could remember in his seventy-three years.

He was always surrounded by "trusted" bodyguards that he didn't trust. His adopted father, Julius Caesar, had trusted his bodyguards, and look where that had gotten him. Stabbed in the rotunda by his best friend, Brutus.

The only one Augustus trusted completely was his wife, Livia. Ah, they'd been wild and crazy once, silly in love. Had an affair. Ditched their spouses. Now, years later, he frowned on the very lifestyle they'd lived—he exiled family members for doing what they'd practiced, not what they now preached.

Today, the day before he left on his Palestine trip, he and Livia were eating lunch. They were picking over their cheese croissants, sipping cabernet. Livia said, "Tavius, running Rome is tiresome while you're out roaming the backside of your empire. This daughter, Rome, is almost as wayward as your own daughter, Julia."

"Both are whores. But I do long to see my granddaughter, Claudia, once more, before my final exit. She's so bright. Why wasn't she a boy? She'd have made such a good successor."

He didn't notice Livia's pained look. Couldn't read her thoughts. What about Tiberius, my son? He's the best choice by far in this game of thrones.

Now, a few weeks later, Augustus stood on the command deck and overlooked his armada anchored in Caesarea's harbor. Gaius greeted him with an obsequious grin when he walked down the gangplank covered with red carpet. Gaius bowed and scraped. "Your daughter and grandchildren can't wait to see you, sire. We're all so honored you would visit us here."

Augustus looked his son-in-law up and down. *Here's cruel cleverness strapped to unfettered ambition. I've given my little tribune a large Jewish rat to swallow. But how else would he learn to be powerful without being mean? His huff and puff, sniff and splutter, will get steamed out of him in this cesspool. Jews couldn't even get along with Jews, much less Romans. You put four Jews in a room and you'll always have five opinions.*

Augustus sprinted into the lead chariot instead of the comfy coach, thus hijacking Gaius' leadership. Appearance still counted. He clasped both hands together to hide his palsy. Imperial guards clunked behind their emperor in gleaming brass jackets for the two-day, forty-mile journey to Sepphoris. The whole contingent climbed the coastal valley over Mount Carmel to the high country of Galilee.

Loyal Romans viewed Augustus as the gods' oracle. But there was much this oracle didn't know. He had no idea why he wanted to visit this granddaughter. He couldn't fathom how Father's wild will would blend his life with the life of a teenage Jewish laborer. And last, yes last, he didn't know at all how this Jew, his granddaughter, and he would all walk hand in hand in the pitch black of night, to the center of a maze, where he would draw his last breath.

7

CLAUDIA

Grandpa and his soldiers appeared through a cloud of dust. The dot on the horizon got bigger. Soon he took up my whole vision, like he had when I was little. When he came roiling into our courtyard, I ran out the front door of our villa. He stepped off his chariot, swooped me up in his arms, and I felt safe once again.

Grandpa twirled me around. "I've not seen you in such a long time! Look how you've grown. Your fine features, cheekbones, mouth, and chin—all very Claudian. And those long limbs and astonishing blue eyes, from your father's side."

I twirled, and Grandpa stood back, with head tilted and hand to his chin. "Yes, Claudia, with my blood in your veins, your mother's figure, and your father's ambition, you're a perfect Roman goddess." He looked down. "But alas, we're both doomed to be mortal."

I bowed primly. "Oh, Grandpa. The Senate's elected you to be a god, or they will soon. You're so full of life!"

Grandpa's attention fizzled off me. He turned to commend my idiot twin for reports he'd heard of his swordsmanship. Then, in a moment, he commanded us, "Go back to your studies, children. Your mother and I have to plan how to get you back to Rome! I can't bear having you so far away, now that I'm racing toward decrepitude." He went inside.

Claud went back to playing at soldiering with his drone friends. I ditched class and went exploring. I'd already explored the fortress next door where we'd been living in the west wing. I knew exactly where those trapdoors were, the secret passages, the escape tunnel that went out with the wastewater. Now I wanted to explore our new villa.

First stop, the kitchen, where everything smelled delish. Antonio's wife, Julia, offered a bowl of icing from her latest cake. I took a fingerful of coconut cream and popped it in my mouth. A world of sweetness exploded on my tongue. I walked out of the kitchen and passed by an azure urn sitting in a puddle of sun, Roman-red begonias twining over its side.

I went to my own bedroom, the place where I'd soon be dreaming of Rome and boys. Surprise! The young Jew was at work there, sanding the bedroom door. A trapezoid of silvered sun from the opposite window high-lighted his hands. They were rugged, strong, and slow, made for touching and creating.

My Aramaic was terrible, but my first words with him stumbled out. "I've been looking for you. And here you are in my bedroom."

He replied in fluent Latin. "Just doing my job, Miss. I'm making sure everything fits well. That's the way Abba taught me—do things right. Do the right thing."

His voice and diction floored me. He spoke with a careful lilting ca-dence, consonants crisp, articulated. At that moment, I knew my future and his would somehow wind together. And the future was not in his hands. It was in his mouth. His voice was delicious.

My bones knew his words would change my life, but I couldn't speak it. Instead, I stuck my hand on my hip and pouted. "I'm not sure I trust you to do right by me. Let's see how tight this door is." I moved to close the door. "Stand here beside me, Jew-boy, while I check the quality of your work."

He moved to stand outside the door.

I held up my arm, grazing his chest. "No, here, next to me, inside the closed door."

He put his hand on the door, keeping it open. His voice excited me. His words did not. "Miss, I can't play with you here, not in this way. It's not right." He moved to leave me.

An annoying twitch, in the corner of my right eye. Men didn't refuse me like that. "If you go, I'll scream, and you'll be in trouble with my father and grandfather. You've been making advances toward me in my *bedroom*, Jew-boy."

His forehead bunched up, and his eyes latched onto the doorframe be-side me. After a moment of silence, he said, "You do have that power. You could have my family and me crucified. Choose what will be, Miss." His knees quivered beneath his short work tunic.

At least I had that satisfaction. He'd rejected me, but at the same time, he'd opened a door into his world. An image crashed into my mind of him *being* a door, a doorway into a huge adventure.

I came unhinged.

A long moment passed, our eyes locked on each other, brown on blue. Tension mounted. Deep rivers flowed from his eyes and drowned my fake scream.

I said something truer than most things that come out of my mouth. "You've opened a door of some kind with your voice. And your eyes, they have these flecks of yellow, like liquid sun in amber heartwood, fixed just on me. Astonishing."

"Your eyes, too, are beautiful. Open them wide with wonder, and your body fills with light. Live squinty-eyed with manipulation, and your body becomes a dank cellar."[2] He turned to leave.

I grabbed his arm. "Airy-fairy mist. Another day, another time will come for us. You'll see."

Ack, there I went, attacking again. Why was I, a royal, so insecure with a commoner? Maybe because he was a treasury of words surrounded by skin and bone. And those guileless, clear eyes that rested on me—and that voice. All that and more I couldn't yet say, made me fall in love with him.

He breathed out a sigh. "I must go now. My abba's waiting for me."

I followed him down the wooden staircase, his musk trailing behind him. My thin slippers slapped the polished wood like the back of a hand might strike a virgin lover's face.

We arrived on the front porch steps of our villa. Both our fathers and my grandpa stood in the entryway. We Romans stood two steps above the Jew. Father's purse was open, heavy with gold coin. The Jew's purse looked empty.

Jesus quietly took his place a step below his father. Columns of heavy light flowed over him. Grandpa's sharp eye looked back and forth between Jesus and me. His thin lips were white, pressed shut. I hurried into the space between Father and Grandfather and held hands with Grandpa as I had so often as a younger child. His hand shook. What was this?

I rose on tiptoes to his ear and whispered, "Breathe, Grandpa."

He grinned at my coquetry, but his huge, meaty hand still shimmied.

Father's ivory-colored toga rippled like spun sunlight. "Jew, why was our home the last to be finished? It's no bigger than the others. I didn't get more for my money." Glancing askance at Grandpa, he fidgeted, then stood straighter and puffed out his chin. His leather wallet remained open. Gold coins, with Grandpa's image, flashed in his hand.

Joe-the-Jew looked father squarely in the eye. "Tribune, you can't see what you're paying for. We Jews believe that our foundations are far more important than our house. If my house rests on rock, I am content, though the house be humble. If it rests on scree, I fall."

Father raised one eyebrow at this comment from a commoner, one that refused grievance.

The Jew-named-Joe continued, "We put down twice the fill—rock and concrete—twice as wide, sometimes more than twice as deep as what others put down. We did this even though Cynico assured me we would not be paid more to sure your home's foundation."

Father weighed Joe's words, sizing up man, motivation, and money in a moment.

I nudged his side and whispered, "Oh, go on, Papa. You do want us safe, don't you?"

Father looked my way and made sure my eyes followed his fingers. He dropped the coins into Joe's hand, plus an extra one. The wages landed, a melody that began and ended in the same instant. Father turned on his heel and resumed talking with Grandpa. They moved inside and I followed.

Before I left, I looked back at Jesus and flash-grinned. Then I entered the door, slow fingers slipping along the sanded door jamb, leaving it wide open.

8

WINDY

At her next-door neighbor's villa, Claudia put down her scroll and turned to her best friend. "Fiery, don't you hate it when Antonio force-marches our brains through history? Like today, that lesson on some deadbeat Egyptian Pharaoh who owned a jillion Jewish slaves?"

Firenza nodded absently and filed her nails.

Claudia thought, *I'm sick, sick, sick of this rain. It's interminable, and what's more, it's blowing the crap out of my dating game.* She stood and looked out the window. She could barely see her villa through the storm. It had poured, day after day, for a whole week. She came back to her chair and slumped over her scroll, head cradled in her arms.

Yesterday, she'd told Grandpa, "The gods' septic tank has broken, and the crack's directly over Palestine."

He'd laughed. "Why are you so unfairly clever, Claudia? You make it so tough on the rest of us." She smiled at the memory of this smooth, jovial intimacy she felt with him.

A sharp cracking noise interrupted her reverie. The floor shifted under her feet.

Firenze dropped away as the room split in two, exactly between their chairs.

The roof fell in chunks, here, there. Firenze tried to grab Claudia's outstretched hand when a slab of concrete hit her in the head. She slid off a sharp ledge, screaming. Dropped down and away, caught in a cascade of building blocks, jagged rocks, and muddy water.

Claudia's chair slid toward the edge. She leapt from the chair a split second before it got sucked into the splintering abyss. She backpedaled her way toward the villa's front door, felt something hit her once, twice. She crawled out the entry and into the half of the courtyard that hadn't disappeared over the cliff.

She watched the disaster unfold as if her life were happening at quarter speed. Blood pumped in little spurts from a gash in her right wrist. More blood gushed over her eyes, a waterfall of bloody rain. She clamped her left hand over her right wrist and limped toward her home. *A dazed wonderment passed through her mind—our villa still stands, all of it.*

The gate to her courtyard opened. Father and Grandpa popped out. They saw her crawling toward them, covered in mud and blood. Mother and Claudius had hunkered down behind the two men. Both tribune and emperor sloshed through the deluge toward her.

Father picked her up and carried her to her bedroom. At that moment, this child-woman felt somehow saved, and surely loved.

Later, she wondered, *Why me? Why was I chosen to be saved, not Firenze?*

9

CLAUDIA

At midmorning tea, the day after the disaster, I told Grandpa, "I had a dream two nights ago. Rain poured down, with sheets of lightning flashing all around. Jesus-the-Jew appeared, hair plastered to his face. He came out of the dark and said, 'Your grandfather is in danger. His fortress will fall, as will his empire.' Those were his exact words. That's why I asked you to leave the fortress and stay with us the last couple of days."

Grandpa didn't believe in visions. His faith was in sharp iron, capable administrators, stern soldiers, and a mail-covered fist of iron—his own fist. But this dream, following this landside, seemed to shake him. His right hand started flopping around, worse than usual.

Maybe to distract me from his shakiness, he prayed out loud to Asclepius, "Cure Claudia's mind, oh god of healing."

Later in the day, Grandpa and I walked together, hand in hand. He misstepped once and fell. I guess he didn't see that rock right in front of him. I helped him up. We moved to the cliff's edge, carefully, and peered over the ragged ridge. Below us were the remnants of the villas, scattered through the forest like toys, many with dead people still inside them.

Where each house had been, only a line of crosses now stood. Each cross was occupied. The builder responsible for that villa hung in a position to view the work he'd done.

It was horrifying. Grandpa had decreed it, Father had commanded it, Cynico had supervised it, and foot soldiers had done it. Roman justice was served. You mess with us; we will surely mess with you.

———— ✁ ————

My only Jewish girlfriend, Abby, was daughter to the richest guy in town. He sold whatever anyone needed. If the stuff was allowed by us Romans, he'd sell it out the front door. If you wanted contraband like weapons or iron that could be made into weapons, he sold out the back door, but very carefully.

I met Abby at the only high-class bathhouse in Sepphoris. Servants bathed us, put almond oil on our skin, and plaited our hair. We were both filthy rich, enjoying the good life. During those times in the bathhouse, Abby had learned to trust me. I'd learned to act like I trusted her. After she started this trust thing, well, she was a fountain of information.

"You Romans breed terror like rabbits breed bunnies. Crucifixions are terrifying. Your rules sprout like weeds, and horror lurks behind closed doors. People can never tell what's going to get them in trouble."

I leaned into her words and tried to act interested. This wasn't about me, so why pay attention?

"When you moved into town," she said, "it was like gourds of silence sprouted from street corners. No one dares *speak* about their hidden rage. Instead, they plot revenge. Sometimes they get by with it."

A shiver of danger ripped through me. I pretended to do a neck roll to relax, but what I wanted was to check my back. *Are any stalkers creeping up on me?* Anger and fear did crazy things to me.

A few weeks passed. Grandpa was leaving today. Before he left, he said he wanted a little chat with that Jew-boy, the bearer of visions in the night to me. I couldn't tell if he was worried about himself, Rome, or me. We all could be shaken. We all could fall.

The grand ballroom at the fortress was crowded. I stayed with Father and Grandpa. Old shields covered the walls, alternating with spit-polished weapons and deep-dyed tapestries smudged by smoke from the fireplace. Servant girls bustled about with flagons of wine and finger food for royalty. They moved through fractured light. Shadowed and golden streams alternated, flecked with dust motes all adrift.

A coterie of Roman officers was present, all subordinates to Father. Jesus walked in with his father and uncle. They were escorted by Cynico and a few other subhuman hulks.

Father introduced Joe the Jew to them. "This is my builder, his brother, and his son. They were the ones who built the only villa that didn't crumble. I've recalled them to rebuild all the villas that fell."

Father eyed Grandpa. He sucked some power from him, puffed up his chest. "The cost of shoddy workmanship is hanging outside. The reward for good workmanship is here."

Father took a thick leather purse from under his military toga and spilled thirty silver coins out onto the floor in front of the Jews. "Joe the Jew, this is an advance. Repair the ruins. Rebuild them exactly like the one you did for me."

Joe blinked, looked confused. Jesus crumbled to his knees.

10

JESUS

When the thirty coins hit the floor, my knees gave way. Images clicked into my mind's eye. A bolt of pain shot straight through my head.

The sound of thirty coins hitting the pavement—a shady payoff given to a shadowy man. A half-recognition shimmied down my spine. I asked Father for help. A breezy silence wrapped around me.

Windy whispered, *not yet time for you to know. Trust Me.*

I exhaled and returned to the room. With new confidence, I stood and whispered in Abba's ear, "Seize the moment, Abba. Make it ours."

Abba used Gaius' formal name and rank, giving him honor in front of Caesar. "We don't have enough workers, Tribunus Laticlavius Gaius."

Gaius harrumphed. Not happy.

Abba said, "We can rebuild only one house at a time from its ruins. If we stretch too thin, then we stand in danger of hanging on a cross—like my friends who now die all along this cliff."

Gaius replied icily, "Your friends reaped what they sowed. As do you. Go, sow more. You are now construction supervisor, responsible for who you hire and what they do. Dismissed."

Abba motioned to me. I crawled about, carefully picking up what had been loosely spilled.

Claudia stood in her grandpa's shadow, watching me.

When I had given the coins to my father, and he'd carefully placed them in his leather purse, the emperor spoke to me. "You, Jew-boy, come with me. I want a word with you."

The emperor wanted to talk with *me*?

Augustus motioned with his hand. The two of us went into an elegant side room off the great banquet hall. I trailed behind. Once the door was closed, the emperor sat in a gilded chair. A table on his left side was laden with food. He commanded me to stand on his right side.

The emperor, an Italian ruler in royal finery, examined my threadbare tunic and mantle. He looked at my muddy feet, ran his careful eye over me—up one side, down the other. "Exactly what kind of relationship do you have with my granddaughter, Jew?" Unrelenting face, granite hard. Visions of a cross flickered, frightened me.

Windy exhaled. I inhaled.

My backbone strengthened, heart softened, vision focused.

Look at his vulnerable core through my eyes, Son. A monarch, but also a mere man who puts his sandals on one foot at a time. And now, see? His eyes dance around you, not at you. Like the sun, like death, he beholds you briefly. And then, he must look away.

I took in her breath, exhaled. "Emperor Augustus, I've had but one conversation with Claudia. I was sanding a doorjamb. We talked briefly, and then we came downstairs."

"You also spoke to her from within a dream. You've invaded her bedroom." Augustus squinted shrewdly, poked with pointy words, an amused look on his face.

Windy, what to say?

Augustus preempted my process. "Speak!"

Windy's words, coming from my mouth, surprised me. "This was the only way we could get your attention. It was not your time to die in this Judean mudslide."

His eyes narrowed. "What do you mean, we?"

"Father and I are one with the Spirit," We answered. "Your death will happen in less than three years at your birth home in Nola. You will then face the God who made the universe. He has given you the time between now and then to repent."

His face purpled.

I was amazed. How could I have known this?

His sword arm twitched. "How dare you talk to your Emperor like that!"

I examined the emperor curiously, without fear.

"Jew, you *do* know you stand before a god and, "he lowered his voice, "and Augustus is his name."

I noticed a few gold coins on the table beside him. My gaze flickered back to his face.

Augustus had followed my eyes. "You want my gold, do you, for seer services?"

I shook my head. "May I pick one up for a moment, Highness?"

Augustus nodded. "You do see whose image is there, don't you?"

I lifted the coin and studied the image. "Yours, sire. But is it not true that the quality of your coin, and mine, comes from whatever metal is in our mint? You rose to your rank, sir, because of your character, not the shiny surface image of public opinion." Windy's blasted gift hit me again. I knew he would be mad before *he* did.

Augustus' face moved from curious to furious. Fury came in clipped tones, steely as the battle-ax on the wall behind him. "You lecture me on issues of *character*?" He waved vaguely toward the street. "You could be tacked up on the empty cross over there for such presumption."

Windy soothed me, *Steady as you go, Son.*

"Emperor, you could kill me easily. But not the truth I speak." I returned the coin to the table. "Your body will return to dust in less than three years. I'm merely a messenger, relaying the truth to you from Yahweh."

Messengers of bad news were routinely executed. A fresh wave of trembling hit me.

Augustus didn't notice. Windy had wrapped herself around him, squeezing air from his frame, even as I spoke the Name. *Son, notice how the forethought of his brevity taxes him. See his forehead wrinkle? Look how his thick fingers whiten beneath the pinch of jeweled rings that once fit him, but now define him.*

Augustus flicked his eyes upward from where he played with his signet ring. He caught me eyeing him, then resumed examining his own hands.

Windy breezed a whisper in my mind. *He's wondering who's in charge of this interview, him or you.*

The sun hit the emperor's face full-on. I noted the emerald color of his eyes. He turned at a slight angle away from me. A shadow sliced him in two. He quietly removed a hidden jeweled dagger, smaller than his hand, from inside his tunic. Light played on the encrusted rubies and opals. Casually he reached out and stabbed the lamb on the platter beside him. The servant had prepared it bloody.

Windy said, *He likes his lamb rare.*

Caesar casually knifed it into his mouth and chewed thoughtfully, sucking strength from the lamb. He took a crust of bread, washed it down with a slug of wine from his golden goblet.

Shadows spiked and clawed across the floor, threaded across his face. Augustus disappeared within himself. His glance on me came and went, ephemeral. I felt his dis-ease slouching my way.

Windy instructed me again. *What you're feeling now, Son, is his envy of your youth and prescience. He wants to shove his fear down your throat and eat your calm. Mark this feeling. You will experience others' envy again and again. I will strengthen you to bear it.*

Augustus abruptly leaned forward, his voice ragged as a gash. "I may send for you later, in Rome. If my granddaughter were not fond of you, I would execute you today. Keep your distance from her, Jew. Dismissed."

I joined Abba. He stood by the exit door of the great room, in Cynico's shadow. The sergeant unsheathed his sword. The tribune, seated at the banquet table, gave a slight shake of his head. Cynico let us pass.

As I walked past him, I glanced at his sword. Cynico had proven to be a true poet of the profane, a legionnaire who could out-cuss the scrawls on an outhouse door. But today he was mute. He pointed to the door with his sword and stood like a sphinx.

Abba, Eliazar, and I walked past the cliff of execution. These good men revealed the terrible blanch and crumple of carelessness. They had failed to work warning into their lives.

Abba whispered in the air, "I'll look in on your families, give your sons work." No one on the stakes heard him, but I did. His heart's goodness leached into me. Abba passed by the empty cross. He saw a splinter along the backbone of the wooden upright and sanded it off with the wood rasp he kept in his satchel.

Somewhere beyond the last cross, a guy with a ratty gray prayer shawl hung in the shadows. I'd seen him before, the day Jabez was executed. A sly tavern grin slopped over his face. One eye didn't wander at all. It bored a hole into me. The other eye rolled around in his head, loose as a spinning top. This man meant evil toward me and all who were dear to me. I was sure of it.

Abba interrupted my feeling of foreboding. He'd been scribbling on his slate. "Jesus, run and get that lazy-eyed man loitering over there. I want him to give your ma this list of builders' sons to come work for me. He'll be glad for the work."

I didn't want anything to do with this man. But I obeyed my abba and approached Gray Prayer Shawl. "Would you like a job as a messenger for my abba?"

"Why, surely, master." His voice dripped with well-practiced sincerity. His head bobbed up and down, one eye circling while the other one looked directly at me without making eye contact.

Abba gave him the slate and directions to our doorstep in Nazareth.

Both Laz and John, my cousin, showed up for work the next day. John was odd, prone to isolate. Laz was more sociable. Guys warmed up to him—he was valued as a fun, loyal friend. Women, so I'd been told by girls in Torah class, shielded themselves from his roaming eyes.

Abba assigned John to framing. Laz joined me in foundations. Most of the building materials for the original villas, foundational material from Caesarea, had crumbled onto the forest floor. We could use these broken pieces to rework these villas' shallow foundations.

Abba approached us. "Son, this will be a hard job and an unclean one.

"The hard part is bringing up rock and rubble from below. The stinky part is that you'll uncover dead bodies in the process."

"Laz and I will need help, Abba, particularly if we have to touch a corpse."

"Right. We'll all do the purification rituals for you and Laz in the mik-vah if you touch the dead. Moshe can recite the *Tumat HaMet* liturgy while you dip in the mikvah. But for today, I need to go home. Laz told me something disturbing when he arrived this morning. That guy with the weird eye yesterday? Somehow, he spooked your ma. I'm going to check on her and the younger ones."

The stench of this evil-eyed man returned, like a shroud for the dead had been thrown over me. Laz and I trudged up and down the goat path all day, carrying bags of rubble, or a dead person on a litter. Head rags, scented with eucalyptus, helped fool our noses.

We dumped building materials by the old foundations and corpses at the gates of the fortress cemetery. This cemetery was running out of space. The Jewish men on the crosses were also long dead, but Cynico blocked us when we wanted to bury them. Abba asked the tribune for permission to take down our fellow Jews. The tribune was resolute. "No. Noses are better teachers than scrolls. Class is still in session."

Stink in the ground below, stink in the air above, stink from the wild-eyed man. Crows, those ungrateful mouths on wings, snipped bites from carcasses at the Crucifixion Café.

11

CLAUDIA

I'd invited my friends who'd survived the mudslide to our villa for class. It was more fun that way. Abby was the only Jewess present. She was different from us. She talked about her devotion to God, carried a happiness with her that felt brightly dense, and cried real tears for her friends. Whatever she had going on made me curious.

That afternoon, Antonio droned on about the Pyrrhic wars while he rambled around the room, stopping at each student's desk to check our work. When he took a break and left the room, we studied history, all right—current events. We crowded over to the window and watched Jesus and Laz pass by, up and down the hill. They were forbidden fruit, but out of reach anyway.

Roman boys my own age were pimply predators, playacting warriors—all of them—including Claud. Besides, they were far too available. I needed someone hard to get. These Jewish workers were not only hard to get, they were yummy to look at—loincloths, broad shoulders, lean, and sweaty.

Jesus and Laz came by just then, with a corpse on a litter. The clothes, that hand flopping out from under the shroud.

Oh no! Firenza.

I flashed back to her outstretched hand, her slide into the abyss. This kind of sadness compressed time. It lodged inside me, like a stuck prune pit in my throat. Too icky to stay with that memory now, but sometimes I couldn't un-remember her. Nightmares floated her, utterly weightless, into my mind's eye. She crumbled me—like all that rubble Jesus brought up from below. Even in pocket-sized daymares, her memory tipped me over. I grabbed my purse. Brought my mirror up from the wreckage in there.

Ha! Dazzling.

The next time the two men came by our window, I stuck my head out and waved. Laz smiled big at me and flexed his chest muscles. Jesus sang to himself and kept his eyes on the path. He was like a focused beam of light, even if the focus was on putrid bodies and rubble. Up and down the hill all day, sticking stinking rocks into holes deeper than men were tall. About as exciting as watching camel turds dry in the desert.

The Jews' camp on the hillside was visible from our roof. In the late afternoon, when the work and school day was over, I would stand behind a post and watch. The men would strip naked and dunk in a pool they'd hollowed out alongside the stream flowing from the hills. Then Jesus and Laz would dunk again while the men muttered some mumbo-jumbo. Something about purification rites. Ritual for them, exciting scenery for me.

After their baths, they ate. Then they would chorus more religious chants to their one pagan god, bobbing their heads up and down. Later, while the older men sat around the fire and talked, Jesus and his friend sat under the apple tree on the edge of the camp, a smudge torch between them. Sometimes a guy with a camel-skin tunic joined them. They studied some ratty old scroll fragment directly torn from a sheep's side.

I was truly and deeply bored with life here in Sepphoris, bored down to my toenails. And what was more, my parents and Claud were leaving tomorrow for a party in Caesarea. Grandpa had sent a delegation from Rome to honor the tribunes. And why wasn't I invited to this party in Caesarea? Everyone who was anyone had been invited. Besides, I was as much a grown-up as those other women father drooled over. He flirted with girls my own age.

I had an idea. I'd organize a rooftop fashion party. We'd have fun, put our assets to work in plain view of the stars. If the Jews in their camp caught an eyeful, well, so be it.

Julia, my governess, would be tipsy by then, well into the bottom of her bottle. Antonio would be deep into his books or asleep. I dodged inside to check my mother's wardrobe and cosmetics. The plot was thickening.

12

JESUS

The next day, Laz and I did our work up and down the trail. Studying scrolls at night became the work of the day. It was this way each day—learn Scripture in the circle of men around the campfire, read it aloud with Laz, then recite and discuss Torah during the daylight working hours.

I spoke out loud the words we had been discussing around the fire the night before and Laz repeated them. Laz wasn't stupid, his attention just wandered. Anything and everything caught his attention, particularly girls, since we'd hit the changes. And whatever had Laz's attention had every bit of him. He stacked up stories like cordwood and his mind flitted from one to another.

We knew each other so well that when Laz's mind started wandering, I knew it before he did. I could sense the distraction, like it was crawling under my skin. I'd turn on the trail and say, "Laz, repeat after me…" Then I'd say whatever the scripture was, yoking his attention to mine, like two oxen in the same yoke. I could repeat no more than a sentence at a time, or he'd lose it.

Today it was one of my favorite passages: "You'll use the old rubble of past lives to build anew, rebuild the foundations from out of your past. You'll be known as those who can fix anything, restore old ruins, rebuild and renovate, make the community livable again."[3]

Laz was not attending to my words. Instead, he said, "Hey, Jeez, have you noticed those girls looking at us from the second story window over there in the Tribune's villa?"

"Laz, bounce your eyes off them. They're sticky eye-candy. I've already mentioned the gorgeous one with blue eyes, auburn hair, and a great smile. She's the chief tribune's daughter. She uses her beauty like Delilah with

Sampson. Don't look at her. Where the eyes go, the heart and hands will want to follow."

"Aren't you being a bit extreme? After all, they're in their ivory tower and we're down here in the trenches. No harm to sneak a peek. I mean, we're regular guys, not pervs."

"A bit of yeast in a loaf of bread grows like magic, even when you're not looking. Apply heat, yeast rises."

Laz whistled a merry tune. "I'm a flirt because I don't know how to talk to a girl. In the flirting game, words aren't as important as bodies. Besides, girls like me because I'm the easiest of Jews to please. All I want is limitless love."

I laughed out loud and turned to look at him. Just as I turned, Laz had lifted his eyes off the path, looked at the villa, and hit a stumbling block of basalt. He fell backward, following his backpack of rocks down the cliff.

I watched him fall, my spine tingling with alarm. He plunged more than a dozen feet straight down, hit a thin layer of crusted mud and crumbling rock. The crust gave way, and Laz fell straight into an old grave. He stopped, tangled with a corpse wrapped in grave clothes. The smiling skull seemed surprised to have company after such a long dry spell. From where I stood, it was hard to tell Laz from the dead guy, except Laz's thighbone stuck up diagonally, jagged end in the air, with blood pumping out in spurts.

I yelled to the others at the top, "Help! Laz has fallen! Bring a stretcher!"

I picked my way down the steep trail into the grave, lifted the bag of rocks off Laz's leg, and sat with him in this place of the dead. His right leg had snapped above the knee. He must've hit his head because he was unconscious. I cradled his head in my lap and looked at his leg. I gently rocked my friend and prayed, *Father, teach my hands to help.* Then I breathed in a healing intention and looked down.

Windy said, *put your hands on either side of Laz's fracture. Pull the bones gently apart, then put them back together.*

I did what She said. I settled my palms over the open wound and watched, open-mouthed, as the bones knit together.

Windy said, *this work is foundational for later work you will do.*

Laz woke up, groggy. He grabbed his head in his hands and moaned. "What happened to me? How did I get down here?"

"Breathe, Laz. You fell. Father came to help."

At that moment, Abba climbed down into the grave with Hez, Laz's father. They carried a cloth stretcher hanging between two poles. Both men positioned themselves to load Laz onto it.

Holding up a hand, I looked down at Laz. "Do you think you are steady enough to walk out of this grave with me?"

Laz nodded, still rubbing his head.

I took him by the arm. "Let's see if we can walk."

Together, arm in arm, we walked out of the grave, a bit unsteadily, with shreds of old grave clothes clinging to Laz.

13

WINDY

Jesus and Laz sat under the apple tree on the edge of camp. Laz faced the roofs below. Jesus faced his friend and their scroll. The candle flickered between them. Jesus tested Laz on his memory of Exodus 22, the passage about welcoming strangers because Jews were once foreigners in Egypt. I reminded Son, *You're all foreigners, journeying Home.*

Laz gazed into the distance over Jesus' shoulder, rubbing his eyes. "Does this mean we should welcome the enemy—not plot to overthrow them?"

Jesus breathed out my reply. "We're to love those who mistake themselves for nothing. Also, those who tempt us—a job for men, not boys. Boys are more interested in getting. Men give better than they get."

Laz massaged his temples again, swaying his head from side to side.

"Your head still hurting from the fall today?"

"Yeah." He raised his arm and pointed behind Jesus. Laz once again became stuck inside his stare. Jesus gave his arm a yank. "Let's get to our tent. Otherwise we'll both get frozen in place. *4*

"El Abba has someone for you, Laz—a beautiful Jewish girl. She's waiting for you to finish your foundational work. When the husband is ready, the wife will appear."

Laz nodded. "Okay, okay. I'll hurry up."

14

CLAUDIA

The sun slipped over the horizon. Fireflies winked off and on, did their jitterbug dance. Jesus and his buddy studied their ratty scroll. Julia was drunk and Antonio slept. Everything seemed normal. But then, so were rot and rust. The roof was mine, and I was ready to bust "normal" into splinters.

The tangerine-orange water clock dripped steadily. Fountains jetted purpled water into the air while servant girls played lyres and tambourines. We maturing women sipped cocktails. Our torchlit fashion show was about to begin.

One at a time, my friends emerged from behind a scarlet silkscreen that fluttered in the breeze. Each danced sultry and slow to the music. The rest of us became a cheesy, sycophantic chorus. We knocked ourselves out, a real giggle-fest.

At last, my turn. I shimmied sideways from behind the screen, hands over my head, swaying, and a-shaking, and a-snaking, the hottest girl on the roof. My mother's filmy negligee folded and unfolded breezily around my body in the hot summer wind. I looked over my shoulder more than once. Jesus had his back to me, but his friend could see us.

I moved in and out of light and shadow as if competing for a prize. My friends thumped and circled me, joining with my music, my rhythms. No question about who won "Most Seductive Woman of the Night." And not just because it was my house and my father was the biggest cheese on the block. Okay. Well, maybe.

❖

The party wound down. Father's guards loaded my tipsy friends into covered coaches. Horses whinnied in the moonlight, trotting toward the end of our street. I waved them away and went inside, lounging in father's chair, catching the scent of this stranger who I called father, this man who was so tantalizing—bringing comfort, but only when I wasn't angry with him. I pushed through his papers. Didn't see any of them.

I remembered walking in on him with another woman, here in this study, a few years ago. I wheeled around, embarrassed for him. Later, when I was next alone with him, he laughed that grown-up-getting-ready-to-lie chuckle. "The other day, I was comforting that new tribune's wife. Her sister had died." *Did he think I was an idiot?*

I was a scorned woman, and not just by this man. *Jesus* didn't look at me once all night. He left me spinning in space, untethered. A passing breeze just might blow me onto one of those lonely stars, way up there. I escaped from my father's study and ditched the family compound, trying to escape my mood as easily as that villa. No luck. I walked into the wee hours, lonely and lost on a goat herder's path.

After a long while, I realized my feet had taken me higher on the hill. I had walked well past the round limestone outcropping that overlooked our villa to the north. The bony rocks that remained after the mudslide looked like a skull, leering down at me. Shivering, I pulled my cloak around me and the sheer negligee I still wore—moved on.

In a grove of oak, sycamore, apple, and eucalyptus, a woodpecker, usually asleep at night, banged her head against a tree over and over.

Yeah, girl. Know how you feel.

Scattered stones lay between trees, bark crumbles strewn like a shroud.

I was a fizzled firecracker, nothing more—less than unimportant. I leaned on a spreading sycamore, looked to my right. And there he sat, four trees away. *Jesus!*

He was alone, facing at a three-quarter angle away from me. He gazed up into the sky and spoke softly to himself. I strained to hear what he was saying.

"Father, I miss you. I'd like to come home. Really, I would. Whatever tomorrow will bring won't be easy. Premonitions break me out in cold sweats. I panic. Still me, Father, as you have since I was a small boy." His voice faded to a mumble.

I was confused. No one was there. Was he crazy?

He shifted his butt. Leaves beneath him crackled. "Claudia, come out of the shadows. I feel your presence, even as you felt my absence, earlier."

I had been so quiet. How had he known it was me and not someone else? "Jew-boy, you're a nutter—rambling on to your 'father' when you're all alone?" The tang of bile was sharp in my throat.

That golden voice rippled through the dark. "My name isn't Jew-boy. My name is Jesus. And yes, I was speaking to my Father, the One who loves Jew and non-Jew alike—even you, a Roman child."

"You are stranger and stranger, Jesus. Is this part of your mystic folk religion? Or have you been consorting with devils?"

"You remind me of your grandpa. But I sense your hunger. Neither grandfather nor father realizes how starved you are for their attention and affection. The more women your father uses, the less important you feel."

His words swept me up like a wave, and pulled me in. I tumbled around in there, feeling naked. I swiped my salty, bubbling tears away with a knuckle.

Jesus faced the lights of Sepphoris below. "No need to hide your tears. Father counts every one and puts them in a bottle."[5]

I hurried toward him, spread my cloak on the ground, and sat close to his side. "You said you were lonely. Can we be friends, or more? Even though we're Jew and Roman, rich and poor, conquered and conqueror?"

He was silent for what felt like an eternity.

I sensed a struggle—maybe mine, maybe his.

White clouds swept over the silver moon, violet skies, and thin cloud layers. The only sound was our breathing. Our elbows almost touched.

Jesus' skin goose-bumped. He put his hand on the ground, elbow locked. "Remember that time in your house, in the doorway to your bedroom? Let's do the same here as we did then—not close the door, but not act on our attraction. Let's go steady into this night."

My body stiffened. I wanted to lash out with my words or strike him with my fists. I did neither of those things. Hardest things I'd ever not done.

"I dreamed of you last night," I said. "It was a confusing dream of pain, desire. I held you in my power. But you were over me, above me—skin to skin, but distant. Then I shrank down to the size of nothing and vanished."

"What do you think your dream means?"

I turned my head to stare in his eyes, inches away from mine. "Before I met you, I felt like a dream, floating above a rental body. If you want me, I'll feel solid. I know I will."

Oh, shut up, Claudia. Never beg for anything. Make boys beg you.

He hugged his knees. "You're the most beautiful, spirited woman I've met. Your dreams are great teachers. Father created you, and Windy is your Dream Weaver. If you want them as I want them, you *will* become solid."

What I heard was, *I want you.* I pulled him toward me and massaged his neck. I wanted what I wanted.

A dark wind blew. An apple hanging over us fell.

I picked up the apple, carefully placed it on his inner thigh, let my finger linger. I remembered a part of the Jews' creation myth. I flashed on Eve, tasting what was forbidden, and tempting her Adam.

Leaves and peeled bark rustled above us. Distracted, we looked toward the noise—a black viper slithering over branches, tongue searching, licking.

Jesus pushed himself up to one knee, eye level with the viper. "Satan, leave!"

The viper bared its fangs six inches from Jesus' face. A drop of venom fell on a chunk of bark between us and burned through it with a sizzle.

Time froze. Then, for no good reason, the viper dropped on Jesus' heel and slid, quick as a wink, over my bare thigh, and into the dark.

"Aiyahhh! What just happened?"

Jesus shook his head. "Satan co-opted that serpent. He wanted to tempt us— 'love sex more than God.' But Father worked that trial for good. Satan became our distraction, not our undoing."

I burst into tears and hugged my knees. "Jesus, I have no headspace for all your words. All I've got is body hunger. Hold me. I need to feel safe."

Jesus wrapped one arm around my back and the other around my knees. I felt solid in his embrace, my head on his shoulder.

Moonlight bathed us.

After some time, too short a time, Jesus unwrapped his arms from around my body and moved away. Maybe a foot.

He sat, arms now wrapping his knees. "You're very powerful. If I had stayed as we were, I couldn't have kept refusing my desire for you."

"Hey, your Father made sex to be good, right?"

"Yes. He made sex better than good. Sex is best at the right time and place. Sex is so hot it's like fire. And fire needs to be kept in a fireplace, or it'll burn your house down."

I pushed the leaves away, making a little clearing. "Looks like a good fireplace to me."

"A good fireplace begins with marriage. Father's told me I'm not to marry but remain celibate. Sometimes, *like now*, I hate that. But my intimacy is to be with Father and His Spirit."

"That's horrible. A rip-off," I spat. "Sex sizzles, makes me feel *something*, not nothing. Makes me feel alive, not dead. Sex reminds me of fireworks, a Roman candle, for instance."

He laughed. "If my life were my own, we could have a blast." Then Jesus turned serious. "But I don't belong to myself. I'm Father's true Son and on a different course than you. Father and Windy make me feel alive, not sex."

I inched toward him and disregarded his spirit chatter. "You talk to all the animals?"

"Father trains me to do what each situation requires."

I picked up the fallen apple, took a bite. Held it out to him. "Tart. Try it."

Jesus shook his head. "No."

I sulked. "Yeah, right. Might have snaky juice on it, huh, Super Saint?"

When he didn't answer, I tried a different tack. "We're alone. We can do what we please."

Jesus turned those heartwood eyes of his toward me and did as he pleased. We sat close, at diagonals. The breeze blew his loose chestnut hair, blowing it away from his face. His gaze penetrated me. Unnerving intimacy. I felt so *alive*, heart thumping wildly in my chest.

I coached myself. *Breathe. He's giving you a different kind of sex.*

"Mm-hmm," he said, as if reading my thoughts. "This kind of coming is better, isn't it? It right-sizes desire, keeps Father first, and us under him." He inhaled, held his breath, released it. "Our spirits will mingle in our journey. Our paths will crisscross time and again, and our love will deepen." He hesitated and looked me smack in the eyes. "You'll grow older, wiser, and marry a powerful Roman ruler."

My spine tingled. The seer was at work. "Who? Tell me who I'm going to marry! And, while you're at it, what else do you see in my future?"

"I tell you what Father tells me, nothing more."

"Well, rattle Father's cage. I want more."

"More will come when you and I are ready, not before. Be patient with your abba. He's still learning. Can't yet see you for the treasure you are. And you don't know how long you will have him with you."

A throb of pain in my head. Drumbeat of danger. I dismissed it. I couldn't know what he meant, but it didn't sound good.

15

JESUS

It was late. I couldn't sleep, and neither could Laz. I asked him if he'd like to know what had happened. Laz was all ears. I detailed all that happened the night before, including my showdown with the viper.

"Holy Moses! You just walked away from her? I mean, just like that? You're impossibly good, Jeez. I could never be you."

"Believe me. I came this close to losing my virginity last night." I held my thumb and forefinger up, an inch apart.

My best friend nodded. "Woody has no conscience whenever he pops up."

"Claudia's real sexy. If I had stopped talking with Father, the night would have ended very different."

I looked at my best friend. We both needed to get our minds off sex. "Do you know how I first learned to listen to dreams?"

He shook his head.

I pounded my words like a nail in a wall. "I was five years old. We'd settled in the heart of Alexandria for maybe two years. The Street of Carpenters was a hodgepodge of colors, creeds, and cultures.

"That neighborhood and those people were my first memories, first friends, first sense of who I was. Way different than Nazareth. Many nations crept into my dreams and ways of thinking. I spoke Egyptian with playmates and Latin at school. At home, we spoke Aramaic. In temple, I studied Hebrew. I also figured out that I was multi-personal. Father and His Spirit bounced around inside me, forming and informing me."

Laz turned over on his stomach, propped onto his elbows, and rested his chin on his hands.

I talked on into the night hours. I told Laz about my first dreams back then. Dreams that came true, dreams that helped me to make friends with a boy named Julius, the Egyptian prefect's son.

"Did you know Father told me in a dream that I'd see this Julius again one day? We'd stay friends."

When Laz didn't answer, I turned to him. A dream had distracted him, I guess. He'd fallen asleep. I too closed my eyes, slept, and dreamt.

The next morning, I woke up in a tangled bedroll—woozy, hands clenched into fists, dream images clanging in my head.

Cynico, with a scythe, racing on horseback directly toward me, leaning down to swipe off my head. Claudia dancing close, hips rotating, pulling me into her. Laz's broken bones spilling out every which way from inside a tomb. *Oh, Father, what is the meaning of this night's puzzle?*

I felt my loincloth—ah, okay, another wet dream. I left our tent, washed out my loincloth in the creek, and joined the others at the campfire.

Abba was surrounded by men asking for direction. His face lit up when he saw me. "Morning, Son."

"Morning, Abba. Could you help me with a dream?"

"Not now. Tonight. After you eat, I need you to take a message to your ma for me. Bring back fresh bread, too, for dinner."

"What is the message?"

"Laz's abba has found him a bride. His betrothal is next month. The girl's father, Achan, works side by side with Hez. Laz doesn't know yet what the two fathers have agreed, so let's keep this secret for now."

Laz was to be married! He'd prayed for his wife to arrive soon. Father said 'yes,' this time—not *wait*, not *no*, like he did a lot of the time. If I was another guy, maybe we could have a double wedding. I gave my longing to Father, for him to hold, because I could not. All I could do was repeat, *marriage is another's life, not mine.*

"What's her name?" I asked.

Abba smiled. "Gomaria. Friends call her Go. I hear from her abba she has a pretty younger sister too." He raised an eyebrow and a half-smile toward me. "The two sisters have been staying with our family while their abba works here. When Achan goes home for Sabbath, they join him at their home."

I sighed and set out for home. Sepphoris and Nazareth were five miles apart, but legions apart in culture. Sepphoris was Jewish but with a Roman flare. Nazareth was small-village Jewish, through and through.

I enjoyed walking through the open farmland. What I liked more, though, wer, the Scraggly Crags along the way. Homeless people from Naz and Sepphoris made their home there: a mix of lepers off at the far end; at the other end of the caves, vagrants, thieves, murderers, shepherds with their flocks, winos, and aging whores. All of them seemed to get along, except when they didn't. Their attitude was wary hopefulness—trust every-one but guard your heart.

When I walked by the caves, Abishag called, "Hey, come over here." She was one of the former whores. She still might barter sex for food or wine, but she hadn't worked out of the main brothel in Sepphoris for a few years. "Eli isn't going to make it through the day," she said. She referred to one of the lepers, a man I'd known for years. "Thought you might want to say goodbye."

My heart sank. "Still in the second cave on the left?"

"Yep, that's the one. He asked for you."

16

WINDY

The stench of decaying flesh almost knocked Jesus out. This cave was only an indent in the cliff face, just enough to provide some shelter from the rain. Soot blackened the overhang. A cooking fire smoldered. One skinny ewe and a white-bearded goat lay huddled together, warming what was left of a person.

Eli was bordered fore and aft by sheep and goat. His disease had whittled him back into child size. He half moaned, half sighed. His face was missing most of his jaw. He drew in a ragged breath. Clawed his way back from death's edge with his one hand's two remaining fingers.

He pointed at Jesus. "I was hoping to see you before I died. Didn't think it would happen."

Son moved Eli's crapping pot, scooted closer, and took his outstretched hand.

The leper broke into an awful smile. "Fitting this is, fittin'—my ending, your beginning. Traveler's inn, you know, the one beside the Tower. I was a sheep tender for the temple flocks there, outside Bethlehem. That was the year before I became a leper." He sank inside himself, fell into silence.

Jesus thought, *maybe he just died.*

Eli surprised him. His chest rose, and he pushed out his few remaining breaths, the same ones Father had allotted to him. "Never forget that night you dropped outta the sky, dropped outta your ma. You had to drop a long way now, didn't ya? That whole whiz-bang gang of blinding Lights singin' in the sky. I think you came down inside their song. Or maybe on the light of that blazing star. Thought I'd lost my mind, thinking stuff like that. Ain't like me at all."

He was quiet for a long time. His breath shallowed.

He startled. "Quite a get-go you had, boy. Made me want to fall down in front of you an' worship. Don't have to fall now. I'm already low as I can get."

Jesus was about to speak, but I braked him. *Smile, shut up, lean in.*

Eli studied Jesus' face. "I grew into my leprosy. It grew into me." He paused. Eyes clouded over, and then welled up. "You're the only one who touches me at all."

Jesus' stomach was in knots. Feelings flooded into his eyes and dripped from them.

Son, I'm stretching you now. Relax. Let me breathe you.

"Few, few years ago," Eli continued, "I saw your ma and pa again. They walked by, you trailin' behind 'em. Must not have been more than eight or nine years old. Knew then I needed to stay here close, close to where you lived. I hung on, going downhill, losing fresh pieces of me every month. What you see, what I got. Sheep, goat, not much of me."

Jesus stroked Eli's patchy gray hair. "Father kept you close to me and me close to you. Today, you will rise up, rise higher and higher, till you are wholly present with Father. All because you believed in me."

I nudged Jesus. Eli's time was at hand.

"Okay, Eli, you can go now, go to Father," Son said.

Eli's last breath whispered out of him and away, away, up, and up the same pathways Jesus had fallen down and down. With Jesus in his eye, his whole self slipped with Me from a planet half in darkness.

Jesus looked toward heaven. He saw the fully radiant man whom I'd wrapped in a billowing rose-colored garment—glowing, flowing upward on the angels' song, the whole crowd of them welcoming him through the front gate of heaven's home into the wide-open arms of Father. Jesus smiled as he watched him go, just as Eli had smiled as he watched him come, bookends.

Abishag caught Jesus by surprise. She and Jabu, an aging thief, had snuck up behind him and been watching. She brayed, "Guess he croaked, huh? Hey, Jabu, get that shovel! Got to get his body ditched 'fore dark, or he'll stink up the camp. He said I could keep his goat and ewe for the milk, you know, if I'd put him down for his dirt nap, Jesus."

Son moved aside as Jabu and Abishag wrapped Eli's cooling body in a sheet. Without a word, they dragged him into the forest and dumped him in a shallow hole already dug.

Abishag and Jabu didn't know what to say.

Son did. He looked with love on their expectant faces, and then he looked up. "Thank You, Father, for giving Eli such a grand journey home. Thank You for his rise, my fall. For letting me down easy—into the love and grief of being human. I didn't know till now how much alike falling in love is with falling in grief. Either way, You catch me. I fall into You. You're my foundation."

When he finished his prayer, Abishag and Jabu were staring at Son wide-eyed, with wonder.

Jesus thought, *lepers, whores, and thieves will believe before most others.* Then he stood up and took a deep breath. On the exhale, I blew him forward. He decided to cut across the hills homeward. There was no path. He made the path by walking.

17

MARY

Jesus busted in the front door with arms wide open. "I'm home!"

James, Jude, Justus, and Miriam danced around him like a tumble of puppies. He looked for his youngest sister, Deborah, not yet two. She'd hid under a corner chair. Her makeup for the day was oatmeal smear, and she'd managed to get it over most of her face. She looked around the chair leg, then hid, playing peekaboo.

Jesus crawled to her chair and played her game. After a few peeks and boos, she came out, arms wide open. He stood and jiggled her high over his head. She showed her love by throwing a fistful of cold oatmeal in the air and erupting a massive fart. He responded with an even louder toot of his own. She threw her arms around his neck. "Wuvs Jesus! Wuvs Jesus!"

Jesus looked away from Deborah and spotted our two guests, sitting against the far wall.

I said, "Jesus, meet Gomaria and Leah."

He greeted them. The younger sister, Leah, stood a step behind her taller sibling. Gomaria flashed her sparkly green eyes at my son. Her hair was the color of honey and framed a face with cheekbones so high and sharp they'd thin-slice angel hair. A cream-colored cotton dress flowed over a perfect figure.

She tucked a loose strand of hair into her scarf. "Hi, Jesus. I hope we can become friends."

Son nodded pleasantly and immediately turned his attention to the smaller of the two sisters. "Hi, Leah."

Leah lowered her eyes, then stuttered a reply that died a lonesome death on the floor between them. She was darker complected than Go— high forehead and thick black eyebrows that wandered uncertainly toward each other. Her narrow face seemed made of rose-colored porcelain, the kind that breaks easy. Tiny ears, almost too shy to make an appearance, mostly hid behind her walnut-colored hair. She was still a child, seriously nervous, who lived in the long shadow of her sister's beauty.

Jesus turned to me. "I only have a few hours here. Abba asked that I bring a half dozen loaves of bread back to camp with me. And I need a word in private with you."

I delegated Go to make the bread, something we had done together quite a few times. James herded Justus, Jude, Miriam, and Deborah into the courtyard. I put together a plate of cheese, rye bread, and dried figs, then pulled Jesus with me out into my vineyard.

I looked up and saw Son studying me. I asked, "Tell me what you see."

"Someone I love. You're so brave. You're only thirty years old, Ma, and responsible for six children, your widowed mother, and Abba. I see a woman who married a man about her father's age, someone who's fond of saying, 'The thing about the past, Son, is that it's not past.'"

I absorbed his words, knowing that our woven past now shaped the present moment. "I got a picture just now—thousands of baby grapes, each rooted in your Father's heart, each gaining strength for the day when they'll be stomped on and pressed." I teared up and looked into Son's brown eyes, flecked with yellow—mirror images of my own. "At first, I thought this outpouring was from me, but then your face appeared. You were the one pouring out blood."

Jesus put his free arm around my shoulders and squeezed. No words were needed. We ambled through the vineyard, arm in arm, feelings swapping back and forth between us.

I asked, "What's happening with you and Abba?" When he told me the betrothal news, I felt alarmed. "I'm not sure Laz can handle Go. She's a mystery, but not a good one. This match may spark more heat than light."

"But there's so much good to be harnessed in her, ma. I suspect she's had to grow up before she was grown up."

I gave him a slight head shake. His comment was a nonstarter with me.

He kept going, anyway. "And you know, there's plenty of room in Father's house for folks like Go, just like there's plenty of room for her in our house. Heaven knows she and her sister get an amazing role model in you."

I flickered a smile his way. "Well, there *is* something else. When you were rolling around on the floor with the younger ones, I looked at James. He was watching Go watch you. His eyes burned with jealousy."

"Ah, so that's what was cooking my guts in the house. You're Father's tuning fork, schooling me with words for the feelings that roost in me—mainly others' unwanted fears or impulses."

I said, "Father tasked me with this part of your training. No time to speak with James today, but I'm sure you'll figure out a way to mingle truth with love when the time is right."

We rounded the last row in the vineyard, a special section where my favorite grapevines were planted. Leah squatted in front of a vine, shaping the steaming compost into fistfuls of fertilizer. A trowel and pruning shears stabbed the ground beside her haunches.

Jesus looked my way, quizzical. I opened my hands toward Leah. *Check this one out.*

Jesus angled toward the young woman. "I'm impressed, Leah! Ma trusts very few people around her favorite vines with pruning shears."

Leah broke into a shy smile. Her upturned face was beautiful, even with a streak of compost on her cheek. She was in her element in my garden, without Go's shadow to beard her beauty.

She said, "Go loves making bread. I love making plants grow. Mother Mary taught me how to prune these vines. We knew nothing of this, living in the desert."

I fingered a delicate branch shooting off the stump. "Most of what I taught Jesus is that a branch doesn't produce a thing unless it's joined with that stubby stick poking out of the ground. If the branch doesn't connect to the vine, and the vine to the root, the whole thing goes in the burn pile."

Leah looked up at me. "I worry my ma and pa gave us no roots worth tending." She lowered her eyes.

Jesus said, "Ma knows about grafting new branches onto these roots. She can show you how."

He and I moved toward the house.

Five loaves of baked bread stuck out of his backpack in a corner. I gathered everyone together and prayed for Son's safety on the return trip to work. He hugged us goodbye and headed toward Sepphoris. We all stood in front of our home, waving goodbye until he rounded a corner, out of sight.

18

JESUS

An hour or so later, I'd arrived at Scraggly Crags midway between Nazareth and Sepphoris. The late afternoon sun slanted through the stand of tall pine trees that I'd stopped to admire. Just then, a stranger with a wolfish face leapt into view from behind a pine, about five feet from me. He said nothing. Instead, he lunged sideways at me, slicing heart high with his stiletto. I dodged, but his blade caught my side.

I threw my satchel of bread at him and ran—straight into a den of thieves—only a step or two ahead of my hopeful murderer.

Someone from the group around the campfire called out, "Rabbus! Knock it off! This is Jesus, Joe-the-Jew's kid."

Rabbus huffed into camp, his mouth full of bread.

Chief of the robbers said, "Sorry, Jesus. New guy." He ripped the satchel out of Rabbus' hands and tossed it back to me. All the bread was still there, minus a hunk the size of Rabbus' mouth.

I put my hand in my shirt and pressed the hanging chunk of skin and muscle back to my ribs. Blood dripped between my fingers, down my legs, and pooled by my right foot.

Rabbus stood there, knife hanging limp at his side, head down.

I held out the loaf to him, the one with a bite shaped like his mouth. "Here, why not finish it?"

He eyed the blood dripping on my feet. "I ain't et in a week. Hungry stomach ain't got no ears." He hesitated. "Got an extra shirt. I'll get it."

A minute or so later, he returned with a stained peasant blouse a size too big, but with room to grow. I thanked him, took off my bloodstained shirt. Rabbus tore it in strips and used them to bind my wound. His hands were callused, a working man's hands.

When he was done, I told him, "You're with a good group—not a faker here. Stay and learn—or maybe you'd like to come with me. My abba's the foreman on some remodels in Sepphoris. He can give you an honest day's pay for an honest day's labor."

This man of few words nodded and grabbed his stuff.

While we were walking, I asked, "Tell me your story, friend. Much or little, as you like."

Rabbus talked in a toneless voice like he was reciting from a boring scroll. "Everyone called me Barry back then. Ma'd say, 'Barry, steer clear of your abba when he's drinking.' Didn't do me no good. He was mean. Beat me a lot." He got quiet. I thought he'd stopped his story, but after a half-mile or so, he started talking again. "Ma and Pa died. I drifted, found work as a stonemason, like my pa. Got married, had a kid. Fever came through town. Wife and kid both died. I busted up pretty good, started drifting again. Days didn't build on each other like stones did."

Windy planted a thought. *Earth always arcs toward morning. When Rabbus feels his mourning, his morning will come—and he'll wake up. Till then, he sleepwalks. Ask another question, Son. It helps with the whole mourning thing.*

I asked, "Your own family, what happened?"

Rabbus spoke between bites of bread. "We're Samaritans. Lived in Gerizim's foothills. Band of Jews came by one night and looted the farm. I was eight. Watched from a hidey-hole inside a hay bale. They slit Pa's throat. Did the same to Ma, but only after they took turns climbing on top of her. Torched the house and barn and the hay bale I was in. Rode off. I escaped."

I sucked up the sadness Rabbus refused to feel. "What kind of man was your father?"

"I complained once about a toothache on my right side. He hit me hard on the left side and said, 'That'll fix it.'"

I talked like he did, coughing up bones without meat on 'em. "We both know how to let go. My family? Refugees in Egypt. Came back a few years ago. Struggled, recovered. You can too."

◆——◆✕◆——◆

We arrived in Sepphoris just as the sun set. Abba's workers ladled chunky, steaming lamb stew seasoned with spring onions and peppers from a scorched pot. But they had no bread. Rabbus passed the remaining loaves around.

"Abba, meet my friend, Rabbus. He's an experienced stonemason."

Abba welcomed the silent man with a quizzical look. "Just in time for supper, you two. We're ready to eat after you wash up and we thank Yahweh for this food."

After dinner, Abba took me aside and wanted to hear my dream from the morning. He'd remembered! He also wanted *all* the news from home. "Don't leave out even one detail!"

He helped me with my dream from the morning, and then I went over the whole day, bit by bit. I saved the stories of Eli and Rabbus for last. I unwrapped my side. Abba smeared honey and wound-wart balm on my wound and rebound it with clean strips of linen.

The next morning about halfway to noon, Laz and I took a break from bagging rocks. We watched Rabbus set a plumb line in place for a courtyard wall.

"Why give him work?" Laz asked. "The guy almost killed you."

"I was listening to Father. He said, make this man a friend. Take him with you. *It's the best way to make a disciple.*"

"Your Father must have been thinking of me too. Heaven knows I need your friendship, with this betrothal news." Laz hung his head. "The one time I saw Gomaria at synagogue, I remember thinking, *She's too gorgeous.* Bathsheba and Sarah made Uriah and Abram disposable. Being married to her might get me killed before my time."

Windy breathed out her response, using my mouth. "Father determines destiny. Doesn't matter if she's beautiful or ugly. Love her by serving her."

Laz sighed. "Like I know anything at all about how to do that."

The rest of the afternoon, Laz worried his way along the path behind me. My side and heart both ached, one ache from Rabbus' blade, the other from my best friend. Laz's fear clung to my heart. Ack. What to do with these feelings? Today, they were way too much.

19

WINDY

Before Laz and Go's betrothal party, the two of them were allowed a get-acquainted meeting while the guests filtered into the front courtyard. They sat on a bench in the garden out back. Mary and Martha chaperoned from a distance, discreetly.

Laz grew dark rings under his armpits. Go appeared as cool and collected as one of King Herod's famed ice carvings. Neither would peacefully survive this conversation, in one piece.

"Uh," Laz said nervously, "what do you think about what our fathers have done?"

She darted a glance his way. "You as nervous in bed as you are on a bench?"

Laz looked away. "Don't know. Not yet been with a woman. Are you as cool in bed as you are on a bench?"

She laughed. "*I'm* not telling. But I don't think we'll get along."

"Probably not at first. Everyone says a good marriage has to grow on you."

"Like an incurable disease. You know what the other girls in town say about you—you never miss a chance to admire yourself in a mirror."

"Ow. Probably true, but only because I'm so insecure. I promise, though, I'll be faithful to you. But I wonder, can you be faithful to me? You know, both my sisters and my mother think Abba made a big mistake. They said beautiful women are dangerous women."

"When people tell me about themselves, I believe 'em. When they tell me about me, I don't. Which sister are you more like, the super spiritual one or the busybody?"

"Hey, careful there. And it'd be good for you to respect my mother too—particularly since she's the only one you have now."

Go heard herself say something *she* didn't want to know. Didn't want Laz to know either, but she couldn't help herself. It rolled out of her. "Don't you *dare* talk about my mother. I'm just like her." She got right in his face, about two inches away, and spat out, "I'll *never* forget how much her husband enjoyed her murder. Execution by stoning, for adultery. He held Leah and me by our ears and made us watch. You husbands are *all* alike—conniving and full of anger."

Laz swallowed hard. They'd turned a corner in their relationship. The future looked unfamiliar, a dark street with no sign postings. "I'm so sorry, Go. I had no idea what I was talking about."

Go ignored his words. She flipped her veil down and grabbed his hand.

They walked past his sisters into the inside courtyard. All the guests stopped their chatter and applauded the new couple while musicians played a traditional tune on fiddle and lyre.

Go plastered good cheer on her veiled, made-up face. Laz led them to their place of honor at the head of the table where Jesus reclined, directly across from them. Rav Moshe called the gathering to order and read aloud the *ketubah*. Go heaved a sigh of relief when Rav detailed her rights of divorce. This wasn't how they played the game in Moab.

Wine, music, and dancing followed the legal bits. Alcohol eased the fright in Laz but seemed to wind Go even tighter. The band was so loud that Jesus' knees vibrated from the inside while he danced hora with his friends.

He spoke briefly with Menachim, one of his father's friends in the synagogue. Menachim, he noted, hadn't spoken to his wife the whole evening. Instead, he stared a lot at Go, who turned away and talked with other young women her age.

Jesus felt a sense of foreboding. *What's up, Windy?*

I fastened my reins in his eyeteeth and turned his eyes to Father. *Go is terrified but faking ease. But don't focus on her, Son. Instead, chew on Father's promise to make everything new because of you. Live in the lurch between the present and the promise. He'll work His plan.*

Uh, okay, but what else is cooking my guts, Windy?

I remained silent. He needed to not know, but live by faith in Father's word.

After the feast and dancing, people began making their goodbyes, *mazel-toffing* each other. Mary, Laz's sister, sat with Jesus on a polished olive-wood bench he'd made some years back. The bench was beside a side gate. Many people had sat when they arrived, so the hired help could wash their feet.

The two young people overlooked the garden. Lichen etched the backyard paving stones. Zinnias and geraniums tangled with jasmine—a color riot of violet, mango, and tangerine. Honeybees wallowed a shaky path toward their hive, their bellies full of pollen. The air was quiet for this moment in time, except for the buzzing of these bees.

Just then, Martha arrived. She loaded a tray with dirty dishes and clattered a beeline from banquet table to kitchen, almost tripping on her own sandal.

Jesus called her over. Martha put her load down, came and sat. She crossed her legs and fidgeted with the worn shoe strap. Mary put her hand on her sister's arm. *Calm down.*

Mary turned to Jesus and wiped away a tear that had started a slow roll down her cheek. She said, "Laz is in deep trouble. Abba did the deal without asking Ma or us what we thought. This is so different than my betrothal and Martha's. Our whole family discussed Ehud and Mordi, weighing all the pros and cons. But what's to be done now?"

Martha heaved an exasperated sigh. She took off her ragged shoe, pulled a needle and thread out of her pocket, and furiously jabbed her needle into the material, worrying with her sole.

Jesus felt her worry and Mary's fear.

He looked at Martha and slipped off the bench. He sat on the ground next to the servant's bucket of water, slipped off her other sandal, and washed her feet. She protested, but he persisted. Mary shut her up with a look. The only sound was dirty water being squeezed back into the bucket.

Jesus put his wet rag down and picked up her worn-out sandals. "Martha, I can imagine you saying to these sandals, 'I love you so much! You've been faithful. You've carried me to this spot. I'll just keep patching you.'"

He put her sandals down and caught her eye. "Let go of your broken shoes. Instead, make friends with the broken parts of you. The first step into a new conversation with yourself, and God, is stopping the old one. Go barefoot, if necessary."

Martha was silent, body tight. Her mother yelled for her from the kitchen. She picked up her tray of dirty dishes and huffed off toward the sound of her mother's voice. She went barefoot.

Mary said, "She's twenty, married seven years. I'm seventeen and already married three years. But you're centuries ahead of us. We just want someone else hurt by that flirt—not Laz, not our family. We talk between us all the time, afraid she's going to put him in an early grave."

"Mary, the new conversation is with my Spirit in you, and with yourself. He, Father, is overall, works through all, and is present in all, even Go. Talk with Him. He knows what He's doing—even with Go and Laz." He breathed out my words. "Be like me. Admit you don't know what you're doing most of the time. Instead, be led by the Spirit, who shows us what to do, even when the rules don't apply."

20

GO

During my betrothal, I settled my eyes on Jesus, the only man in the room I didn't think would sleep with me, if given a chance. His quick smile carried an unstoppable bias in my favor. But when he left, and when I left, that grown-up part of me disappeared.

After the betrothal, I was grateful for Mother Mary's kindness. She walked me part of the way home. After her goodbye hug, I continued on alone. A stray rapeseed had lost its way and given birth to a field of yellow flowers in the mud roof over his house. These blossoms bobbed back and forth in an uncertain wind.

Inside, Leah lay on our bed in a fetal position, facing the wall, snuffling. Achan waited for me, fire in his eyes. I smelled the alcohol on his breath and didn't argue. Did property have a right to talk back to its owner? He spoke slurred, like he had a bloody condom wrapped around his tongue, not where he needed it. I left my body, floated over to Leah, circled her, hoped she was thinking faraway thoughts. Hoped I wasn't being made pregnant.

When he was done, I crossed the crawl space between his bed and the one I shared with Leah. I lay on my back next to her, stiff as a board. Leah lay still, face turned to the wall.

Ach began snoring. I cleaned up, changed clothes, and slipped out the back door for the steamy, seamy side of the next town over. Getting money for doing the same thing Ach took by force? What a relief, even though I didn't get to keep *any* of it.

Two of the Sepphbro's guards waited at the corner, holding a horse the brothel provided for its best earners. My face was veiled just as when I'd been betrothed. The guards and I kept to the shadows as we left Naz. I loved riding this horse down dark roads. This was the only fun part of my job—men before me, men behind me, men not able to touch me.

I thought of my sister. She'd learned to act invisible. Maybe Ach wouldn't see past me to her, his ugly daughter, his only daughter. Did he know I wasn't his? How could he not?

He'd said, "Just givin' ya on-the-job training, girl. My way o' being generous—an' for your own good." I could still hear his voice.

My wages went into the wooden box with the Sepphbro label that Ach kept under his bed in the earthen floor. He wrapped the box in a silk robe a client from Shinar had given me as a present.[6]

Ach counted the silver every day, letting it trickle through his fingers while he cooed, "Look at you, my precious." He'd told me once, a devilish glint in his eye, "Be real careful, girl. Don't want to come to your stoning. One's enough. Your ma was 'xactly like you. You're just friskier. I have my family name to think about."

Memories flooded me. *Mother buried up to her neck, terrified, wild-eyed. Righteous Jews reining judgment on her head, one rock at a time.* Ach, sly Amalekite that he was, wanted to fix those images in my mind—what Jews do to Jews. And it worked. Barbed-wire memories went straight through my eyes, down my spine, and jumped out every time I was anywhere near Leah's father. Betrothal to brothel in one small hour.

We were almost to Sepphoris. The brothel butted up next to Priapus Gate. The gate, made from marble, was named after some Greek god and shaped like a huge erection.

My best customer, Menachim, waited for me. He and some other hyper-religious Jews from Naz had just been at the betrothal. Awkward.

Torchlight flickered in the dim hall. Third door on the left was my room. Animal noises came out of the first two. Soon they'd be coming out of mine. I'd become a pro at authentic passion moans. They were the best way to jack up a girl's revenue stream.

After, the better ones would lie there, feeling bad for cheating on their wives. Expected me to use my words and make it all guilt-free. Tell them how they deserved what they'd just had. Men! Such boys.

My next customer was a different kettle of fish, Roman style. He was partial to rough trade. I bound him with straps, knowing he could snap 'em if he wanted. Later, he bound me with ropes I couldn't break. "No marks on the merchandise, Cynico," I reminded him, with a sly smile. He went about his business, grunting like a boar. He could do what he liked with me, even kill me, and no one would blink twice, including my Jewish bodyguards.

This Sepphbro goldmine was going to be hard to leave behind. I'd yet to figure out how greedy Laz was. Probably he and Ach weren't all that different. But Laz was best friends with Jesus. Maybe, just maybe, Jesus had rubbed some kindness into Laz. I'd wait and see.

21

JESUS

A whole group of us walked to work the next day. When we got to the Scraggly Crags, Abishag sat on a rock beside the road and motioned me aside. I called to my buddies, "Catch up with you in a minute."

"Hey, what's up, Abishag?"

She smiled in a frowning sort of way, worry twizzling her good nature. "Living in the Scrags with these men ain't 'xactly dull, Jesus. The odds are good, but face it, the goods are odd." She'd stitched her own logo on the peasant smock she wore: "Faded Sparkle."

Nailed it twice, Abishag. Faded but sparkling with Father's glory.

"Heard you went to a betrothal party last night."

"News gets around."

"This is for you and me, Jesus, not your friend over there." She nodded toward Laz, his back to us. "His betrothed works the same room I used at the brothel. Been there almost four months. Popular with the locals, and some of the Roman guards in Sepphoris."

Passing storm flickered through my mind.

She kept going. "Word on the streets, you the one who gets him ready for her."

I nodded.

She gained strength in her voice. "You're gonna have an awful time with this girl. Not sure she's marriage material at all. Nope, not a working girl like her. Know what I mean?"

"How'd you suggest that I go from here?"

"Well, now, Jesus, ain't sure." Abishag scratched her head, eyes up and to the left. "Might require wisdom of the good Lord, his own fine Self."

"Well, we're on speaking terms." I gave her an affectionate, sideways hug, then trotted off.

The first person I caught up with was Achan.

He walked alone—head down, not looking left or right, not inviting conversation. He'd loaded his mule with tools, food, and supplies for the next six days.

I fell in step with the silent man, struck up a conversation. "Quite a betrothal for your oldest last night. You doing okay, morning after?"

"Yeah, it wuz time. Been old enough for a while now."

I felt dizzy for no good reason and reached out to steady myself. Ach looked over the mule at me. I looked back and nearly freaked. Vapors of dark stench fingered off all of his exposed skin. He smelled like an outhouse, and his face looked like candle melt.

"Too much to drink last night, eh, Jesus?" His voice deepened, slurred, slowed.

I shook my head. "No, sir."

This is definitely weird, Father. What's happening here?

"I want your help. Laz asked me to be the bridegroom's friend—the one who helps the bridegroom get ready for the chuppah. Not an Amalekite custom, I take it?"

Ach shook his head. "Nope."

"I know Laz and his family pretty well. But I don't know you or your family. You haven't been here all that long, have you?"

Ach's skin and speech were still stinky-slurred, a thunderstorm in an outhouse. "Yep, four or five months. Couldn't stay in Moab. Weren't working out for me an' the girls."

"What happened?"

"Wife died a year or two ago. Complicated. I was left t' raise them girls. Couldn't find work after she died. Someone in a bar said t' try up north. Packed up and left town next day."

I'd been staring at my feet, hoping to regain my balance. Overwhelming distrust congealed out of the stink.

Windy breezed in, schooled me. *What would I be feeling in his shoes? Ask yourself that, Son.*

I took her breath in, exhaled. "How'd you cope?"

Ach smiled sideways. Smelled like diarrhea slipping out of a goose. "Not sure. It were a stink hole."

I held onto my breakfast, barely. Felt like my feet were stuck in syrup. "And the girls? Must have been tough losing their mom so young."

"Don't know. Not much for talk, me and them. Far as I see, just more of what they already wuz—mad Go, crybaby Leah. The wife'd been playing me. Didn't think I knew about her screwing around. All stuck up, her, singing and screwing in the castle. She earned what she got. Dragged her in front of those hotshot Jew judges. Stoned her lickety-split. Made the girls watch—a warning, don't cha know?"

He looked over at me and continued, with all the insight of a boxed mushroom, "Might have marked the girls a bit, bad blood 'tween their ma and me." The odor coming out of his mouth mixed with foulness coming off his skin.

Amazing, Father. Help.

I opened my mouth, and wind from my own lungs shaped these words, "I'm sure they had feelings about their mother's death. Your girls seem real smart."

"Leah's the bright one. Takes after me. Got her letters down too. Just like I got my Amalekite letters down." He puffed up his chest. "Glad to get Go gone, for sure. Ripe for some stud to pump her."

Once Ach's words were trued, my nose, eyes, and feet got more normal. Father sighed his grief. Windy picked up His exhale and inflated my lungs. His exhale, my inhale, synced more regularly now. "Your own family?"

"Moabite. My line goes back to royalty—King Agag was my ancestor. Before him, some guy called Haman. King's right-hand man in Persia.[7] Girls' mom, a Jew like you."

"Your father a carpenter too?"

"Nah. Learned that from the wife's father. My pa was into joinery." His hips thrust back and forth, and a sly smile slopped around his face. "He weren't skilled with nutin' but buying and selling stuff on the street, ya know what I mean?"

The stink of trafficked people invaded my senses. *I don't know what to ask. Keep me steady, Windy. What next?*

Windy exhaled Father's words. "Ach, tell me more about your daughters."

"Go's tough as nails. Spank her as a kid, she'd just get meaner. Leah's squishier. Look at her sideways, she collapses in a puddle. Go's more physical, know what I mean?" He hee-hawed out loud. "Yup, we get along all right—like fire and oil."

We arrived at work. Finally! Felt like a camel took his hoof off my chest. We joined up with the other workers from Sepphoris, broke into work crews. I walked with Laz toward the foundation's crew, looked up toward Gaius' house.

Claudia stood in the window, arms crossed over her breasts, scanning the landscape. She saw me, grinned, and ducked back inside, curtains flapping through the wide-open window.

22

CLAUDIA

I'd just finished my literature analysis for the day, Plato's *Symposium*. Antonio popped his head in the door of my study room and asked, "Finish your lessons in geometry, literature, mathematics, and philosophy, Claudia?"

I nodded, but then put on a pout. "Do you really believe this stuff from Plato?"

"Which part?"

"The part about where we all were two selves in one body, got separated, and wandered around looking for our other half." I flipped a short scroll to him. "I just finished telling you why I think that's a crock."

Antonio scanned my report, furrowed his salt-and-pepper brow, and played with a silver ringlet on his forehead. "I'd always believed Plato was truer than not, until Julia became more interested in her good Roman wine than her good Roman husband. And you, my precocious pet, have you found your other half?"

I stared at the closed window and waved my hand vaguely in that direction. "Well, since we're being so honest, I *have* found him—but he's not found me. He's busy pouring quicklime over little rocks in big holes. Then he and that other guy tamp it all down, so our houses don't crumble into bits when it rains." I took another shot, testing our trust foundations. "I'd love to have him in my bed, but he'll have nothing of me!"

Antonio took my frustration seriously. Angst was his mother country, even more than Italy. He ate doubt and pooped jaundice. "Do I know him?"

"Yes, Antonio! Joe the Jew's son, Jesus. He's my other half, if Plato's right. My friends change boy idols like menstrual rags, in one day and out the next with our courses. Jesus and I aren't like that."

"How are you different, my dear?"

"He's got this thing going with his Father. Crazy in love with a guy he can't see. Claims Father loves him desperately. Feels incestuous, right?"

"So, he's a religious-sexual nutcase?"

"Not sure. All I know is I'm banging around inside a sharp-edged love triangle that cuts every step I take. I love him. He loves Father. And supposedly, his Father loves not only him but me too. Somehow I got looped into this mess."

I could practically hear Antonio's prodigious memory click over, sorting solutions. Everything anyone had ever written was recorded there, dense, elegant, cataloged. He remembered the words of people who'd forgotten they'd even written them, the birthdates of people who'd practically forgotten they'd been born.

"Antonio, when I see Jesus' face in my mind's eye, I feel at home, in a house of belonging. He answers questions I don't know how to ask. He believes the best of me—a person I've yet to meet."

"Most 'love' is infatuation, dear. The cure for this kind of love is to know the other person better. Expectations for *pure* love are premeditated resentments, that's it. But if *this* love, *this* Jesus, is your other half, I'd not let him go."

"Antonio, I've tried. Believe me, I've tried *hard*. But he won't have me. He speaks of a 'higher destiny.'" I stabbed the air with quote marks.

Antonio raised his eyebrows, quizzical.

"For a peasant bagman who carries rocks and dead bodies up a hill, he's literate, Antonio. He speaks, reads, and writes perfect Egyptian, Latin, Aramaic, and Hebrew. He seems to understand what he's reading. Which is more than me, most of the time."

Antonio pursed his lips. "Hmm, and you're a quintessential smarty-pants, Claudia."

I soaked in his praise and kept talking. "On the other hand, he talks to an invisible Father and snakes, who listen and obey him! Really, do we have potions to cure this?"

Antonio shrugged. "Snakes didn't obey me when I was a boy."

I scratched an itch. "He might be crazy, but he's crazy like a fox. He sees right into me, like he can read my thoughts sometimes, and weirder yet feels my feelings before I do. He said Father made us all from clay and breath. I think his piece of clay and mine were side by side in a primordial clay pit when Father blew us up. Time passed, and our clay pieces found each other. Zap! We combusted into separate fires."

Antonio shook his head. "More likely this, he's an incarnation of Janus, the double-faced god of endings and beginnings, transitions, doorways. You could write this play. Even be the female lead. You're so *good* at drama. You'd become immortal!"

"You've been dipping into Julia's wine, tutor. At best, he sees me as some bit player in *his* play. Breaks my heart. I want to make him love me! But he's very sensitive to anyone devious, so I don't know why he gets within a mile of me."

Antonio actually laughed. "At least you're being honest about being dishonest. Lot to be said for that. Why not use these skills to twist Grandpa around your little finger?"

Hm. He had a point.

"Maybe this peasant could make himself valuable, prophesying time and place of uprisings across the empire, time and place of life and death. Perhaps he could go to Rome with you, perhaps marry, until he becomes inconvenient. Suck a share of immortality from this god, then divorce. As they say, 'If pleasures fly, let marriage die.'"

I closed my eyes. The lesson had changed from Plato to family politics, with a side lesson in devious fidelities. *We Italians were hopeless.*

23

JESUS

It was midafternoon, hot enough to fry an egg on the rocks. Our switchback goat path up the cliff face topped out directly past a shade tree where Cynico had planted himself. The sergeant scowled each time we went by. After a dozen trips up and down, Cynico called Laz over. "Hey, you, Jew-boy, come here!"

Laz walked over to him, a bag of rubble on his back. A fret was stitched into the smile on Laz's face as he lowered his bag to the ground. "You mean me, Sergeant?"

Cynico matched Laz's smile but added a slit of slyness. "Yeah, you. You did some Jew rite with a half-caste Go-Go girl, huh?"

Laz appeared oblivious to danger. "Indeed! I'm betrothed to be married in six months to a lovely Jewess, sir."

I stumbled against Laz, discreetly trying to push him out of harm's way, but harm had blocked our path.

Cynico taunted, "You know your little whore's been screwing half us guards in Sepphoris and most of you Jews at SepphBro? Mighty generous of you to settle for sloppy seconds, maggot."

Laz gulped, a fish out of water. His face turned beet red under his bronze tan. His fists knotted. Neck cords popped out. He looked ready to swing.

Cynico's sausage-sized fingers gripped his short sword. A wild boar on a long leash.

Heat radiated toward me, through me, front to back, back to front. I felt one demon's grinding presence in particular, a spirit called Serpico. I'd seen him floating around the patch. He now gyrated in and out of Cynico, below his navel.

Windy beamed hate through me directly into this demon, speaking words I didn't know I knew. *Get gone. Not Laz's time to die. Not yet.*

The spirit howled out and away, his shriek heard only by those who had ears to hear. Cynico's rigid shoulders slumped into sullen meanness.

His boss rounded a corner and called, "Sergeant, get over here. I have a job for you!"

Before Cynico left, he grabbed my wispy beard with his ham-sized fist, spraying spit onto my pimply cheeks. "I remember you. That row of cruci-fixions… Naz. Yeah, you worked some whacko magic. One guy died way too early. Now you're at it again, doing weird stuff." He shoved me over his outstretched foot. I sprawled on the path sideways.

Laz helped me back to my feet. "Is what he told us true, Jeez?"

I looked my best friend straight in the eyes. "Abishag told me the same thing today on the way here. Two witnesses, Laz—truth. Even if we don't like truth or the witnesses."

Laz shook his head woefully. "Sure sounds like Hosea with Gomer. God called him to husband *that* whore. And now me, with Go? Is that my destiny too?"[8]

Windy feathered a touch on my shoulder. I said, "Your destiny is Father's business—revealed just to you."

"Oh, come on," Laz said. "Finagle Father's will outta Him with some divine doodah. I need to know."

I ghosted a quick smile at him, then Windy spirited away my humor. "Hosea had his own life, and so do you."

Laz stared into the mid-distance, shaken. "So … Go or no Go?"

"Laz, I don't know. I doubt my visions, even for myself. My own thoughts often feel out of my control. Father and His Spirit talk to me, through me. When I'm down, I wonder if I'm deranged. Other times I know what I know."

He looked at me thoughtfully. "You've always been different than my other friends, Jeez. You're often preoccupied. Then you're the life of the party. That's always been your way ever since I've known you."

"Yeah, you're right," I said, suddenly shy. "Strong winds blow through my thoughts, pull me into the ether. Other times I see faraway things, like a hawk, and swoop to ground, nailing my prey. Like with Serpico, the demon, just now. He wanted to use Cynico to kill you."

"Ah! So that's who you were talkin' to, quiet-like?"

"Yes. The more I fast and pray, the better I get at throwing out demons. Better than I was, not as good as I'll be. We all have to practice our gifts. Works in progress, both of us. And hey, we're barely seventeen."

"You're a different piece of work than me."

I nodded. "But Father's given you gorgeous Go, not me."

"The law commands me to have her stoned."

A memory flashed. "This is different, but you know my mother was pregnant with me during her betrothal to Abba. You've heard the taunts about her being a whore, right?"

Laz's ears got red. He studied his feet.

"When she started to show, people were telling Abba to have her stoned. But he had a dream, put him on a different track."

"Well, tell me, what happened?"

"An angel in a dream said to him, 'Mary's not had sex with a man, but God.' Abba believed what the angel told him in the dream. Pretty incredible, huh?"

Laz whistled. "So. Let me get this straight. A beautiful fourteen-year-old woman comes to her thirty-year-old fiancé, tells him that God had sex with her? He was in his right mind, still believed her?"

I grinned. "Maybe God will speak to *you* in a vision or dream."

Laz wrinkled up his brow. "God does strange things in strange ways. A few minutes ago, I wanted to kill a man. Then I thought of killing my betrothed. Then I learned you came from a woman who'd never had sex with a man. Then you implied I might want to husband a woman who's had sex with every man in town."

He bit off the top of a thumbnail. "Today's been so weird. I'm relieved no one got killed. Like me, for instance. That would have wrecked my whole day."

He paused to see if I was listening. "What we learned today is cause for killing her."

"You're right, Laz. But eye for eye and tooth for tooth leads to a blind and toothless people. It's the path of death. Our warrior training is different."

Laz looked interested. "I'm pretty good with a bow and arrow, but not much with a sword."

"El Abba's training is different—inner warfare, different sword. Windy's razor-sharp sword slices garbage out of our heads, scalpels out old regrets, future dread."

"Jeez, hard to stay focused on that kind of battle."

"Focus on what Father is doing right now. Kingdom work requires absolute attention.[9] Windy's always doing her work, and nothing's never happening."

24

GO

Day's drizzle grayed into night and skipped the sunset completely. Rain beat a feathery rhythm on our mud-block shanty. I kissed Leah good-bye but left her with no candles, no lanterns. Light was expensive.

I went to work and waited only a few minutes for my first customer. Cynico stormed into room three and yelled, "You'd *dump me* for that moron Jew?"

Before I knew what hit me, I'd been hog-tied. Starbursts of pain spread through my head from his hob-nailed boots. Jaw and cheekbone busted, ribs cracked, hand stomped on, back lashed.

The last thing I remember was wailing, "Mercy, Cyn, please, mercy."

Maybe Leah was praying for me, maybe Jesus. Pain hazed mind-fog through me, sounds of Cyn slamming out the door. I laid on the floor, snot streaming, trickles of blood running across the floor. I rocked back and forth between the bed and wall.

Sepphbro's madame checked in, saw how bad her merchandise had gotten busted up. She took a few coins out of my pay and threw the rest my way.

"You're giving us a bad name, girl. I took the cost of repairing this mess out of your wages. Now that it's good and dark, I'll have 'em pull a cart up behind the back door. Don't come back."

I threw on my street clothes, veiled up, and slipped out the backdoor.

I'd gone from money maker to money loser in one hour.

I felt each rut in the road on the way home. The guard dumped me at the front door of our hut. Ach wasn't home. I crept in, lit a candle. Little sister was horrified when she saw me. She tended my wounds and put me to bed. She held my head in her lap, stroking my hair with her hand.

The only other thing I remember from that time was a nightmare—not one I *wanted* to remember, but the only one I couldn't forget.

Ma, at heaven's gate, holding her own bloody head in shackled hands, her neck just a ragged stump. She rapped her own head on the gate. *The head asked, "Can I come in?" Gabriel stuck his flaming angel head out the wicket door, looked her up and down, then slammed shut the needle's eye. The sound of bolts being thrown echoed off heaven's gates and bounced down the path sign-posted to hell.*

Heaven knew Ma and me were made of dirt. Pretty dirt, but still dirt. Ma didn't live to be a memory, but that's what she'd become. She'd stamped my memory with her image and passed on.

Before she died, she'd showed me how to milk rage bulls like Cyn. She taught what she knew—music and bedroom skills. She also taught something else—a bred-in-the-bone rage for men.

I was a good student, huh, Ma?

And now, today, my birthday—sweet sixteen. Two choices dangled in front of me. Chase Laz's snot-nosed kids around a hardscrabble backyard and die like other pruned-up desert women at thirty. Or sneak out the back door and join Ma and other long-lost ghosts wandering through hell.

A knock on the door interrupted my private bitch session. Leah answered the door while I watched a cockroach weave its way in and out of cracks in the wall.

"Surprise!" Laz brayed. "Jeez and me, we've come to visit. Glad to see us, li'l sis?"

Leah asked them to wait. She whispered, "Guess who's at the door?"

Like I hadn't heard, right? No other exit from this roach coach, no handy fig leaves. So, I got out of bed, every muscle screaming.

Leah helped me to a reclining position on the dirt floor along one side of our table. She invited the two men inside and served tea, thin-sliced rye bread, and slivers of hard cheese.

The others also reclined around the low table. I sat up, stiff-backed. Not gonna take this lying down, no sir. I felt their eyes boring into me— my purpled-shut right eye, stinging, rope-burned neck, a jagged jaw that didn't want to work, busted hand, fat lip.

"Go, we know. We know about Sepphbro." Laz rested his hand on mine. "Abishag, the woman who worked room three before you, told Jeez. And Cynico himself told me yesterday. No more hiding that. But what happened to you?"

Image of a cut glass, dropped on a stone floor. I hid my broken hand under the table, said nothing.

Leah said, "Cyn caught up with her." She told my story for me, even mentioned where Ach kept my earnings in a box under his bed wrapped in a silk robe.

Jesus shook his head slowly. His eyes puddled.

Laz looked squarely at me. "If you'll have me, I still want to marry you."

The shock I didn't show, Jesus did. His mouth dropped open. He faced Laz with what seemed to me like wonder. No one here was over seventeen, but it seemed to me we were all playing way over our heads. The silence was broken only by the sound of Leah's fingernails getting a raggedy chew down.

I stared at some point beyond Laz's head. Then I said something that surprised me, 'You don't know me, Laz. I'm already spoken for. Married. The first time Ach took me, I was eight or nine. My body... she married Shame that day. I looked the other way. I knew Shame so much, so many times, he split me into many."

I looked up. My eyes skittered around the circle. Then quick, eyes down again. I barked out a laugh. "I'm royalty now. Queen of my own walled state—many burrows. We all dug in, rooted, had Shame babies."

One of my younger me's, Escape, floated up beyond those talking people. Became air, twisted memories. A little older part of me, Cutter, pulled out mother's paring knife, and scratched open a vein. This red line joined all the others, making a crosshatch, filling up the inside of our left forearm. We felt calmer now, calm enough to remember our rules—*Don't feel the stain. Act out your name. Don't stay, just Go.*

25

JESUS

Four of us teens sat in a square around their rickety table—twitcher, sniffler, weeper, stoner. Laz twitched. Leah whimpered. I wept. Go froze.

I sat on Go's left and sucked in frost from her cold front. Leah's hot grief slammed into my body from the opposite direction. I felt the whiplash of one sister's denial and the other's lament.

Go made a face, cussed. She checked for my reaction and kept talking. "Don't screw with me, Laz. We're done. You know it. No future. Not now, not ever. Never. I'm already taken."

I popped a full, hot pimple on my forehead and wiped away the goo. Checked with Windy, *is she demon possessed? Do I cast them out?*

Windy said, *no, Son, not demons, not this time. Just a fractured self in need of healing. But not like Laz's fractured leg. More complicated. I'll say more later. Right now, be present.*

Laz sat up stiff, lips tight. "I still want to marry you. We'll work out all this Shame stuff as we go."

Go ranted. "My darling betrothed! You can't take my cutting, much less, all my me's."

She held her left wrist with her right hand, blood seeping through her fingers. A blood-stained knife clattered to the floor beside her. "I'm not here for your saint parties. Mother taught us Torah—in between screwing Moab's king and chief rabbi, believe it or not. I will *not* make you look like Hosea-the-Hero. Hosanna, Hosea!"

She fake-bowed in his direction, and her voice elevated into a falsetto, sarcastic serenade. "Oh! Did you hear how wonderful, kind, generous Laz scooped up whoring Gomaria off the street and married her? What a wonderful human being he is!" Go skipped a beat, eyes rolling. "But her, poor dear, what a sad, sad story. And did you hear what happened to her mother?"

As she sucked in a sharp mock breath, her hands now waving in front of her, a spray of blood landed on my face. "Why, no! Tell me all about this, so we can pray for her, of course."

I felt my cheek. My tears and Go's blood fingered down my face.

Laz's lower lip kept twitching.

Leah's hand covered her mouth, and her ears pickled purple.

Windy breathed into me, *Son, you feel what Go refuses. She sees your your tears, and they soften her soil. Your love, one day, will meld her pieces together, slow by slow.*

Go stormed, "Nope, Laz. Not copping to your pretty pimped-up, pumped-up Shabbat-the-Saint act. Let me be my straight-up, screwed-up whoring self, without a savior in sight." She wound down a mite. "May not live long, just like Mama. Won't go slow, either. I'll be quick about it, go in my own decent, skanky way."

Leah started sobbing, wrapped her arms around her big sister. "Don't, Go. Don't go."

Go's shoulders melted like wax in a furnace, softened by Leah's sad love for her. They collapsed into each other's sadness—no room for men inside that huddle.

We men took a few steps and bent low over the two sisters. Laz gently lifted Go. I carried Leah. Together, we tucked them, still weeping, into their shared bed.

Laz and I reclined back at the table to consider the best path forward. We talked in murmurs. A plan came into being.

Laz and I walked to Moshe's house, knocked. No one answered—a rainy night, and late. I kept knocking.

Moshe looked out the window. "Can't this wait till morning? Esther and I, at last, have some time together." His eyebrows raised twice in a little jerky motion.

I persisted. "Moshe, if this weren't an emergency, we would not bother you."

The Rav wavered, caved, shut the window. A minute later, his front door swung open. Laz and I ducked under the low lintel and made our way into the kitchen, sitting on a low bench around the family's dining table. Buttery light from a single lantern spilled over the table's center. Rav poured each of us a glass of leftover Shabbat wine.

I was quick, dished out the dirt in thin, clean lines. Soldiered facts forward, one after another. Mentioned all Go's earnings were kept in a SepphBro box under Ach's bed.

Moshe commented, "Another Achan, another Valley of Achor, eh?" He lapsed into silence. "What do you want to be done with your betrothed?"

"I'm not pressing charges," Laz said. "As you said yourself, we all have had adultery in our hearts even if we haven't acted on it."

Moshe nodded, staring into his drink. "Witnesses surely heard and saw the goings-on at SepphBro last night. Gomaria's identity was made public. Elders will likely vote to stone her."

Laz countered, "Can't stone someone who's not here. Give Go and me time to disappear tomorrow—no, later today, in an hour or two."

The Rav's face was solemn, textured in the candlelight. Shadows filled valleys between his ridges. Light glinted on his eye closest to the lantern. He hunched over, absolutely still, weighing his choices.

I broke the silence. "Laz, Go, and Leah need to leave town very soon. Cyn injured Go so badly that she can't walk. She'll ride our family's donkey. Laz and Leah will walk alongside. Can you stall a final decision tomorrow? Allow time enough for them to get gone down the road?"

Moshe seemed to measure the crosscurrents of conviction and desire within him, sifted between our streams of light and the shadows we cast. "Don't tell me where you're going. I don't want to lie when they ask me if I know where you are. Sometimes a man has to hold two opposites in his hands and not drop either of them. This is one of those times. Mitzpah."[10]

26

LEAH

An hour or so passed. Go drowsed. And, I packed. We had to get out of this dump. Had to.

A knock at the front door. I opened it. Laz and Jesus stood there, along with a mule loaded down with stuff. A moon shadow fell on the ground behind them.

Pa had arrived from the opposite direction. He moved to their side and slurred, "Hey, whatcha two doin' here this time of night?"

Drunk-walking, drunk-talking man.

"Get yer ass gone."

Jesus put his right hand on Laz's back.

Laz said, "Ach, let's go inside. We have an emergency."

Pa was defiant. "We'll talk after I've sobered up. Get outta here."

Laz approached Pa, eyeball to eyeball. "You've heard the news about Cyn beating the crap out of Go?"

Pa dropped his head. "Ain't no secret now."

"The elders meet soon. Most likely, they'll vote to stone Go, and you know, maybe you too—for incest."

Pa's tone escalated into panic. "Nobody said nutin' 'bout me sexin' Go! You got no proof. No proof! Only proof's Go's a whore, like her ma!"

A neighbor followed his candle out of his front door, nightcap on. "Ach, shut up with your bellyaching, will ya? We're trying to sleep."

Laz stepped back, out of Pa's personal space. A good move. Pa was a street fighter from way back. Even drunk as a skunk, Pa could probably thrash him.

I was surprised when Laz braved forward. "We can do this the easy way or the hard way. Hard way is to get into a big fight. Or we go inside, work it out. What do you want?"

I felt like we were teetering on the top of a steep hill.

I heard Jesus whisper, "*Father, invade earth. Do your will. Here, now.*"

Pa backed up a step, opened the front door, and walked in. He left the door open a crack.

Laz and Jesus came in behind him and closed the door. Laz went to Go, who'd come up behind me at the door. He took her a few steps away, against the wall, and positioned himself between her and Pa. She sighed, used the wall for support. Jesus stood between Pa and me.

Pa sized up the situation. "I see how 'tis. You's turned my precious girls against me."

Jesus looked at Pa. "Remember our talk on the way to work?"

"Maybe. Make it quick. I'm wasted."

"Your ancestors Agag and Haman … sexual predators. Your father trafficked women. Your wife died in that trade. Your daughter could be next. Generations shamed and sacrificed by sex."

Pa flinched and looked down. Didn't argue.

Laz said, "Go and Leah need to leave town with me, now, or she'll be stoned later today. You can seek your future here or elsewhere. Choose."

I couldn't stand the tension, so I looked at a fly crawling on the ceiling, watched a roach scuttle into a corner, and smelled Pa's wine-reek.

Pa fell to the floor, banged his head on the floor, over and over. "Go. Get gone."

Sister took a tiny step toward the door. Go and I picked up the two ratty bundles I'd packed.

Jesus spoke into the darkness.

I dragged my eyes to where he was looking and saw what looked like a ripple in the air.

Jesus said, "Leave this man. Leave him to his own consequences."

A foul stink, like poo, blew past me and disappeared in the night.

Right before Jesus swept out the door, he spoke, "Turn around, Ach. Repent. Then the Father will be with you."

Pa was *not* listening. He was crawling to his bed and rooting around under the mattress in the dirt floor. Checking to see if we'd thieved from him.

Outside, silvery light from a new moon poked through the scudding layers of cloud. The road to Bethany was silent as a new tomb. Sister rode sidesaddle with stuff stacked up fore and aft. She leaned sideways on cloth backpacks, dozed, then jolted awake, moaning. Laz and I supported her on either side. Jesus led Betsy, the mule.

We came to Scraggly Crags. Shadow of a man suddenly shot out, scaring the willies out of me. That man was quick as moonlight and disappeared if you looked at him sideways.

Jesus grinned. "Nearly pooped my pants just now, Rabbus."

He said, "Sorry, Jesus. I heard what happened at SepphBro. Abishag thought Go might beat it outta Naz. Thought you might need a bodyguard."

Laz spoke up. "Love to have you join us."

"Where ya going?"

"Hometown, Bethany. Ma's sister lives there with her family—settled, richies. They'll probably have enough work for two of us, I think, if you care to join."

Jesus told Rabbus, "The law kills. In this case, Go, if she stays put."

"No problem getting around the law," Rabbus said. "Love bein' a thief and murderer on the right side of the wrong laws, protecting sinners from the self-righteous."

My spine tingled. I felt relieved to be in bad hands. He seemed like the man for the hour, a thief with a conscience.

Rabbus picked up his backpack. "Good thing I travel light. Let's go."

Satin skies toward Nazareth fringed barest hints of light. Dawn wasn't far off. Ahead to the west, Sepphoris inked sheer black. Jesus sidled up next to me, looked up, and then back down again, gazing into my face.

He breathed out these words: "Go needs you and you, her. Rabbus needs you too but doesn't know it yet. I'll pray for fruit from your root."

I took a deep breath and smiled, even though I didn't know what he was talking about. A curious image flickered—Jesus, serving as a midwife during a delivery. A voice whispered, silky smooth in my ear, *Jesus is delivering your soul, birthing you into the life Father has waiting for you.* I shuddered, felt new born—like I was being born again into a wild new adventure.

I turned my attention outwards in time to see my "midwife" clasp both Laz's shoulders. He stood looking at him in the new moonlight. "Maybe your chuppah will be at Passover. Love to be present."

Laz looked confused. "Is that a hope, a command, or both?"

"All of them. Remember your warrior weapon, the one we spoke of earlier. Practice using Spirit's sword to hack away dread and worry. Walk well into night's not-knowing, brother."

Jesus also said to Rabbus, "My Spirit will be your guard."

Jesus turned around and headed back to Nazareth. We kept moving into the dark.

27

JESUS

I got to the outskirts of Nazareth, a town not yet awake. I rested under a gnarled oak tree. I was alone, except for the steady Wind that faithfully circled this dark world. Gradually night unwove itself and the light poked through. Sunflowers woke up in the field next to me. I felt one with them, our heads following the sun from morning to night, life from light.

Father materialized out of nowhere and sat beside me, his right arm draped around my neck. He kneaded my neck. His love flowed through his fingers into hollow places within me as he listened to me blubber along, unpacking my anger about Ach and Go.

Then he nourished me with strong words. *You are My beloved Son. You please Me so much, all the time, without fail.*

I shifted my position and laid my head in His lap. Father's words sang within me and I soaked in them. I felt my need of Him, bred in my bones. I felt my purposes renew, intentions seal, homesickness ebb, and resolve harden. Father revealed only the next step or two in my journey.[11]

I said, "Father, I want to know more. And then again, I don't. Please stay close, even if I can't see you. Be my forcing bed for faith."

Father squeezed tighter, enfolding me.

Spirit whirled around the two of us, a flaming tornado. He fed Father and me angel food cake in the still eye of the swirl. He kept the funnel in place while shapeshifting into a mother Lion, who circled her lair, keeping a protective boundary in place for me.

Windy whispered to me, "See over there? Hear that guttural howl? That's Satan roaring. Today he's mimicking a lion. He roars because Father pulled his teeth. All he's got left is his roar that he uses to intimidate. Can you see? Now he squinting in Our direction. All he sees is a whirling, white-hot furnace inside a tornado, under an old oak tree."

Moshe sat in the stone chair beside the ruined village gates. Behind him, cerulean skies stretched forever, broad as Sinai's massive western flank. This was Nazareth's place of judgment. The synagogue stood in front of him and the half-burned gate behind him. A minyan of nine other male elders sat with him. Younger men milled, their mouths buzzed, waspish with indignation. Temple guards loafed on the shady side of the stoning pit, leaning on their shovels.

Moshe convened the meeting by looking to the elders. "We all know why we are here today at this special council. One of you speak it aloud."

A senior graybeard spoke. "Gomaria, the Jewess-Amalekitess, shamed our community by whoring for hire among the heathen. Bring her for judgment!"

Seven elders brayed agreement—vociferi with bugles. Only Abba and Moshe sat silent. Abba caught sight of me leaning against a column of the synagogue and nodded in my direction.

I listened to legal words pour through broken pots. Moshe was an exception—he was a whole, double-spouted pot, pouring grace and law from the same vessel at the same time.

He asked, "Who witnessed her actions?"

Elders fell silent, eyes hooded.

Menachim called out, "Common knowledge. Everyone at SepphBro witnessed with their ears what was happening upstairs—breaking furniture, screams of lust and desire. Sickening!"

Everyone in our village knew his marriage had devolved into desert bake, icy patches, and flaming eruptions, with paid sex on the sly. No one spoke what they knew. This was Nazareth's unspoken code, with very few exceptions. *We'll overlook bad behavior as long as you don't shame us by making it public.*

Menachim said, "I was in Sepphoris on business. Her father and I passed by Priapus Gate, opposite sides of the same street. A piece of furniture flew out the window, almost hit me. Go get him, along with Gomaria. He can be the other male witness."

Moshe motioned for the two burly temple guards to come. He whispered in one guard's ear. The pair left. They were gone for a long time. Finally, Achan appeared, but without Gomaria. Menachim asked where she was. The guards shrugged.

Menachim shoved Achan to his knees. "Tell us, Amalekite, what your Jewish daughter has been doing at SepphBro."

A pile of stones, about the size of a man's fist, rested beside each elder.

"Yes, yes. Go worked there," Ach gibbered. His face shifted a bit, became more hopeful. "I had her mother stoned for whoring. Go's *just* like her mother. You could stone her too."

Moshe held his head at an angle and raised an eyebrow at one of the guards. The guard nodded. Moshe returned his gaze to Achan. "Do you deny profiting from her prostitution?"

"Oh, my lord," Ach cried out, "I would never do that to any daughter of Israel!"

"Well then, what of this?" Moshe pointed at a wooden box that the guard then handed him, a box wrapped in a silk, purple robe. He took it out of the robe. The box bore the SepphBro logo. He emptied its contents. Silver coins showered the ground.

"The two guards testified that they found this buried beneath your bed."

Ach shrieked loudly and fell on his back, spittle flying, mouth foaming. Then he snapped to his feet and stared wide-eyed, pointing directly at me.

28

WINDY

Everyone's eyes followed Ach's pointing finger. Sudden swirls of air from my fingertips whipped dust angels all around the synagogue. Ach was mystified. His forefinger now pointed directly at an empty spot where Jesus had been standing only a moment before.

Ach panicked. He shouted, "God's own Son, Jesus the Messiah, claimed my girl for himself!"

A Roman tribune galloped by toward Sepphoris, roiling the wind. The elders heard only the sound of those hoofbeats, as well as inchoate rants from Ach's mouth.

Ach howled louder, louder, "Jesus the Messiah! He took her to his bed!"

By the time these words fell on elders' ears, they too had become gibberish. Ach's ranting caught fire, sparking indignation through the public square. Rogue spirits, Satan's local mafia, had joined the gathering. They drooled over human heart meat, stropped butchers' blades.

The same two temple guards trotted back to Mal's house at Moshe's request. They renewed their search for Go. Many in the crowd joined them, combing the village in vain. This took a very long time. Men paced, nostrils flaring, bulls scoring the ground with sharpened hoofs.

Ach writhed. Once he popped off the ground, as if spring-loaded, to see if they had found a substitute for his sins. Alas, no savior was in sight. The guards also returned, empty-handed.

Moshe circled Ach, called for silence, and then spoke. "Your daughter is missing, along with her betrothed. You pointed at another to take your guilt, but only you saw him. We cannot convict the invisible. You, on the other hand, have admitted to capital crimes in our law—incest and sex trafficking. Do you deny this admission?"

Ach bounced about on the ground, flopping this way and that. Demons within him screamed, "No, no, no!" His own, softer voice, murmured, "Not me, not me."

Ach's flagrant foul begged for retribution. Elders gripped their rocks tighter, gaining energy from consensus. Ach's dance changed course, inexplicably. He aimed himself toward the stoning pit. All mortals present speechlessly eyed Ach as he jitterbugged straight to the edge, tumbling himself into the pit.

The villagers' chant escalated. "Stone him. Stone him! *Stone* him!"

Menachim led any who'd caught the killing blood lust. He held up a scroll head high, then opened it to the verse that commands stoning for sexual sin.[12] He grinned through his hatred. A righteous echo chamber boomed within and around him. He scratched his nose with the pointed end of a glittering shale stone in his right hand, his throwing hand. Scroll and stone rocked up and down in either hand, a feverish rhythm. Both amulets guarded him against the energies of Love.

Menachim's strident tone splashed urgency over the crowd like a thundershower. His words didn't need to make sense. What counted was his spellbinding cadence of surety, waving hands, and bulging neck blood vessels. Such oratory served to ensure agreement of even a wholesale massacre of innocents.

Temple guards had never been so well assisted. They ricocheted between amusement and amazement. They looked at Moshe, inquiring.

He nodded.

They dropped into the pit, bound Ach's hands behind him, and shoveled dirt back into the pit up to his neck. Tamped the dirt down. Only Ach's head was exposed. It whipped back and forth, mouth frothing, senses evacuated.

A fast-moving cloud passed over this wild-eyed stalk, sticking up from the killing garden.

"May God have mercy on your soul!" Moshe cried.

Father and I had mercy on him, but the crowd did not.

Bone fragments flew, tangled with goo. Skull shortened on its stump. Bits of Ach stuck to Menachim, who stood on the pit's edge. Ach's spirit flew into outer darkness. He zoomed past where I waited for him, not yet ready to accept My mercy.

Guards dug him out of the pit, wrapped their hands in rags, and collected shards of Ach's skull. They re-formed the goop into the shape of a head and reunited Ach to his body. Together they wrapped his body in burlap and trundled him on a cart to an unmarked grave. They tipped Ach's body into the grave and threw the cloth over him, followed by dirt. Once he was covered, each guard lit a smoke and leaned on his shovel, exhausted by Love's absence.

29

JESUS

I was confused. Only Windy and I were present, walking on high chaparral. She wore a swirling set of gossamer veils over shiny red dance shoes. "Where are we, Windy?"

"Loud-mouthed demons were blowing your cover, Jesus. I had to dance you out the back door."

"You're as beautiful as you are quicksilver fast."

"That I am. And always willing to fling away my seven veils, but only for those desperate to see."

"You're like a diamond dancing in the root of a tree, or twinkles dancing in the stars."

"Yes, and *you* have a way with words. Either way, whether you or Me, one show ticket per customer, but no expiry date."

"Where's Father?" I asked.

"Father, ah, you know Him. He loves to stay hidden behind all the gifts He throws our way."

We enjoyed the quiet.

After a while, Windy said, "Take a squint on the horizon. See who's coming our way?"

Four tiny figures headed toward us, walking on a ribbon of a road along a flattened gash in the earth.

"Yes! That's them! Rabbus, Laz, and Leah steadying Go on Betsy. Thanks for watching over them, Windy."

"Ah, watch-care is Father's job, dear boy. He's so good at keeping you humans safe from yourselves and the devil. He speaks. I make it happen. He's such a joy, hanging whole galaxies on tiny threads. Keeping this quartet safe is child's play."

She paused. "And Rabbus, such a stitch, thinking that he's the hulking bodyguard!"

Windy changed into a stormtrooper and blew around the desert hilltop in a cyclone of impersonation, dragging his knuckles behind him, whipping his head back and forth with a twitchy, glazed gaze—a stiletto stick in his hand he'd snatched off the ground.

I cracked up at the improv, hilarity in harmony. My tension drained out of me. His joy flowed into me.

He laughed at my laughter, a perfect mirror. "You gotta love that Rabbus. His heart's in the right place these days, now that you befriended him."

"Yeah, I wonder what's going to happen with him."

He became She and shrugged. "Dunno. That's Father's gig. Just trust Him to do Our plan His way. We planned our work, and now We work our plan—each of Us in sync doing this whirly-gig dance we do. But I got to hand it to you, Son. You got the hardest job right now, doing your part blindfolded and walking a cliff's edge. Faith in Father's rhythms and my stepping your feet. We offer you minimum protection and maximum love in this dance of life."

"If I didn't do this here and now, Windy, how would all those others in our plan, before me, behind me, ever have a chance in this dance?"

"Simple, Son—they wouldn't." She hugged me, with a flash in her eye. "We three divide and conquer for the Kingdom—one in heart, three in function. But for My money, honey, you've got the toughest donkey ride!" She goosed me a good one, tuned up some music from within her, and upskilled my hora.

It took a while for my lesson to take, but when Father joined us, things sped up. He and Windy linked left arms with me, right arms stretched up and out, torsos leaning back, and right legs stretched straight out—a kaleidoscope of perfect, flashing triangles.

The setting sun, a warped tangerine crown, shimmered behind us. Each of us showed the others off to best advantage. Anyone looking from a distance would have thought a star, pulsing light, was visiting a dark planet and teaching its creatures how to dance.

I was quickly exhausted, but Father and Windy were just warming up. He looked at Her, beamed a thought. *Let's take a break, for Jesus' sake.*

She replied with a wink. *Amen.*

We settled down on the desert butte, stars thick as shattered crystal chandeliers sprayed across the cosmos. Father's heartbeat sounded like joy thrumming from a cosmic kettledrum.

Windy gave me a jug of ice-cold tea, laced with honey nectar. I chugged it.

"I know you're dehydrated," Father said, "but you're also thirsty."

"For you, Father, thirsty for you."[13]

Father and Windy said nothing further for a long time. They leaned into me, one on each side of me—a God sandwich looking into the night sky. Twinkles of light scattered across the night's tapestry, enough to fill a trillion darknesses.

"Windy, Father, You're so kind to all of us on this earth."

Father held both my shoulders in his hands, solemnly looked into my eyes. "We are. We are what you need Us to be. We journey with you, whether you see Us or not. Most people in the middle won't see you or stick with you. Those on the edges will see you most clearly—the blind, poor, foreigners, even the demons. *Pay no attention to creatures* who praise you, whether from the edge or middle. What counts is this—We who journey with you."

Windy looked at Father. "Enough of our Trinalogue. Jesus, you and Me, gotta blow. Only Father's totally in the know, and earth time's a tickin'."

Immediately I was absented from Father's overview, blown by Windy's mobile view, and woke up to my under view—inside my worksite tent. It was morning. I yawned, looked up at the sun slanting through the canvas flap. I got up to go pee, then followed my nose over to the campfire to see what was for breakfast.

30

JESUS

Cousin John and I worked the last villa in the row of collapsed homes. A gentle wind rippled the wheat fields, their sheaves whitening toward harvest. John was compact and a bit surprised looking, wild-eyed, like a possum that had tripped over a lightning bolt. His jet-black hair was untamed, no matter how much he splashed water over his head to smooth it back. Coarse strands of thick hair poked straight out from his skull at odd angles—brilliant thoughts gone ballistic. His ideas, under pressure, seemed to blast through tiny hair follicles without benefit of social timing.

I had just gotten back from Egypt when I first really got to know my cousin. I remember the day when Beninah, my friend, pulled me aside at recess and said, "I don't know how John memorizes Torah so fast! I'm only halfway through some boring genealogy in Leviticus, and he's already chanting the imprecatory psalms."

He mimicked John's head bobbing up and down. "'God, hurl my enemies' children off the highest walls!' The way he said it, eyes boring holes in me, I felt like chopping off his head—just to get him to shut up."

Beninah's younger sister, Tamara, spoke up. "His uncle Zeb, the Essene, is so weird. And John's just like him—smart-weird. He got that way after he came back from those years in the desert with his uncle after his parents died."

"And one more thing," Beninah said. "John leaves. I'll be talking to him over lunch, take a bite of my falafel, then look up, and he's gone. Ghosted. Maybe you can help with this, Jesus. I mean, what to do?"

I shrugged. I didn't know what to do with John any more than they did. I had no memories of John's abba, Zachariah. Ma mentioned he was "socially challenged," with a priestly flare.

Not that I was any better than John. For example, like John, I didn't know what to do with girls. I was a complete idiot most of the time in seventh grade, particularly with cute girls. Like that time in seventh grade when Tamara caught me popping my zits.

She'd said, "Eww. Gross!" She flounced off, but the next day she sat next to me at lunch.

So here we two were, in the trenches, trying to figure out how normal teenagers should act.

John asked me, "How do you get girls to like you? I can't figure that one out."

"When you dress in skins—you know, the ones you've liberated from their prior owners, they give off an odor of rotting flesh that arrives before you do. Girls might not like that."

He looked up and to the right, considered. "Really? Hadn't thought about that. I thought they were the coolest ever."

I added, "Also, your diet's a little weird. When you catch locusts and lizards, fry them up in grease, and pull them from your pouch for snacks? Girls don't think that's awesome, as a rule."

John scratched his head. "Locusts are very yum. Crunchy."

I said, "Locusts might not be high on their go-to snack list."

At some point in late morning, I got the strange sensation of strength being drained from me. I whirled around. I felt like someone had stuck a tap in me and started sucking strength from my bones. Where *was that* other smell and sucking coming from?

Windy breezed a thought into my inquiring heart. *Son, did you ever think that this drain might be your cousin? John doesn't have enough skin. His heart's been skinned. He doesn't know how to identify, feel, or express emotion. He needs other skins for protection from rejection or scary attachments to people.*

Huh. Hadn't ever thought about that. How to help?

Love the sprout inside the seeds, Son. John ignores all his feeling seeds. Help him feel felt.

I waited for more. Nothing else came.

I said aloud, "Okay, Windy, I'll try."

John looked over at me. "Say something, Jesus?"

I looked inward and upward, answered outward—all with one inspiration and exhalation. "I've never come right out and asked, but how did you feel about your parents' deaths? You were only four when your abba passed, then a year later, your ma."

John looked like he had a case of locust indigestion. Then he weirded me out with the tone of his answer. He launched words in the air, disembodied, like Rabbus had done when I asked him about *his* past. "It was their time. They were old. I was born out of season."

I listened in my best sprout-assisting posture. I wanted to speak, but Windy said, *Quiet now. Even you, the Word, must learn how silence speaks. Wrap Father's kindness around all your unspoken words. I'll breathe them out of you at the right time.*

John's stiff face softened after a while. "One of my only memories of Abba is sneaking up on him when I had just turned four. He sat cross-legged, facing the window with a pool of light on the scroll. I came up back of him, put my hands over his eyes from behind, and said, 'Guess who's here, Abba?'

"He made up names. 'Is this Jonah?'

"'Noooo.'

'Is this Moses?'

"'Noooo.'

'Is this Sampson?'

"I giggled and came out around from his side. 'Yes! See my big muscles, Abba?'"

John was silent for almost a full minute, eyes closed as if remembering. One eyelid quivered.

I leaned forward, said nothing.

"Abba fell over laughing and held me close. I climbed onto his chest, held him down, a four-year-old Sampson.

"He looked into my face. 'Your name is not Jonah, Moses, Sampson, or anybody else. No, your name is John. Yes, John. That's your name. Let's not forget that, you ... or me.'"

John cleared his throat, then turned half a face toward the wind rippling through the wheat fields. Tears trickled down his cheeks. "Abba died soon after that. I found him, almost same spot where we had wrestled. His head was on his chest. Sunlight streamed through the window, angling down on the Torah on his lap.

"You were still down in Egypt, Cousin."

I felt a fundamental kindness for him. "Thanks for trusting me with that."

His eyes misted at that moment, like mine. "Most people would dog me with sympathy. 'Oh, what a poor boy!' Or maybe use my story to talk about their lives. You didn't do that. I feel like something got fixed."

We went back to work. Most of the energy suck was gone. John was back in his part of the hole, and I worked the other end. Dirt flew up and out of the trench from both of us. We sang a worship song together, harmonizing.

Windy intoned, *Well done, Son. You're helping him sprout. And, by the way, that energy suck was more than just John.*

31

WINDY

Claudia circled the last villa, playing hooky from her classes, devoutly seeking trouble. She sat in the wheat field, watching Jesus. Who was this creepy specimen with him? Totally disgusting. Worse than the last horn dog. Well, at least Laz wasn't impersonating a hyena with a loincloth. This new guy was beyond weird.

She smoothed the soft silk tunic with its pink and purple floral pattern, the one she'd borrowed from her mother. A size too big, but the floppy front left more than a hint of cleavage. Checked her mirror and sniffed her pits. Added a dab more perfume. Okay, not bad. She made her move, sashaying out of the wheat field from two rows back. She headed for Jesus like her homing beam had just turned on—and he was home.

Jesus leaned on his shovel, watching her advance.

Claudia wrinkled her nose. "What's that smell around here?"

He played back. "Not sure, other than whatever perfume you're wearing. You've overwhelmed the flowers of the field for the past half hour."

She flinched. *How humiliating!*

He eyed the scroll sticking out of her bag. "Studying agriculture over there?"

"Very funny, Mr. Foundations. That is Socrates' play, *Antigone*. We get tested on it tomorrow."

She leaned in and whispered, "Who's Zoo Boy with the dreadlocks, down in the hole?"

John catapulted from the trench, wide-eyed at Jesus talking to a goy girl. He reached into his loincloth, pulled out a roasted locust, and popped it in his mouth with a loud crunch. Claudia struggled to manage her gag reflex.

"John, meet Claudia. Claudia, John."

He looked at Claudia. "His mother was my mother's aunt—known him since before dirt, really. Nobody in my book's greater."

"Hi there, John. Great hair. Don't know if I've met anyone with your taste in snack food. Unique."

"Th-thanks," John stammered. Dropped back in the hole. Dirt began to fly.

Jesus gazed down over the town below, shimmering in the noonday heat. He asked, "Aren't you supposed to be in class with your tutor now?"

"Well, of course. But I'm on a field trip—flowers of the field, that kind of thing. My friend Cress is going to join me soon for a picnic up there in the willow glade. Join us? We could use a Jewish point of view on these Greek guys."

"That would be fun. But your abba's not forking out good coin for my insights on Antigone. He wants these foundations dug deep, sure, and on time. Besides, this flirty game you play, way too scary. Even the appearance of evil and your father could stick me on a stake."

A shovelful of dirt grounded Jesus' feet. John, in the trench below, gave Son a thumbs-up.

In a blink, Claudia flipped her flirty face into a serious one. She looked around for prying eyes, then reached out and rested her hand on Jesus' shoulder. "Let's us two be careful with others. But please, let's not lie about what we feel for each other. That'd be a serious form of lying, huh, Mr. Truth Speaker?"

Claudia raked her eyes over Jesus, like a farmer scything a field.

"I really don't want to talk about homework. Grandpa spoke to me before he left. Something you said to him. And also, there's this dream. Can we talk? What about tonight, same place as last time?"

Jesus shot a request my way. *What now, Windy?*

I blew a bit of counsel his way. *Breathe. Get your skin back in the game here.*

I'm jittery.

Do you see how John and Claudia are alike?

They're anything but alike!

Really, Son? Both try on smells and clothing to see what defines them. John uses a pickax, and Claudia, tweezers. But they both change moods in a mo-

ment. Both are hormone-driven. Both are desperately trying to get comfortable inside their changing bodies. Remind you of anybody else you know, Son?

Okay, got it. We three are more alike than different.

Mm-hmm, Windy said. *And yes, by all means, meet with Claudia. Do you see the empty town square below you? And the town well there in the middle of the square? No one is there at noon. Tomorrow on your lunch break. An excellent time and place to meet for a drink!*

Jesus roused himself and looked over at Claudia.

She was staring at him. "Back again? You seemed otherworldly, for lack of a better phrase. But your silence did put a plug in my mouth, so I didn't keep blathering out into the world."

Jesus smiled. He wasn't the only nervous one in the field. "You know silent and listen are spelled with the same letters? I was silent, listening to Windy. He mentioned maybe we could meet this time tomorrow, down there at the well. Sit in the shade and have a drink?"

"You know how to pick your times and places."

"Safe spot. Probably nothing snaky hanging from an apple tree."

She rolled her eyes. "Okay, I'm dying to connect—even if that time is stinking hot and I'll smell like a rat drowned in its sweat, but all right. Tomorrow, noon, town well."

32

GO

A ll four of us travelers were bone tired and cranky. I begged to stop.

Rabbus said, "Nope, not safe here. In this Judean wilderness, men, snakes, and coyotes all fight for survival. Everyone does what's right in *their* eyes, not yours."

We had melted into a large caravan on the King's Highway, heading south. On this third day of our journey, we cut off the highway and took a goat trail west. I sat sidesaddle on Betsy, rolled with her slow amble beneath me. Fumes curled out of thick mud crusts. Sinkholes burped up hot, stinky sulfur.

Rabbus said, "Miss a step, you'll drop into the quick of that sand or boil to death in the bubbling sulfur."

We took an even fainter goat trail that led into a shadowed wadi. At the end of this narrowing canyon, under a waterfall, a jutting rock face hid a cave—cool, dark, and deep. The cave entry was marked by the smoke of many fires. The pool beneath the waterfall dropped a few ledges, each level with its pool. The stream disappeared underground after maybe twenty yards or so.

Rabbus told Laz, "Let's stay here a couple of days. We all could use the rest. Then we make the long climb into Jerusalem."

"Only if we find food," Laz said. "We've got nothing to eat. Let's go kill something."

Rabbus told the two of us, "Get a fire going. Settle in. We'll be back with dinner." He took his slingshot, and Laz took his bow and quiver of arrows. They walked into another arm of the wadi.

Leah and I meandered in different directions, gathering olives in the grove, herbs on the hills, and firewood. I found a gauzy white web forked between two low branches. A tiny, slick wing poked through the gauze, pulsing.

I heard these words come out of my mouth, "Go, girl. But tell me. How should all my me's get free from the web *I've* woven?"

A voice, not unkind, said from within that web, "It helps when you can't run. Try hanging upside down, in the dark. Stay still. But if you'll excuse me, I have work to do."

I looked around to see who was talking. Another, softer voice, in my inner ear. *Let the butterfly struggle. Strength comes with that struggle—for both of you.*

I sighed and scooped stream water with my dipper from the top pool, the deepest one. I filled Ma's iron kettle, the same pot that had been my pillow the last few nights on Betsy. I put Ma's pot next to an old fireplace and then studied the hills and woods. No staring eyes. I sat poolside at a lower pool, struggling out of my clothes, trembling into nakedness. When I lowered myself into in the cool spring, I cried out when a boulder scraped a cracked rib. Once in the water, I floated spread-eagle in pure, clear water beneath a mossy chute. Then I used my thin bar of soap to scrub dirt and the stink of fear off my skin. I also beat my pile of clothes into submission on the rocks.

Leah returned with a basket of olives, wild onions, mushrooms, eucalyptus leaves, and a few figs that were almost-ripe. She held up her goodies with her right hand while her left hand rose in a fist pump. She looked me over. "You're healing, Go! You look great in purple, yellow, and green."

I thought, *time won't heal what's in this web. It's a wonder that a heart so broken could go on beating at all.* I put on a bright smile and twirled for my sister, showing off my new colors and not my fracture lines. *Yeah, this is how it is. Better to hide my me's than be them. Much safer.*

Leah got naked, like me, and washed herself and her clothes clean under the waterfall. While our clothes dried, I showed Leah the cocoon and its occupant. We watched the creature flicker and flail, fail, rest exhausted, and try again. I watched her one exposed wing shudder with the rhythm of her beating heart. We left her to her struggles.

After we put on our damp cotton smocks, I rested. Leah gathered more firewood. Together we fired it with flint and a small pile of dry moss. I blew the flame gently, nursing that tiny spark into crackling fire. *God, help the men find food. Rat, rabbit, bird, snake, hedgehog—doesn't matter.*

Shadows lengthened. We listened for footsteps.

I began to imagine things that go bump in the night. I said, "I'm getting scared. You too?"

Leah nodded once. "I'd like Laz and Rabbus back. Now would be good."

She scooted closer to her mother's other daughter. We both stared into the fire. Fear simmered to just below a slow boil. Goose flesh rippled up and down my spine.

When two strange men crashed out of the underbrush, I wasn't even surprised. Much. Not with my luck. Even so, none of my me's peeped. We were all stunned into silence.

Leah and I jumped behind the fire, keeping it between the men and us.

Leah picked up the cool end of a fiery branch and held it in front of her, waving the flaming brigand back and forth. Cutter brandished mother's paring knife.

The men played a bit with us, jigging left and right. They quickly tired of this game and made a dash for us from both sides of the fire at the same time. The one man's grip bent my right wrist double, dropping mother's knife at my feet. His strong fingers wrapped around my throat.

Gasping, no air. Please, God, help me live.

This man, while choking the life out of me, undressed me with his eyes. That was when the sharp end of an arrow shot out of his chest, stopping a few inches before it entered mine. His eyes rounded. His last lungful of exhaust blew up my nose. I pushed him away, hard, with my left hand. He turned as he fell, facedown, in the fire.

I looked for Leah and her assailant. In the moment of my looking, sound of a *whump, stone striking bone.* Man's arms flew out to either side like he was being crucified in thin air. In the next moment, he fell backward into the shadows, with a sputter and a sigh. *Maybe he met the other guy on the way to Hades.*

Rabbus and Laz stepped into the circle of light, brandishing bow and sling. They ditched a few dead animals and their weapons. Rabbus kicked the first guy out of the fire. The dead man's hair and beard were blazing, skin already bubbling, crisping black.

Rabbus rolled him in the dirt. "This guy looks about my size. Never say no to a new suit of clothes, right?"

Laz followed suit, stripping the other man's garments. After, the men hobbled the robbers' two mules to the same tree where Betsy stood, eating leaves off that tree.

Once done, Laz wedged himself between us and became our arms of comfort. Together we rocked back and forth, breathing, gazing into the fire. Leah and I shallow-shook, our bodies quivering with what must have been feeling.

Rabbus, for his part, appeared unmoved. He stalked the dark perimeter, stiletto in hand, before he returned, muttering to himself. He sat and skinned the non-human prey he and Laz had killed, but from the look on his face and the speed of his knife, he could have skinned all the prey in a jiffy. His knife flew, like it had a mind of its own, making short work of skinning, gutting, and skewering rabbits and birds. *Nice to have a practiced skinner on your side now and again.*

Our resident murderer-skinner-cook sat on his haunches, turning the spit. Soup in the iron pot, next to the skewers, simmered. He stirred Leah's mix of spring water, mushrooms, spring onions, and herbs. Carcasses dripped fat on the fire, sizzling. Fragrance of roasting meat and soup filled the air.

Laz fed us words of comfort. "I knew you were in danger. Someone, not sure who, warned me. Happens to Jeez all the time. He gets visions from outside the box or below the scroll. Invisible stuff that's weird, really weird. And the more I've hung with him—"

Rabbus held up a hand, cutting off Laz's talk. He took four skewers off the fire, filled four tin cups with soup, and passed the food all around. We all got greasy, tucking in rabbit meat and bird breast with our fingers, slurping soup from the cups.

Leah, mouth full, said to Rabbus, "Did you get the same funny feeling Laz had?"

Rabbus cracked open a rabbit leg and sucked the marrow out. "Nope, but when he spoke, we moved. Glad he listened to whoever, and I listened to him."

"I was so afraid when Jesus left," she said. "But seems His Spirit is weaving his story into ours."

Rabbus glanced sideways at her. "Not sure where to put this bit of Jew talk, but I'll see if there's a spot for it in my saddlebag."

After dinner, we walked past the naked corpses. I looked the other way, not wanting to see another naked man, ever. Leah stood between the two mules and soft-talked 'em, stroking their long noses. Rabbus took the saddles off while she soothed the animals. Together they opened up the bandits' packs.

Dried food, clothing, tools, and a heavy leather pouch full of gold coins were now in our care—more money by far than what had been in my Sepphbro box. We voted the most conscientious, focused person in our group to be treasurer. Leah hung the money pouch between her breasts on a thick leather cord.

We moved back to the fire, added wood, and rested. "What's the story about this place and your past?" Leah asked.

Rabbus looked at her out of the corner of his eye. "You serious? You *really* want to know?"

Leah leaned toward him. She pulled her knees together under her sin-glet and opened her hands in invitation. I watched my sister slowly pull speech out of vapor, reeling in this murderer-skinner, bit by bit.

33

WINDY

Rabbus spoke into the night air while he fiddled with a rabbit skin and patch of straw that he'd left beside his feet. "I once lived in this cave. I was a child then—a very mad boy."

Go said, "Huh. Guess we had that in common when we were children, Rabbus."

He recovered from her interruption. "By dumb luck, *Leah*, after my parents' murder, I found this wadi. The group of killers who lived here didn't kill me, 'cause I wasn't worth killing. They took pity on me, turned my rage to the gang's good. The leader called himself Rip. He taught me the art of the double-cross. Others taught me to cook, heal wounds, and track the spoor of wild things. And they all taught me to fight."

He worked the rabbit skin around the straw. Put a stitch in here and there. "They didn't call me Barry, like my folks. Rip named me Rabbus."

Laz, so full of book learning, asked, "What were their training techniques—you know, the art of the kill?"

Rabbus mouth crooked up at a corner. Leah might have said it was a smile. "I had three choices: foot soldier, slinger-archer, or horseman. Each protected the others. In my case, horses weren't an option. They'd eaten them all."

Leah cleared her throat as if to say something, thought better of it. She stirred the fire, leaned back toward Rabbus—not crowding him, but her eyes all bright and seeing.

"The knife brother, Badu, was a slippery, skinny Bedouin. Skin baked black. He'd no need of tattoos—already had more scars than skin. He'd circle with me, crouched over, knives in either hand, one long, the other curved and short, both stinging sharp. He'd lunge, swirl, and strike—little poke here, little nip there. Left the main bleeders untouched."

He paused. "Nothing killin' in Badu's lessons, just enough for skin to remind head. I didn't make the same mistake twice, but a lot of mistakes to be made. I started lookin' like my teacher." He stood up, stripped off his shirt, and showed a tangle of scars. The other three sucked in their air, all together.

Leah traced the line of a thick scar between his shoulders in the dimming firelight. He liked her cool, light touch—a lot.

He looked at Laz. "And Bado taught me how to skin animals, all in one piece, and stuff them—a hobby that filled up spare hours."

Laz asked, "You practice warrior stuff with each other in camp?"

"Yes and no. Raiding parties, more like it. Practiced murderers watched me practicing murder. Stuffed darkness into me and stitched me up around it."

Leah's smile understood him, just as far as he wanted to be understood. Good-lookin' woman like her, touchin' a man like him? Huh, a real head-scratcher. He shifted his weight, leaned into her side, barely. "Those of us who lived through those early raids got born again under a full moon—rite of passage. I'd seen others go through it. My turn now.

"The gang stripped me naked, blackened me with potash, danced me in a fast circle inside this man-womb. Bare to the moon, blindfolded. Labored me down a slope, right toward this six-foot spill gate."

He gestured toward the waterfall behind us. "They twisted me round and round on my back, pushed me through two men pouring sheep guts over my head. They sloshed all that on me, then shoved me between their legs out into the dark, with a whoop. I slid down *that* birthing chute.

"Two others caught me at the bottom. Took off my blinders, dunked me in the pool, rolled me over and over. Cleaned off the afterbirth. Carried me over their heads to creek-side. Two others wrapped me in linen strips, head to toe—swaddlin' clothes, ya know?

"Once I was mummied up, they took me back to the circle of bearded brother-mothers. Right where we are now. Rip pronounced some ancient mumbo-jumbo. Badu flicked his knife here and there. Loosened my wrapper, like cutting some cord. Got new stuff to wear, new weapons. We all got drunk."

Rabbus looked at Laz. "That's how ya get born again when you're a thirteen-year-old Samaritan—gang-style in a desert whirligig. Boy dies; man arrives."

Leah looked at Rabbus. "What happened after that, Rabbus?"

"My gang became my family, the one I'd always wanted—a little bit of Ma, a little bit of Pa, a lot of brothers. They all packed a blend of Bedouin, Philistine, Ammonite, Edomite, Jewish stuff into me.

"And then, one night we looted a Roman guard post and killed everyone, took their stuff. Partied and whooped it up. It was after midnight when everyone flopped down, right where they fell—here, around this fireplace. All of us, skunk drunk.

"Another gang leader, Rastus, had been spying on us from those woods out there. Those murderers crept in and murdered the lot of us murderers—all except me. I'd woked up, walked sleepy-eyed into the bush to pee. I was finishing a long pee when they attacked. I couldn't see 'em. Just heard 'em from where I hid. I imagined them doing to us what we'd done to the Romans—slittin' throats, slidin' daggers under the third rib, with a twist."

Leah's eyes were huge.

"I'd hidden in the hollow of a rock and pulled tumbleweed in front of me. Hardly breathed. Still as a mouse under the full moon when the owls are out swoopin'. Rastus' murderers tromped back and forth, less than three paces from my hiding place, turnin' the livin' into the dead."

He paused. "Rastus. Yeah, I remembered that guy from other skirmishes. Small build. Jet-black beard, wicked, glittery eyes, droopin' eyebrows."

I brooded over this small group of four. Watched them bed down in the cave, men in the front, women in the back, each in their own bedroll. Predators' yellow eyes winked from the trees.

I sat on the circle of time with Father, in the eternal now. I shifted my gaze to a tiny Moabite village, thirteen years earlier, on the same night Rabbus was born again. A few hundred miles away, at the same moment he was unbound from *his* wrapper, a baby girl was born to an Amalekite tradesman and a Jewess musician-singer.

The father said, "Let's name her Agatha, after my ancestor, Agag."

The mother looked at her older, two-year-old daughter. Such a beautiful, secret gift from Moab's chief rabbi. Then she looked at this new daughter from her tradesman husband. The child's cone head angled down into frantic eyes and a screeching mouth. Plain, at best.

The Jewess hummed a lullaby in a soft, lilting soprano voice with golden tones, soothing her squealer. Then she said, while easing breast milk out of her nipple into the searching mouth, "Dear, let's call her Leah—the lesser sister."[14]

Both this newborn girl and newly reborn Rabbus began their predestined trajectory toward each other, at that moment in time.

34

CLAUDIA

The day dawned hot and clear. It was going to be a scorcher. I wore a gauzy, ankle-length flamingo-red dress, set off by a royal-blue silk scarf, colored to match my eyes. No perfume. Definitely, no perfume. How could I know my mother's fragrance was that strong? I mean, really, why was I cursed with a mother who had such poor taste in perfumes?

On my way out of the courtyard, I grabbed a water jar from the servants' shed—one of those ten-gallon jars with a flat base, curved body, wide lip. The glaze was so good I stopped to admire myself in it. This one had a thin crack down one side, but no matter. I carried it under my arm. After a few steps, since no one was around, I gave it a try on my head, balancing with both hands.

The whitewashed paver steps were shallow. They wound downhill in switchback Z's for about a mile. Late-morning sun, behind me, pushed my shadow before me. I practiced my humble, peasant girl shtick—three steps forward, one step down, graceful swaying of hips. Curated my new image. I'd seen squatty local women carry water jugs on their heads. How hard could this be? If Jesus wanted water, water he'd get. I'd carry this numbskull jar on my head like all the local girls he knew and liked. I'd find a servant to fill it at the well. Not going to break my neck or my back, no sir.

Every few steps, the jug did a shimmy, sliding sideways first one way, then the other. I couldn't keep the friggin' thing on my head. I had to work at what the servant classes were born with. Just when I thought I was in control, it began a run to the edge on invisible wheels. I cussed a blue streak under my breath.

This stupid jug would shatter into a million pieces, but really, who cared? How did these provincials do this day after day? Earth Girl was definitely not in the cards for me.

The blaze of the noon sun produced mirages in the open town square. Heatwaves reflected off the empty piazza. Everything looked wavy with vertical lines. Wavy mud-colored storefronts and warehouses, wavy synagogue, wavy houses. Sun-waves looked like they were holding hands high in praise to Sol, the Sun God. How much of what I saw was real?

I sat on the well's ledge under the wooden canopy, amused myself by counting all the subtle shades of tan in this sweatbox solarium—dauby tan, shiny eggshell, flat ochre, dun, buff, sandstone, sun-yellow flecked with bright white, white-yellow swirls. The heat and sand didn't stop. Sand grit wedged between my toes, blew up my nose, swirled through my clothes, whipping hot air around my head and settling it in my earlobes.

If I hold still for more than two seconds, this kiln will bake me into a sand sculpture, guaranteed. Centuries from now, they'll unearth an Italian goddess in Jewdonia, wonder how the heck I got here.

There I was at the well. No Jesus in sight. Was he going to stiff me? Dark sweat stains crept from my pits to my waist, dripped off my chin, matted my hair. Here I am, a rat basting in her own juices. I don't need perfume from Rome. I'm making my own. Then my gripe session was interrupted with the sight of two men in thawbs coming toward me. Had my vision gone wonky, blurred? Coming through the heat blast, angling toward the well from my left, was a man robed in black. Coming the other way, off to my right, another man angled toward me, draped in white.

They looked exactly alike except for the color of their robes. The closer they got, the more confused I was. Once they were practically on top of me, I swore that both were Jesus—identical. Each showed only half his face. The other half hidden in shadow. I wasn't being stiffed by the one Jesus I knew. Now, I had a double date with the same guy.

I turned to the guy in white on my right. "Jesus?"

"Yes, it's me. The person you see on your left is also quite real. Claudia, meet Satan, your enemy. He's here to tempt both of us like he did under the apple tree. He inhabited that viper back then, and now he's morphed into my mirror image."

"Hi there, Satan. You really a snake?"

Jesus-White cut in. "He'll try to fool you into thinking he's just my un-developed half, my evil part that I've split off as unacceptable—you know, me being a good Jewish boy and all."

I turned back to Jesus-Black. "He tag your storyline?"

"I know, confusing, huh?" Jesus-Black smiled, shook his head, and motioned to Jesus-White. "Jesus denies his not-so-holy self. He pushes his *oh-so-sinful* urges onto me—like wanting you, for example. I feel sorry for him. He's not given up on his adolescent ideals—you know, pretending to be a super-spiritual saint. I accept this abuse from him all the time. Honestly, I just want to protect him from himself."

I did a double-take. This guy made sense, even if his smile was an it-ty-bitty shade off sincere. Maybe I could appoint *him* guardian of my body, and White, the guardian of my soul. At least with him, I could compare down, not feel like such a loser.

Jesus-Black continued, "We're both different halves of a whole person. We both love you, want a life together. Together we can return to Rome and take over when your grandpa dies."

Black again pointed to White. "Believe me. He wants the same stuff. But I can be truthful with you in a way that he can't be. Truth is so precious I surround it with a platoon of lies, like those soldiers who guard your grandfather. White's not grown up enough to tell nuanced truth like I do, with all the shades of grey. He's stuck in the 'all good-all bad, black-or-white' stage. But I'm leading him out, slowly. Don't want to rush him."

My head couldn't handle all this full-truth, half-truth stuff. My body felt like she was swimming in the deep end of a pool filled with desire. Hot longing blasted up and down my body, in and through me. I desperately wanted to believe Jesus-Black. More than that, I wanted him. I wanted Jesus in me.

I murmured quietly, "God, help me." I didn't know who I was praying to, but I sincerely prayed in my own sincere-insincere sort of way.

"I heard your prayer just now," Satan said. "It's perfectly fine to doubt. All saints do that, or else they lie about it. Have faith in me, Claudia. It is written, 'The just shall live by faith.'"

I turned into a projectile of desire and threw myself at him, falling to my knees in front of him. "Jesus-Satan-Black-White-Lucifer-Snake, whoever you are, love me, don't go away. Complete me. I do have faith, sort of."

Satan answered, "According to your faith, be it unto you."

Jesus answered him, "Lucifer, do you really think rubbing some scripture on your lies makes you God-pleasing and street credible? Please. Get real."

Lucifer ignored him. "You know, I am the Son of God, Claudia, His full expression of love, not just the pure white-light half. Not just one of those minor, made-up Roman deities like Sol. We two Jesuses were separated long ago. I lightning-bolted down to earth, unacceptably honest to the ruler at that time."

Jesus-White replied, "Your arrogance, Lucifer, separated you from Father's love. The weight of your *own* pride cast you down, Angel of Light. That's the truth of the matter."

Things were getting more and more blurry. Lucifer, Angel of Light, Satan, viper, White-Black. Would they just settle on one name? Ack. Make up your minds, will you?

Black jerked a thumb over at White. "He's stayed above it all. He will *not* own his shadow, so now his shadow owns him. He's more treacherous than me. We two are alike, Claudia, you and me. We're both dark and light, lie and truth, test and temptation, *all* mixed together. Perfection is barren. All her children are stillborn. We, the broken, have many children. White's perfectly, purely unbelievable."

"So, Plato got it mostly right—maybe imperfect, but close?" I said. "We're all split down the middle and looking for our other half?"

Satan tendered me, stroking my lathered brow. "We two, White and me, have traveled out of time and now through time. Finally, we found each other here, well united. United with you, dear, here at the heart of Sepphoris. Now we can all … *come together*."

Come together.

I felt his words as a command. Come. Together. I kept repeating it.

35

JESUS

Windy said, *look how Lucifer feeds on Claudia's adoration—she's a steak sizzling on his grill. He gazes at her with the pity a chef feels for ground beef that was once tenderloin. She's blackened food over his fire.*

Windy, what now? I shuddered, intimidated by Satan's fierce power.

My shudder shifted. A hot wind whipped through my robe and blew my hood down around my shoulders, revealing my whole face. My robe didn't hold onto the wind, even though it was full of it.

Windy, fill and flow. Fill with Father's power, flow into this moment.

I looked at Satan. His arms rose on either side, wings of a peacock. His legs were strong, spread wide in conquest. He held Claudia to him, his frame backlit by the sun's blaze. Claudia held on as well, her body trembling in waves, a leaf in his maelstrom.

Satan never looked at her. His lips hardly moved. "I'm as needful as night, Claudia, as necessary as sex. White's too perfect, too pure to do this dance with us."

His pupils, wormholes of darkness, aimed point-blank at my heart.

He smiled faintly. Sexual funk radiated off of him. None of us spoke. Everyone screamed.

Claudia, at last, collapsed in a heap at his feet. She lifted her face to Satan. "We're now one, aren't we? One. Life. Together?"

Satan knelt briefly to stroke her. He used no words.

Windy whispered, *Son, see how sex welds two people together like a torch. Most teens get this right away. Words get in the way.*

Satan stood and took a step back. Claudia looked squarely at me, edge of bitterness in her voice. "And you, White? You're too good for us?"

I breathed in a fresh breath of wind. Turned to Satan, with the full sun on my whole face. "Hurt one of Father's children, and you hurt Him, and me."

Satan wrapped his cowl around his lower face.

Windy said, *see how he protects himself from the energies of love.*

Strength blew through my voice. "Lucifer, your 'love' is a self-serving mirage."

I pointed away from us, out into the desert. "Go!"

A furnace blast whirled around the well, spraying fine grit. I squeezed my eyes shut and then, when the blast subsided, I wiped them clean with my knuckle. He was gone from view.

I reached out to steady myself on the well's ledge, suddenly drained of power. *Father, protect Claudia and me.*

Claudia slathered sweat off her face with one hand and chirped, "Jesus! Do you do magic sex tricks like that for *all* your friends?" She bounced over to the shady ledge and sat, arms hugging the stone jar in front of her. First, she peeked at me around the left side of the cracked jar, showing half her face, then peeked around the right side, hide-and-peeking, sing-songing, "Now you see the right me. Now you see what's left. Will the *reeeal* Claudia please stand up?"

I felt a little like Solomon. But my job was to unite a divided child, not the other way around.[15] Windy overheard my thoughts and replied, *no worries. Father and I are always interested in unity. My Spirit sword is so sharp that it cuts people together, not apart.*

I didn't have a clue how this worked, but I believed her. I also knew our work here was not done. Claudia moved from behind her jar directly toward me, sly smile on her lips, hands rising on either side, inviting me to join her for a dance of our own.

I said, "I think I'd like that drink we mentioned yesterday. I'm thirsty, and exhausted."

Windy, cut me into your deal. What's up here?

Jesus, remember? Satan entered her. He's still inside, lurking.

Do Your work, Windy. And tell me my place.

Claudia slid her feet closer, her grin lingering. She watched me like a hawk.

Windy cut into spirit—convicting, comforting, and emptying Claudia of whatever energies no longer served her well.

We're almost there, Son. Watch now.

Claudia's shoulders drooped, and she dropped to her knees before me, face dazed. Brief shudder. She lifted her head and stared at a point somewhere between me and a black coil of rope on the well's ledge.

I opened my hand to her. "Let me help you up, Claudia."

She refused my help and stood on her own, wavering in the hot, whipping wind. She took a step into the shade, toward the well. Her hand quivered in mid-air, floated toward the coiled rope. The rope rose to meet her hand, snaked itself in a flash around her wrist, her waist, tangling around her torso, moving toward her neck.

She stared down at what she was holding, what was holding her. She struggled, frantic, trying to free herself from what she had done. She whimpered, "No!"

I wanted to help but heard a voice within me. *This is her struggle. Let her do it.*

When she resisted, the hemp went inert. Then it changed colors from black to a mottled brown, grew fangs and scales, and hovered in front of her throat, poised to strike. She stared at it, round-eyed. Shifted her gaze to my face directly opposite her. She paused a brief moment, seemed to remember something.

She took a deep breath and then shouted at the serpent, "NO!"[16]

The viper slithered down her arm, down the outside of the well, and out into the piazza. Dissipated into gusts of dust. We stayed on the well's ledge and slumped toward each other. She put her head, slick with sweat, on my shoulder. Now, things felt right. We were both exhausted with this battle.

A bucket swayed from the well's crossbeam, attached to a rope. The shadow of that crossbeam covered the two of us.

Claudia tumbled the tub down with a flick of her elbow. The spinning axle paid out the weighted rope. *Sploosh*, way down there.

Claudia closed her eyes. Rested. Our breaths, inhale and exhale, synced. When she finally opened her eyes, they were clear and totally focused on me. I reached for the rope. She did too. Together, arm in arm, we pulled water out of darkness into the blazing light of day.

36
GO

We were packing to leave the campsite that Leah and all-my-me's had named Rape Escape. The men were burying the two corpses, using the dead men's shovel. I looked at the place where Rabbus sat the night before, around the campfire. A perfect little rabbit sat up on his hind legs, front paws up in the air. His eyes sparkled, and his fur was soft as velvet to my touch.

I realized we had eaten him the night before. When I showed him to Leah, she said, "he looks real enough to eat again." Cutter didn't want to leave this place. She wanted to settle in, and take lessons from Rabbus.

The four of us, with our three mules, made our way south toward Jericho. I rode Betsy, Rabbus led. Laz and Leah led our new mules behind us. Laz had decided to name them Goodness and Mercy and prayed they would follow us all the days of our lives.[17]

My fingers told me that my face was healing. Eye, once swollen to a slit, was now reopened for business. Loose teeth had re-rooted, more or less. Leah told me my fractured face looked exotic, one cheekbone slightly flatter and lower than the other. She probably meant 'broken,' and it came out of her mouth wrong.

I was homesick. But for who? Maybe stoned Ma or always absent Abba. Maybe the life I'd not yet found. For sure, not Ach. Maybe this man who walked behind me. I looked over my shoulder, time to time. Laz talked with his hands, laughed easy, listened well. He made fun of his own bow and arrow exploits. Told Leah how scared he was to shoot that guy last night—afraid he'd miss and hit me, or his arrow would go through both the guy *and* me.

Can I reform, God, be a faithful wife? I'm sixteen, so old! I don't even know if I want to reform, God. Escape hid behind Fragile while she prayed and handed the prayer to Bruise. She hurled the prayer at heaven, and we watched it disappear together. Our pain felt as sharp and straight as the blade of Cutter's paring knife.

Jericho's city walls grew out of a smudge into life-size. Rabbus looked at Leah and me. "You two, use your veils. We don't want these men to see how pretty you are." We pulled down our veils, and Leah leaned toward me.

She whispered, "He made me tingle. I feel almost pretty, whatever that feels like." I thought about this little sister. Over thirteen years she'd lived, and it had always been me who was pretty.

God, did you rearrange my face for her to feel pretty? No one answered.

Rabbus led us through Jericho's southern gate into the bowels of that teeming marketplace. It was fun, if you like sticking your nose up bowels. I kept my eyes straight ahead, breathed through my mouth. We led our burros through crowded streets, keeping the town's wall on our left. We stopped at an open gate with a scarlet cord hanging above the entry marker:

Rahab's Rehab
Rest, Work, Worship

All four of us walked through the gates into the open-air courtyard. Leah and I took our mules to the stable, watered and fed them in a stall where a stack of saddle blankets lay over the wooden rails.

When we wandered back into the courtyard, Rabbus and Laz were speaking with a man dressed like a rabbi—tallit, dreadlocks, and a shabby black robe held together with a rope belt and an aura of calm. A woman stood next to him, stirring a steaming black kettle over an open fire. Her blue eyes were the color of my own eyes.

Laz introduced us. He said, "Ladies, this is El Roi.[18] His friends call him Roy."

El Roi pointed to the woman beside him, "My wife, Lydia." His hair, jet-black and flecked with silver, was combed straight back. His weathered face looked like it had been etched with fine shades of judgment. His black eyes were the color of fertile soil. He looked like the kind of person who'd have stories stacked up inside him, like horse blankets in a stable.

Laz said, "Is this the place Rahab lived long ago when the walls came down?"

Roy nodded. "That's why we bought it. Our local synagogue meets here." He pointed to the large room on our right.

He faced the street and pointed over his shoulder. "We keep our faith close to our flaws. Our red-light rooms for the city's working girls are behind me. Customers enter from outside the walls, through that gate over there. Sex workers who're not yet self-supporting learn other trades here. We let them take a few months to switch from what they've known to what they have yet to learn."

"You don't stone whores here?" Laz asked, amazed.

Roy shook his head. "Nope, that's up in Jerusalem, if you'd like a good stoning. I used to work beside Herod's temple up there, close to the place of judgment. After a while, suffering exhausted me of judgment and I left, came here in the wilds of Judea. We work goodness and mercy into our lives and don't just have them trail after us." *Huh, how did he know our mules' names?*

Laz asked Roy, "How does day to day life go here?" While Laz waited for Roy's answer, he looked to see my face but saw only my veil. I wondered to myself, *who is this man?*

Roy did not answer Laz's question, but instead he answered my unasked one. "I am one who sees. I see Him who sees me. And the look in that face is Love."

Laz slid his hand in mine and squeezed some excitement into it.

Roy continued, "Lydia and I retrain sex workers as seamstresses and potters. Lydia directs our seamstress workshop."

Lydia chimed in. "When we work, we usually sing. That way, women learn to make garments of praise from the shrouds of mourning. We also make a pretty decent choir."

Laz asked Roy, "And you?"

"I do pottery training, other end of the workshop. We have a wheel for throwing clay, a kiln, and some workbenches. We take crushed pots and put them on the wheel again."[19]

Roy paused. "We had another couple that helped us with practical things like growing the garden, cooking, doing repairs, and so on. They left a week ago when the wife finished her pottery course. They're in Jerusalem now, setting up a pottery shop."

He looked at me pointedly, as if he saw me clearly through my veil. "But you know, Gomaria, each woman knows her needs better than me. I only know how to remake broken pots that come to me."

His weighted comment required me to wait, before I got it. *He saw names, like my name, in the same way I felt gloom, effortlessly.*

He continued, "I don't think there is any other place in Palestine like Rahab's. Sex workers' bodies are either used like toilet wipes or stoned—if the wrong people catch them at the right time."

Laz replied, "My best friend says people aren't bodies with add-on souls, as an afterthought. We're souls, with bodies thrown in for good cheer."

Roy and Lydia threw their heads back and laughed. Sounded like a kettle drum and flute, in harmony. An unfamiliar voice blew into my head and said, *laughter like Roy's and Lydia's? That's earth's expression of Heaven's hope.*

Roy took a hard-right turn. "And our hostel rooms? Well, they're behind you, over our storefront where we sell pots and clothes. So, when you come into Rahab's courtyard, sleep's behind, work's left, worship's right, and sex is straight ahead. Everyone gets to choose."

37

WINDY

Rabbus negotiated the tariff for two rooms, one night—sisters in one room, men in the other. Leah counted out the money to Lydia. Rabbus guarded her back. Rabbus checked on Mercy and Goodness before he headed out for a drink, alone.

Laz looked at both sisters and offered, "Like to see a bit of the town?"

Leah begged off, claiming fatigue. Truth was, she was desperately looking for a mirror.

Go sent Harlot out, as her envoy. She said, "Let's be streetwalkers together, Mr. Betrothed."

They wandered through the open-air market, bought fresh fruit, and sat on a bench inside the wall. Both leaned back against the black stone wall and let their backs collect heat off the friendly stones. They watched vendors hawk their wares and shared a banana. Go took a bite, then Laz. People came and went.

Laz asked Go, "Did you know these walls were rebuilt after their collapse, fourteen hundred years ago? At least, that's what they told us in Torah class." He retold the old siege from the book of Joshua, voice rising and falling with dramatic spice. Then he added, "Rahab was a woman of great faith."[20]

Go said, "A faith-filled madame? Really?" She thought of Sepphbro's madame kicking her to the curb.

"Probably why Roy and Lydia have this amazing place here now. It's a marriage of more than just husband and wife, Go. It's a marriage of brothel and faith."

Harlot was dubious. "Faith in the ringing till, maybe."

Laz seemed suddenly distracted. "Go, look over there. See that old pile of rubble?"

Go stood up and strained to see what he was looking at, over the passing crowds. Laz stepped behind her. He put his left hand on her left shoulder and pointed with his right arm over her right shoulder, directing her eyes up and to the right. "There, you see that huge pile of rubble on the edge of the marketplace?"

Escape put space between herself and Go's skin. Harlot nodded.

"That's tomorrow's building materials … disguised as yesterday's walls. New lives build on old failures."

Hesitant, Fragile leaned back into Laz, resting on his chest. She felt his warmth, his racing heart. Go surfaced. She said, "I never thanked you proper for the other night. I'm not sure how to repay you. Sex has been the only way I've known."

Laz was quiet. "I've been changing. I hear God's voice. I learned how to listen as I worked with Jesus in the trenches. Go, God will grow us together, build our faith from the inside out."

They did a turn around the city's walls. Go's heart did fluttery, scary stuff. She asked, "Do you think I could stay with Roy and Lydia? When I think about the road between here and Bethany, I get this gut twist, and my head throbs." She didn't mention that Cutter had poked her with the paring knife.

"I get scared thinking of you working at another brothel. Even if it's a faith brothel."

"I could be like the others. Wean off the old, try out the new." Harlot tugged her veil down further. "Like Rahab, I could choose my life … and that's what counts for me, Hosea."

Harlot continued, "I have a whore's heart. I'd be a wretched wife and mother. I'm too fragile for you. I leave a lot, so why don't you leave first—go to Bethany. Find a better woman, better wife, better life." Agreeing with these lies was a lazy bit of work, but she slid right into it.

Laz gnawed a knuckle. "Any reasons to stay clear of whoring, Go?"

"I don't want the crap beat out of me again. That could happen. But then again, it could happen anywhere."

Go's next words bubbled up and babbled out before Escape could leave again. "I've had the craziest nightmare for a long time—I turned into devil's food cake, and Satan was eating me. He started with my feet and hands and worked his way up. But since we left Nazareth, I haven't had that nightmare."

Laz whispered, "God's turning this bit of devil's food into a daughter."

All Go's-me's heard him and smiled to themselves. They walked silently. I blew some glue into Go and saved a dab for the connection between her and Laz.

When they arrived back at Rahab's, Laz asked Roy and Lydia if they had a minute to talk. Rabbus also loitered and listened.

Go took Lydia's long metal spoon from her and stirred the stew pot.

Lydia smiled, grateful, and joined Roy a couple of steps away. Both listened as Laz told them their story, Go's story. Roy's head slowly tilted back and forth, Laz to Go. Laz seemed so unaware, how exposing her dirt would crumble her.

Go felt Shame detach, ready to float off with Escape and Fragile. Roy moved a step closer to the stirred and stirring woman, earthed Shame with his solid presence. Escape stopped her departure moves, started rubbing Cutter's scars on her left forearm.

Laz kept talking. "Go and I were thinking of starting over in Bethany. But when you told us about your work here, and your helper couple leaving last week, we wondered if you'd allow us to stay and work with you."

Go's head jerked toward him. *Who said anything about 'we'? This was about me.*

A movement above. A curtain scooched to one side of an open window, and Leah's side profile slid into view, ear to the courtyard. She didn't want to be left out, even though she had said to her sister just yesterday, "I'm a wafty soul drifting through a changeling's body. I belong nowhere and to no one."

Laz didn't notice Leah or Go. Mr. Unaware kept bubbling over, like an iron kettle over too hot a fire. "Go could learn a new trade. I could help you garden, cook, mind the stables, learn Torah. We'd be so grateful to help and be helped."

An afterthought, it seemed, "Maybe Leah should live with my uncle and aunt in Bethany."

Rabbus stepped in, a moment never to forget. He glanced up at Leah's window, raised his voice a notch over the general din. "Laz, don't know what you'd think of this, but I have a simple plan."

He swallowed hard. "Maybe Leah and I could make a life together. Even though I'm twice her age, she is of the age to marry. She's so beautiful. Maybe we would even learn to love each other. What do you think?"

Here's a twenty-six-year-old Samaritan asking a seventeen-year-old Jew for permission to marry a thirteen-year-old Jewish-Moabitess, in front of a mysterious Pharisee rabbi, who saw more than he could possibly know—all inside a 'faith' brothel in Palestine. Nothing simple about this.

Laz and Go said at almost the same time, "We'd have to talk to Leah, of course."

At that moment, a changeling bolted out the inn's door into the courtyard. She made a beeline for Rabbus. He saw her coming, turned with open arms, and each wrapped the other up, spinning around.

Laz said, "Maybe we won't have to talk to Leah." At the same time, Laz moved toward Go and held his arm out to her. She slid under that right arm—a brittle bit of off-shade genuineness. He let his arm settle there, lightly.

They waited till the rapidly tilting twosome—the newly beautiful girl and a newly softened killer—slowed their whirl and faced them. Leah positively glowed. Rabbus struggled not to look happy. He failed, maybe the first time in his life of disappearing sadnesses.

Laz turned to Leah. "Your father has to approve this, you know. Why don't we return to Nazareth and get his permission?"

Go turned to Laz. "You'd trust me to stay here without you?"

He nodded. "The three of us will leave for Nazareth. We'll return to you later. Until then, guard your heart."

The next morning, Laz and Rabbus loaded all their worldly goods on Goodness and Mercy. Leah rode Betsy, sidesaddle. They made their way to Jericho's northern gate. Go looked at Roy's face, felt seen, safe. Then she looked sideways into the face of her betrothed. She caught his fear and love. It felt to her like each was trying to cast the other out.

Laz confirmed her thought. "There's room here for both disaster and delight, I suppose. But Go, there's plenty of space in my heart, and God's family, for you."[21]

She said, "Go to Jesus. Come back with Leah and Rabbus. We'll see how my life will go. Perhaps, just perhaps, how *our* life will go."

Roy, Lydia, and Go stood at the city gates and watched the others walk away. Leah and Rabbus had turned toward each other, talking to each other with words and their hands waving in the air. Laz turned, more than once, to wave goodbye.

Go didn't know how to say goodbye, so she didn't. Shame froze Go's heart and hands. The rest of her handled the goodbye thing ten minutes later with a bout of diarrhea.

38

CLAUDIA

Jesus sat next to me under the well's sheltering crossbeam. The piazza was still an empty, baking oven. The sun's heat wicked water from anyone who dared sit still, even in the shady side of the sear. The skin suck was almost audible. We'd filled my jar with cool water and set it between us. Each of us leaned over, tipped the jar right and left, and drank from the smooth lip.

If I said he was staring adoringly in my eyes, that would stretch the truth more than I usually do. But in my mind, we were a young couple on a hot date having a cool drink in metro Sepphoris. "Jesus, are there two of you, black and white?"

"There's more than that. I'm one in three. But the Satan you saw isn't part of me. Satan is a sort of trinity within himself—murderer, thief, and liar."

I stared at him, chin cupped in my hands. I tucked a stray strand of hair back of my ear, like I'd seen women do with my father.

Jesus spoke soft and slow. "Satan weaves a lot of truth with seed packs of lies—like when he said he'd fallen like a lightning bolt from heaven. That was true. What he didn't say was that Father threw him out. His arrogance and envy undid him."

I jerked my head up. "Aha! Antonio was right! You are a god. Were you lightning-bolted down like your buddy, Satan? Or did Zeus lay you down, more gentle-like?"

Jesus shot a half smile my way, said nothing.

"I bet you're like one of our Roman gods on the prowl, visiting humans to mate with the one he finds most attractive … like Cupid."

Jesus took a deep breath, exhaled. "Who I am will become clear later. Right now, what you see is what you get—a Jewish apprentice-carpenter interested in foundations."

I was quiet for a moment, then spoke. "So, mystery man-god, we don't get to marry, have babies, and a wonderful 'ever after'? That part was a lie from satin-smooth Satan?"

"Half-lie. You can choose a wonderful 'ever after', but first, you must choose who to believe, him or me. You can't choose both. It's a black-and-white issue."

"Seriously? Cute, White. Okay, I *want* to believe you. You feel more credible, even though he's more tangible. I've not felt *anything* that good, even though..." I took one look at Jesus and shut up.

He tipped the jug and drank in silence, as if listening inside, then told me about myself. Again. "You've been with five other guys, and the one you're with now is your twin. You and Claudius started having sex when you were eight years old. You've dumped the others after having sex with each of them once."

I steadied myself and looked down to see if I was naked. No, my red dress was pulled back down to my ankles. I said, "In my brave moments, I want to shout out to my friends, 'A God-man's told me everything I've ever done!'[22] But in these seen-through moments—"

"I speak, not to hurt you, but to love you. Father gives me insight, hindsight, and foresight. Wraps it all in love. Loving Him is way better than fooling around with just sex."

I arched my back, pushed my breasts up, and said, "Don't knock it till you've tried it, White. Satin Satan was amazing, but I bet you'd be better."

He looked kindly my way. "I love you, but I won't *make* love to you. I'll show my love by laying down my life for you.[23] Our lives will criss-cross without me double-crossing you. You will marry another. And here's a mystery. I dreamt I will remain single until I turn into a lamb and marry a flock so large only Father can count and name them.[24]"

I was deflated yet curious. "Here you go again, talking crazy. I'd say you're a real nutter, but my own dreams are even whackier."

Jesus leaned in. I felt in my bones, even those devious bones beneath my breasts, that he saw the best in me, the me I had yet to be. The shadow of the crossbeam above us landed right across his face and chest.

I offered a new thought. "Satan made me feel happy, found, beautiful, and sexy. You make me feel happy-sad, lost-found, beautiful-ugly, and a virgin-whore. How do you do that?"

"Simple. I inhale Father's Spirit. Exhale his words. Opposites emerge. Father's Spirit feels like I'm holding the reins of wild horses."

"I've got that wild horse thing going too. And to top that off, this weird relationship with you is *really* high maintenance."

"If you don't leave family and fortune for me, you don't deserve me."[23]

"Really? You're that hot, god-man?"

He raised one eyebrow and offered a half nod. "I believe that one hundred percent—about half the time. The other half is a mix of doubt, duty, and moodiness."

Okay, I thought. *Here's something I can relate to, finally.*

Jesus was on a roll. "I'm also high maintenance in other ways. Part of me wants to act out my desires, but Windy contains me. She tells me my sexual feelings for you are normal."

I thought, *who is this Windy? Maybe I could send her for a long walk on a short pier.*

I said, "So … I give you the big horny, honey? You're not all saint, just mostly, plus a little sinner mixed in—for spice? Like back under the apple tree a few nights ago, I was going to grab you when that snake showed up. If I'd gone for it, what would you have done?"

"Don't know. I'm a normal guy. But Father sent me to redefine normal. Part of that new normal means containing my heat, not squandering it. That would sear my soul."

I shook my head. "I must be seared … and your normal's not in view."

Jesus seemed to be listening to music from another planet. "All of us were designed to live whole and holy. *That's* normal. And, by the way, do you know the ancient Jewish story about how 'wholeness and holiness' began?"

I said no. Inside, I coached myself, *lean forward, Claudia. Try to look interested.*

He drank from the jug. I took it, turned it to the same spot where his lips had been and had a drink myself after I'd licked the jug's lip.

Kissing, once removed. Better than nothing, but not much.

I struggled to focus on his holy thing. Instead, I said, polite-like, "Uh, like a myth?"

He shrugged. "Rav Moshe said it this way: A dream is to a person what a myth is to a culture. This Jewish dream isn't too different from yours."

"Oh, that reminds me, Jesus. My dream…"

"Ah, hold on, hold on. I'm not ignoring you. But contain your dream— for a few moments."

He rambled on about light being created and breaking into a billion bits. I sopped my brow. He kept talking, a man of way too many words. I'd been Satan-fried. Words weren't what I wanted.

I whined. "I don't get it, and I don't want to."

I surrendered further thought, wanted only his touch. "I just want you and want you to want me. Hug me close." I reached out with both arms to him.

About this time, the smell of camel poop wafted our way. Crunch behind us, lips smacking.

I dropped my arms, pouted. "You just got rescued again from the embrace of a seductress, oh Sainted One. First a snake, now a whole zoo in a pair of sandals."

Jesus turned and greeted his cousin John. "How did you know where I was?"

"I saw you from up there." He pointed to yesterday's wheat field on the ridge above us. "Joe said lunch break was over." He popped a deep-fried lizard in his mouth.

I was not done with my date, but we got up and joined John for the walk up the hill. The paver stones still quivered with heatwaves. I donated my water jar to the town well. *I was so done trying to keep balanced.*

"John, mind if Jesus and I walk upwind of you? I have a private question to ask him."

"No problem," John said. "Happy to get his foundations ready."

He turned to his cousin. "See ya in the hole."

Jesus gave him a thumbs up. John loped up the paving stones like a mountain goat. He seemed happy to see and be seen by Jesus.

I turned to Jesus. "My dream. Please listen."

Jesus stayed in step with me.

"A circle of silent witnesses stands in a jungle, at midnight. They surround a blazing sacrifice of deer on an altar. Drummers are beating their drums in a second circle around the witnesses."

I stopped and looked to see if he was listening. He stopped with me. I was his total, immediate focus.

"A girl walks through the two circles, drummers and witnesses. She pours out a full jug of frothy liquid on the fire, trying to put it out. Instead, the fire gets more intense. She delicately puts down her jug, takes off her clothes, transforms into a deer, and walks into the fire. She lays down on the altar between the other two, on her back, legs flopping open in the air. After some time, she raises her head and tastes her breast meat. Then she puts her head down and continues to cook. I wake up in a sweat. My heart is racing like it's going to burn out of my chest."

We started walking again. Each stayed in step with the other, two steps across a paver stone and then up a step—each a witness to the other's walk. My face burned, and my eyes felt buggy. My hair was slicked flat and I smelled like yesterday's underwear. I looked to Jesus, anyway. "What do you think the dream means?"

Jesus stopped and regarded me as if I were still beautiful. "If you could speak for any part in your dream—circle of persons with their burning torches, the torches themselves, drummers, flames beneath the altar, or one of the deer trinity—what would you say?"

"Why do you always answer my question with another question? Can't you have the decency to *divine* it for me?"

"I grew up with dreams. My Father schooled us to take our dreams seriously. We all spend about six years of our life in dream school, but most of us sleep through it."

I thought, *hmm. Where'd he get that info? A cloud take a dump on him?*

"Dreams can be a great *foundation* for understanding God's Word. Ask Windy for insight, as I do. She blows through the trees, through our dreams, in and out of our lungs."

"You're dodging the dream arrow, God-man. Don't get me all worked up and then leave me hanging with no climax."

"Sometimes, even sexy dreams aren't about sex. They require waiting and wondering, without a big-bang climax. Go back to my question. Who or what would you be in your dream?"

"No question. The middle deer. The one that was there before me, and the one I became. She's me."

"What would she say?"

I whispered, "My heart's not yet tender."

"Who does she speak to?"

"The girl who dreamed her up."

"There's your answer. Stay on fire without trying to extinguish yourself. This fire, your passion for life, was sent by Father to transform you, grow you up. Don't look for a quick exit off that altar, particularly when you don't yet know the two beside you. The others in both circles are there to see and celebrate your courage in the middle of suffering. That's the answer to your dream."

"It'll take a long time to un-see that dream."

He said, "Wake up and dream a new dream with me. What's a tender-hearted you look like?"

Image flickered of a seven-year-old girl, innocent, sleeping peacefully between clean white sheets. Jesus stood guard at the bedroom door.

I smiled as sweet as a roasting deer could smile, half-done, and said nothing. The two of us strode arm in arm up the paver steps toward the cliffs above. I leaned on Jesus, and he didn't push me away. We walked, together-apart, toward the fires we'd each been given to fuel.

39

GO

I chose pottery, or maybe it chose me. Roy got me started. All Rahab's newbies began by working the garbage dump.

He said, "Go, let's take a walk. We can pull the cart together." Each of us took a strap, hooked it over a shoulder, and headed for the back gate past the chicken coops. A laying hen clucked an egg onto the straw beneath her, announcing her new arrival.

We walked through Rahab's back gate and took a hard-right turn toward the dump. Two she-mules stood there, facing the back wall. Their tails were tucked between their legs. A patch of shy, blood-red anemones bloomed between two rocks in front of them—blossom heads tucked just below where anyone could get at them.

The sound of squeaking bedsprings sighed from the windows above.

Our path intersected a stream of raw sewage flowing beneath the city walls, running down a defile, and then angling toward the Dead Sea. I lifted the hem of my smock and tried to jump the stream. I missed. Sewage splashed on me, up to my knees. Stink roiled the air, thick with what used to be.

Roy and I wandered through the dump, mucked through the discards, getting filthy. He said, "Aha! Here's one." He handed me a pale, pink pitcher from under a maggoty skunk carcass. The pitcher was cracked straight down the middle and hung together, barely.

He said, "Plain ones are the best. Fancy glazed porcelains where you can admire your face? They're the worst. Harder to crush into something usable."

Together we filled our cart with whatever people no longer wanted. Each helped strap the other into the traces. We scrabbled past Trash Row, that long line of shanties outside the city walls. I didn't even try to jump over the stream of sewage on the way back. Instead, I kicked my way past chunks of poop flowing around my ankles.

Back at Rahab's courtyard, Roy got down on his knees. Lydia handed him a rag, and he washed my feet with clean well water out of a bucket. I struggled with this new kind of intimacy as I washed his feet. Didn't look either of them in the eyes. Felt like the right thing to do and not do.

Once we were clean, Lydia went back to alterations.[25] Roy knelt and showed me how to take the bones of broken pots and crush them to powder—creation in reverse, something into nothing. He took a hammer. I took a hammer. He smashed the pot in front of him. I too smashed one in front of me.

But why were tears mixing with my clay? I kept wiping them away. Glanced sideways, checking to see if I was seen. Roy saw me all right, but he didn't stare.

At some point, Master-Smasher Roy decided tiny, sharp shards weren't small enough. That's when the grinding started. A heavy stone roller and paving stones provided a rock and a hard place for further humiliation.

Shame and Cutter fought within me over this grinding thing. Cutter liked it. Shame shrunk back inside herself, complaining, "this is way too sharp. Why put our life on display?"

Cutter kept grinding. She triggered Shame some more, who flashed back on Cyn tearing me open down there. Fragile started screaming, but I shoved a rag in her mouth. I told her and Escape, *when you live in the mouth of a lion, stroke his whiskers and shut up!* She did, but Bruise growled and grew huge. Put one finger in this dam and five more leaks sprang up just out of reach.

In spite myself, I shiver-shook, sobbed hard, streamed snot. I knew down deep, in my own bones, this had to be done without Laz, without Leah. Roy's eyes dripped too, but he looked straight down. Didn't eye-crush my privacy.

I saw my own jagged journey to and from the trash dump—hammered, rolled, ground, scooped into a bowl—so I could be spun around and around into someone I was yet to meet.

Roy left. A few minutes later, he brought back a beautiful, worn woman, the color of mahogany. She carried a funky smell, and her face was slick with sweat.

Sound of men mounting mules, slapping them on the butt. "Ah-ya!" Departure moves back to their caravan.

Roy told me, "Cornelia's done upstairs for now. She'll work alongside you here on the grinding floor. I need to get back to the wheel."

We kept our heads down and our words scarce. Sun inched over the courtyard wall. Finally, Cornelia said, "Roy done bought me off 'en de aukshun block from slavers. They dun steal'd me from Afric'."

I was pulled out of my own little orbit into her story. "Where's Afric', and what's in it?"

"Long way off, chil', lots 'n it. I out de bush early mornin', walkin' to the wader hole, fillin' my jug. I hear chil'en cry. Go lookin'. Two whitey, dey jump out, gag 'n drag me off. No chance for me to do no good-byin'."

My mind wandered. I remembered trying to say goodbye to Ma before they pulled the hood over her head. She never saw me mouth the words, *I love you, Ma.*

Cornelia'd been talking, but I'd missed some of it. Focusing on another person's story is such hard work. "What happened after they stole you?"

"Uh… I 'scaped. We be down Egypt by den, 'Alex-*an*dria."

Slow as honey drizzlin' toward Jerusalem, she spoke her story. "Night, night be dark-dark, moon a scythe. Dey be all drunk afta they done us slave womens. I snuck out de outhouse, lost myself in de big-big town. Four-day walkin' it side ta side. Never see'd so many peoples in all m' life."

I stopped listening. Looked down at blood dripping on the paver beneath me. A tiny slice of stone had slivered under a fingernail. I bit the sliver out, lips pulled back, teeth angling for purchase.

Cornelia saw the blood. "Here you be, clot' strip for m' flow."

I accepted the gift, right-sized the strip by biting off a rip, wrapped my finger.

She sighed. "Slavers cum'd again, nighttime. Gag and truss' me like a pig. Slung me over a camel, all woun' up in de ropes."

She barked out a laugh. "Worsest thing? Dem whiteys. Dey tink a crawlin' swamp be under black skin, screamin' hyena ready to eats 'em up.

Dey jus' scared of de baboon crouchin' under dey own whitey skin, if ya ask me."

She stopped and traced the web of scars on the white skin of my left forearm. "'pologies, missy whitey."

I reached over and gave her a side hug. Went back to work.

"We fed ever'ting that got hungry, missy. But dey fed us. De top dog, he say one night, 'Wit your ol' saggy boobs, no one gonna buy you. Gotta plump you up, bitch. Nice, huh?"

I nodded. "Trying to build you up."

Cornelia shook her head. "Non' dem wantin' me. They'd jus' horse-laugh, buy someone else. Know how humiliatin' dat be? Tryin' to *im*-press people you don' like? Gettin' reject' by folks ya don' want? Wears a body down."

I moved forward by staying put. Felt Corn's life, like it was my own. I must have learned this from Roy, even in the silence between us. I hadn't known how to do this before this very moment. The afternoon wore on, wore me out.

Toward quitting time, Cornelia asked, "Wha' be yo' story, girl?"

I lapsed into quiet. Cornelia matched my silence. Didn't interrupt what wasn't being said. I gut-measured to see if the silence would hold us, then stutter-spoke my story, bite-sized the chunks, and dropped into black holes in between. Quiet held what was unspeakable.

I unraveled myself, thread by thread. I finished, with this memory, "I hid baby Leah's eyes one night when her pa was doing Ma, two feet away."

Quiet. Grinding.

"Den what happenin'?"

"I heard Ma say, 'No, Ach. Not now. The girls are still awake.'

"He went ahead doing what he was doing. Ma hadn't healed up yet from giving birth. She screamed, shoved her fist in her mouth. Blood ropes bulged on her temples."

Cornelia cried for me. I stayed wooden outside but gained strength inside. Her tears gave me words, helped me grind a horror story into a history lesson. Shame and Cutter brought the others, even Harlot. We joined together and sucked out the bitter.

"When Ach was done, he slept. I didn't. Instead, I peeked at Ma from behind my fingers. She slid her paring knife out from under the mattress, hand trembling. She held it over his throat. Was going to push it into the side of his neck, right where he was a-pulsin'. But just then she looked up and saw me see her. Put her knife back under the mattress, laid back, and bled quietly. Her stain spread across the hard-packed dirt floor toward me—a tiny river of red. When she fell asleep, I rolled over and grabbed the edge of her knife still sticking out from under the mattress. I stole that paring knife and hid it. A new part of me, a cutter, got born. That's my first memory."

Cornelia put her roller down, crawled over to me, and rocked me slow, back and forth. "Shh, my baby. Shh, Mama be here." I fell on her shoulders, wrapped my arms around her, and wept. White on black, hush-hush, comfortable. First time since Ma died, comfort-able.

40

LEAH

We'd traveled up the Jordan Valley for two days out of Jericho, hit the main crossroads south of Shechem, and filled our water skeins at Jacob's Well. We kept traveling lonely dirt roads. Late in the afternoon, we came to a cluster of twenty or so adobe homes, some rambling up the hill with add-ons for their grown-up children. All those homes circled a well and general store. A few gravestones were clustered together opposite the well—an overgrown, weedy village cemetery.

A man leaned against a gravestone playing a hollow reed. The music was mournfully off-key and fit his smell, a nose-wrinkling odor like what you'd expect off a gravedigger's boots. I couldn't tell the difference between the smell and the sound, but I knew if this man disappeared *now,* it wouldn't be too soon.

When Rabbus turned to get something out of Mercy's pack, Stinky Mouth Organ let his gray prayer shawl drop. One black eye rolled around in its socket, the other dragged itself all over me, real wanton like. I wanted to run shrieking into the hills. Instead, I walked ladylike into the store with my fiancée.

The wizened wisp of a guy behind the counter squinted as he studied Rabbus. "You look familiar, boy."

"Farm's a couple of miles up the road."

"Gilboa place? West of here?"

Rabbus nodded. "Yep. My pa, Abbas, had a scar like a new moon over his right eye, black hair thinning on the top. He smiled real rare, like it might bankrupt him."

The old man chuckled. "Yep, that's Abbas, all right. You'd stop on your way from school every day or so for a sweet. Scared of your own shadow back then, Bar-Abbas. Anything changed?"

Rabbus scratched his beard. "Not much inside, but you'd never know it from the way I act."

I listened from a few steps back. Trust grew for my man, tingled my spine. I bolded up with a question of my own. "What do you remember about his ma?"

The shopkeeper called his wife from the back room, "Liza, get out here! We got a question."

A white-haired woman with sparkling blue eyes crisped around the corner. Sunlight trailed behind her like spilled milk.

Ben asked her, "Remember Abbas' wife?"

Liza piped, "Sure do, cutest twitch of a gal. Surprised us all and busted out a baby boy. Hardly showed at all. In danger of disappearin' if she turned sideways."

Rabbus said, "That boy would be me. I've grown some."

She stood, hands on her hips. "Well, well, now! You done growed *way* up. An' that girl you've got looks just like your ma come back from the dead. Both of you girls, feathers in the breeze."

Ben asked, "Coming back ta homestead the place? Be real nice to have you here."

Liza added, "Ben and a few others found their bodies and put 'em in that cave facin' Gerizim."

Rabbus' eyes sprang hot tears. He knelt, bent his head to their feet. "I'm so grateful for your kindness. Always imagined them left in the fields for vermin to eat."

A new voice cut through the air like a dagger. "Get off yer face, crybaby, Barry."

Stinky Mouth Organ stood behind the flour bin.

Liza called out, "Crispus, you've no call to be rude to your old classmate. Apologize to him right this minute, young man."

Crispus walked toward us, stood with arms crossed, legs splayed. He didn't seem overly eager to apologize.

Rabbus wiped his eyes dry with his sleeve, then turned to his childhood playmate. "Your pa was the lead defender at Sebaste when the Romans took it down."

"Course he was. We wuz kids when the legionnaires killed him. Ma too after they raped her. Threw my two-year-old sister off the fortress walls. Soldiers made bets which one could catch her on his spear."

Crispus turned and kept talking. "They cut Pa's head off, boiled it clean, and made it into a goblet. Forced me to drink from his skull 'fore they let me go. They knew I'd talk—be their warning not to mess with Rome.'"

He flicked a malevolent look at Laz, who stood by the wall, with his tallit and arm band phylactery. "Jews taught me to hate. Romans spun me up from there. Got real good at it."

Rabbus asked, "Your wife helpin' your hatin'?"

"Na, she ain't helpin' with nothing. Divorced that bitch."

Ben punched a gentle hole in that darkness. Let a little light into the conversation. "Crisp, easy to hate. Anybody can do that. Knowing the right way, right reason, right season, for mad? Well, now, *that* be exceedin' hard."

Crispus paid him no mind. He picked his nose and wiped the bugger on the countertop.

Rabbus' voice sounded to me like he'd dipped it in iron. "Jews and Romans didn't need to school you in meanness. You were that way as a kid—pulling legs off of frogs, diddling baby girls over there in the cemetery, setting cats on fire after you'd tied their tails together."

Crispus rolled his right eye up and around while he worked his jaw. "You always wuz a pussy. Plain weak, Barrie-baby."

Rabbus whipped out his knife. A blade also appeared in Crispus' hand. I stepped in between them. "You two! Don't kill this guy, Rabbus. He doesn't know you anymore, all that trainin' in killing you got. How easy it'd be for you to gut him. Have mercy on him, for my sake."

Crispus looked suddenly unsure of the proceedings.

Liza, the peacemaker, joined forces with me. She smiled and said, "Interested in killin'? Try the goat out back, Crisp. We'll have him for dinner." She seemed to know good peace would come from bad blood only by sacrifice.

The men went out back and went about the business of bloodletting. Rabbus protested Ben's extravagance—this was his only goat.

Ben said, "Ain't getting' my goat, no sir. He's mine to give. I've wanted to get rid of that mangy creature ever since he ate my grapevines."

Crispus drew his blade slow and jagged across the goat's throat. He gurgled with glee as the goat's head lifted off his skinny frame. "Ha!" I shivered my way back to help Liza.

We ate goat and memories for dinner. Ben could remember stuff from Rabbus' childhood, but not what he did yesterday. Crispus reclined at the table's end, half in shadow. He barked contradictions of others' recollections. After dinner, when he finally wandered away into the dark cemetery and beyond, I felt like a camel's hoof had been taken off my chest.

This old couple stood outside the next morning and waved good-bye till we crested a hill. These two enjoyed a tender loyalty that waits for the lucky on the other side of passion, smack in the middle of widow's hump and half-a-memory. Ben remembered enough to sweet-hug the woman inside the hump, and Liza rested her head inside his arms at about his belly button.

Laz, Rabbus, and I took a lonely side road up into the hills toward the top of Mt. Gerizim, the Samaritan's holy mountain. We passed deserted farmsteads with no animals in the paddocks, olive trees gone wild, and fruit trees withered. Long, thin, black clouds scudded north. A cutting wind seethed from out of the south. Tumbleweeds lived out their name.

All three of us pulled our cloaks across our faces, slitted our eyes. The higher we climbed, the more we saw of the Jordan River valley. The river far below reminded me of an emerald-green snake uncoiling itself through this Promised Land of promises that hadn't yet arrived.

We finally arrived at what was left of his folks' homestead. Charred timbers lay in patches around a collapsed roof. Wild weeds twined their way out the windows. Fields lay fallow. A squall swept in, switching the land with spitting rain.

Rabbus wept. I took his hand. "What Jesus said's true—good grief needs big boxes. One body's not enough to hold all your crap."

Rabbus ambled quiet-like beside me, his tears mixin' with God's sky-tears. "I've been walking around with my parents' corpses on my back. That's the way we Samaritans used to punish murderers—bound their victims to their backs till the murderer died too."

I held Rabbus' hand all the way to his parents' cave grave. The great, heavy clouds swept over the homestead. Lightning flashed across the desolations, where earth had torn away from red rock like flesh peeled back from the earth's body. We sat cross-legged at death's entrance, facing the Holy Mountain.

Rain splattered Rabbus' face and dripped off his nose. He turned to me, sitting inside his rain slicker he'd given me. "You're my bigger box. You help me hold my sad and mad, so I don't spill out on folks like Crisp does. Ma did that for me when I was a kid. Now, you. You not only look like my ma. You sound like her. Smart like foxes, beautiful as gazelles leaping on Gerizim."

I secreted a smile to my newly beautiful, and now smart self, my covered woman self. I might need this new me someday, maybe even today.

A quiet voice crept inside my slicker, cocooned in my inner ear. *I'm Jesus' Spirit, breathing your man and you. Pay attention—the sound of Yahweh's vowels are the sound of your own breath. My little wind moves in and out of your body, unseen, unrecognized, about sixteen times a minute. Get conscious.*

I sat still in the spitting rain, cocooned, eyes closed, listening to the Wind. I listened in this land where old memories of violence still prowled, and new memories hadn't yet been born. A time of in-betweens.

41

JESUS

John yelled from down in the hole, "Jeez, you sure you should be talking to that goy gal down at the well? She's loaded *way down* with lechery, crammed with concupiscence, slammed with salaciousness—you know what I mean? She's like the twitchy, bitchy Witch of Endor."[26]

I laughed out loud, joined his dance and song, dancing down in our foundations—way, way down.

John didn't let up. "I mean, wickedness rolls out of her like she could butter you up and wolf you down. Infect you with lust. Torah teaches light should *not* cavort with darkness, right? Guard your rep, cousin. She's bad news, double trouble."

I glanced at him. "Folks who didn't love you might feel judged."

I mixed a bucket of quicklime drippings with small rock, handed it down to John.

"Cousin, you do know judgment drives people away from you."

John rested an elbow on his shovel handle.

I kept on digging with my words. "I can't keep from wondering something. Okay if I tell you what I'm thinking?"

"Sure. You were going to tell me anyway."

"If you want your judgments, smell, clothes, and diet to keep people at arm's length, you're succeeding."

"Hadn't thought about it, Jeez. Just who I am. Like me or leave me. Besides, I don't have the money to buy cool clothes. Uncle Zeb and I, we don't wash much."

"But you *can* be tender. For example, the other day, you let yourself feel and share sad stuff with me."

"I only do that with you. You're heart-safe. And my head's chock full of the Book. Believe me, Law and Prophets tell me that goy girl's packed full of the wrong stuff."

I admired his zeal. "I love you trying to help me. Maybe I could help you too? I could help you deliver the goods, kindly like."

"I'm already in good company," John said. "Jeremiah, Isaiah, Amos. They all got killed telling people to repent. I got wood to chop for God. If they don't turn around, they're headed straight for hell. If I didn't tell them to repent, how loving would that be?"

He danced out a zippy tune he'd created on the spot:

> If God's law you spurn,
> You'll scorch, you'll churn.
> So, turn, you sinners—turn or burn.

John bopped to the sound of his own music, collapsing a side of the trench where he'd laid concrete down the day before. I grabbed his shovel, jumped down in the dirt, and shoveled it out for him. I saw the concrete he'd put down, once I'd cleaned it. He'd drawn a stick figure in the concrete. The man's arm extended, with his forefinger pointing down at a bunch of smaller stick figures. The word 'REPENT' was scribbled into the concrete in block letters above all the stick figures.

The concrete had cracked all the way through. The crack extended one side of the trench to the other, right through the bigger figure's body, separating his head from his torso.

John stood at the top of the trench, looking down at what I was seeing. He had a fresh bucket of concrete in his hands.

I said, "Gimme that." John lowered the bucket down.

I got down on my hands and knees and said, "Come down here with me."

He threw off his work sandals and got down on his hands and knees next to me. I poured the bucket of concrete over his work from the day before, smoothed all the edges and cracks.

I put my hand over his. I moved our hands together, using our forefingers to write the word, 'LOVE' into the concrete. I signed it with our initials, mine over his.

John realized what I had done and broke into a familiar song from the Proverbs. Together we sang how love covers all offenses[27]—not because we'd resolved any differences in our approach or style, but because we loved each other.

I put my arm around my cousin's shoulder when we finished our song.

I said, quite solemnly, "Father creates and judges. Windy convicts and comforts. I love. In the same way faith in Father is my foundation, your faith in me will make an excellent foundation for you."

Maybe it was the confined space in the trench, or maybe I got too close. Don't know. But suddenly, John's eye twitched, and he jammed his big toe in his mouth, right there in the footing. He ripped his big toenail to the quick.

Windy, what's up with this biting stuff?

John popped up to his feet and climbed out of the trench. He breathed deep and rested his hands on his knees. "Got nervous. Needed some air. I gotta chew on your words some more. But I felt loved by your touch. And I'm not ready to stop telling people to repent. I like that... *a lot.*"

I climbed out of the trench and hugged my cousin. "Sin is a wound, not a stain. Sin needs kind healing, not hard judgment. Judgment often covers cracks in character. Besides that, well-lived lives are far more compelling than well-preached sermons."

A light, persistent breeze soothed his wild hair, as if kind thoughts from Windy were filtering back into his head, down into his roots, and thawing his heart.

A week or so passed. It was a Friday, around one in the afternoon. Sweltering heat. Payday. Our whole work crew was leaving soon for Shabbat.

Grandma, who lived below the fortress in Sepphoris, had arrived with Deborah to get a few coins from Abba. Ma had let my littlest sister overnight with grandma yesterday. Now they stood just inside the main gate. Deborah bounced up and down—more liveliness in that girl than a tumble of new puppies.

I stood behind the fortress wall, looking up. Abba straddled the third story wall above me on the fortress ledge. Getting a roof on a fort was no light matter. The triangular trusses had been prepared carefully on the ground.

Abba had sured walls to footings. The footings fit the foundations. The foundations rested on the rock. All that remained was this one, heavy truss, hanging from a hoist and a pulley. Put me in mind of a gallows, drifting in the wind, rope tied to a scaffold.

What's up, Windy?

Breathe me in, Son. Breathe, receive Our love.

Uh, okay. But why am I so scared? No answer.

The wind freshened. Heavy, dark clouds gathered. A tiny bolt of lightning hit the tallest tree on a hill to the north. Dust devils swirled in the sand. Claudius and a group of apprentice swordsmen stopped to see what was hanging over their heads, up there in the courtyard.

The monster frame dangled close to Abba, waiting for him to secure it to the far wall. He rested for a moment, both hands in his carpenter's apron, oblivious to the eyes that gazed at him. He saw me outside the back gates with my feet planted on the cliff's edge. He waved, and I held my arms up to him, passing him my love and loyalty. I leaned back, shielded my eyes from the high sun.

I knew Abba's micro-rhythms of work and rest—focus, work, stop, and soak. He drifted into a gap. Most times, a word or vision followed, and Abba returned to work, refreshed. I felt his tidal rhythm in my bones.

I knew even now that whoever I gazed at most, was mostly who I'd be like. Abba and Father took up most of my vision.

Everyone else was out of focus, except for the wild-eyed, gray-shawl guy. He stood under the fortress entrance behind Grandma and Deborah, resting his hand on Deborah's shoulder. He rubbed her neck softly. She looked up and leaned her little head into the massage. His one wandering black eye rolled back and forth between Abba and me, gazed at us both from a face that was both hungry and cold.

I bolted across the crowded courtyard, wanting to wrench his grubby paws off my sister. But that's when something else happened.

42

WINDY

Joe sat three stories up, mulling a dream I'd given him the night before. I splashed eidetic images around his mind's eye—Jesus, mummified, stalking a grave from inside the grave's cave, swinging a cross beam like a gladiator, cleaning house.

Joe dream-blinked. Jesus, unbound, leapt out of the same grave and ran toward him, radiant, yelling, "Victory over death, at last, Abba!"

I'd trained Joe to act on what I gave him in dreams and visions. He mixed inner dreams with outer life. He saw Jesus looking up at him and raised his arms to celebrate his son's victory.

Behind Abba and his raised arms, Satan rode the hanging truss, lips like split liver in a rictus of howling glee. He whipped the wind around him into a microburst. Truss swirled like a wild, horned bull that he rode, one arm flying behind him. His vicious self darkened the day.

Jesus saw Satan in a flash. His body tingled with adrenalin, top to bottom. "Abba, watch out!"

He was too late. The beam clocked Joe in the head at high speed. Satan's knockout punch blew Joe ten feet out from the wall before Satan projected himself straight into Crispus on the other side of the courtyard.

Joe's body hung motionless in midair for a microsecond, arms raised high. Then he dropped like a rock.

Jesus absorbed rat-a-tat-tat, those three things—impact, projection, and his plunging Abba. Joe hurtled headfirst, a few inches beyond Son's reach, into the gorge below. Joe made no sound. The final crunch of head on rocks ended his life on this earth. I held his spirit close, so he could see what unfolded.

John and Jesus raced to the bottom of the gorge, carrying an empty litter. John led the way, kicking scree off the path. Together they found him. John wrapped his arms around Jesus briefly, tenderly.

He became self-conscious and stiffened. "Let's get him out of here, Jeez."

John stripped to his loincloth and wrapped Joe's shattered skull in his camel skin. They laid Joe's body on their stretcher and John led up-trail, Joe's cooling earth-wrapper stretched between them. They arrived in the fortress courtyard. Distracted, Jesus looked for his grandma and baby sister, panicked heart thudding like a cut truss hitting ground. *Where is that man? I'll tear him apart limb from limb.*

Crispus had vanished.

Antonio, the twins, their father and mother, hovered. Soldiers, at tribune's order, stood at attention. Claudia searched Jesus out, desperate to connect. I turned up the heat on her dream altar a notch or two. Sharp-toothed Grief edged her way into the edges of Claudia's world.

The Roman reached out and touched the Jew as he walked by. Jesus drifted by her, fingers slipping over hers as he went by, eyes cradled in shock absorbers.

Jesus and John began their two-mile journey to the cemetery. A cortege of well-wishers walked beside them. Crispus loitered behind and in back of these supporters, arcing thin needles of hatred through the air at Son.

Jesus' grandmother and Deborah walked closer to Jesus. Deborah didn't understand who was under the shroud, but she had caught the contagion of sadness, Jesus' and Grandma's shock. She cried, shaken but safe, and for now, she was alive. So unlike Joe.

Every so often, pallbearers changed. Abba's work companions wanted to help. When Jesus wasn't carrying Abba's body, he walked beside it, his hand on the litter.

When they arrived at the cemetery, Jesus asked John to run to Nazareth. "Take Debbie with you. Tell Ma the news. I'll stay with Abba's body." John trotted toward Nazareth, Debbie on his shoulders.

Jesus lay next to his abba on the ground. He didn't see the green hills above him where mist fingered along the slopes and fed the grass.

Jesus silently complained to Father. *Everything's rattled loose in my head—I can't figure out what's real and what I'm imagining. Real or not, I feel like You designed life poorly for happiness to have a chance on this planet. None, no chance. Nothing to slip-knot soul-wrench.*

Aninut, this most intense period of Jewish mourning, poured him out like new wine. He ripped the tunic over his heart.[28] Then he lay still, a steady drip of 'if only' acid dripping from Son to Father and Me.

If only I had seen Satan earlier…

If only I called out louder…

If only I sat with Abba on the wall, between him and the wooden beam—and the beams of hatred from Satan.

Jesus wanted to jab lightning bolts at Satan. *Vengeance is mine. I'll repay. I'll twist you in your own typhoon!*

He did none of that. Instead, he lay still as a broken corpse. Still as the broken corpse his abba had become. No energy even to sit.

Jesus sensed angel swirl. Seraphim fluttered curious heads, tipped sideways, two of their six wings covering their eyes. They murmured *holy, holy, holy's*. One small seraph uncovered one eye, peeked at Jesus, and busted out sobbing.

Father and I sat on either side of Son, wordless. We didn't intrude, didn't lighten his load with resurrection reminders, didn't argue with him like Job's friends. We let him sit silent, sift in the suck, be stuck. We gave him dark gifts—unalloyed grief, severe mercy.

Our plan, so long ago, was *not* for Jesus to save folks from suffering, but to show people how to *bear* suffering. He hated Our plan, perfectly. He now knew-felt, with all children of men, the grief of a gone father. Sadness and madness played havoc in his heart. Some, a few, could bear this grief. Others got drunk, got laid, got gone.

John burst into the compound where Mary played in the courtyard with Miriam. Deborah crawled off his shoulders and went to play with her sister.

John braked himself from blurting, "Joe's dead!" He thought, *I've got crummy social skills! Why did Jesus ask me to do this?*

I schooled. He listened. *How would a reasonable person, John, want to find out that her husband's brains just got splashed all over a bunch of rocks?*

John asked Mary, "Aunt Mary, could you come with me for a walk in the olive trees?"

Mary sensed something was up. "John, where's Joe, where's Jesus?" she asked.

"Uhh, could you come with me out back, please?"

She came. They walked to a bench Jesus had crafted, by the garden wall. John carefully wiped the bench down with the hem of his tunic.

John said, "Will you sit with me?" She sat.

I whispered to him, *you're doing good. Steady now, John.*

"Joe just died an hour ago," he muttered.

He thought, *I can't get these sissy tears gone. Elijah would be calm as a judge.*

Mary listened, frozen, until a wave of pain, like hot light, poured through her, top to bottom. A chunk of it stuck in her throat.

John kept going. "A microburst came out of nowhere, blew a hanging truss right into him. Long fall, third-story wall. Gorge ... way down below. Hit head-first. Sorry."

I planted the whisper of a thought in his inner ear, *Jesus sent you as a messenger of death to help you heal from your abba's death over a decade past. It's okay, John, to be the sovereign of snot and sucky social skills.*

John rearranged his stiff body, breathed in my counsel, and had himself a think.

43

MARY

John stopped talking, thankfully. The ground beneath me felt fluid. My garden seemed like molten pitch, swirling me down. I held onto John's arm to keep from disappearing.

John put his hand over mine, and we rocked in the wind. He was silent. Finally, I was able to feel his hand on mine and my feet on solid earth.

He said, "We need to bury Joe before sundown."

I said, "Thank you for telling me the news away from the children. You've become so sensitive." John's eyebrows popped up, surprised looking.

He said, "Me?"

I said, "Yes, you."

Together, we moved inside the house, and I called my children to the dinner table. I took my place, opposite Abba's empty chair. "I have some very sad news, children. Abba fell while he was at work. He fell a long way. Jesus is with Abba's body at the cemetery. We must all bury him before Shabbat starts at sundown. Please help me."

Wide-eyed, not understanding, Miriam and Deborah trailed close behind me, hanging on to my skirts. We swathed shock in busyness—rushed about to collect linen strips, spices, and shreds of sanity. Justus and Jude slowly gathered these burial supplies, as if in a stupor.

I walked by James as he stared in a mirror. His lower lip trembled, but then he saw me and hid his face. I stopped and wrapped my arms around him, weeping softly. "It's okay, Son. It's okay to cry." He wiped his tears away, and we went about the business of dealing with death.

Two hours later, we all arrived at the cemetery with death's implements—sweet-smelling spices meant to fool the nose, strips of linen for wrapping his body, sober men with sharp shovels, women with water to wash my lover's body. Busied people, desperate to slow the passage of putrefaction.

I didn't know where to house this loss within me, so I tucked my beloved in a little box and slid him on a secret shelf next to my own abba, and Jesus. Two done deaths, and another on the way. These three coffins shimmered, buried within the numbing, dumbing business of death. Mind and heart would later find a marriage within me, a way to deal with this death. But today was not that day.

We washed Joe's body in the prescribed *taharah* way. Moshe's wife, Esther, and Beka helped. I couldn't cope with his crushed head. Beka did that, laying aside John's camel skin and tying Joe's skull together with linen strips. We then gave Joe's body over to the men, who carefully lowered him into the earth.

The dipping sun gilded cloud's edges, slipping lower toward the ground, also ready to be swallowed by the earth. A growing company gathered around my man's grave—Abishag and the robbers, lepers standing beyond the fringes, announcing themselves unclean, like death, the golden, gilded Tribune Gaius and his family—hemmed on all sides by soldiers. The inner minyan of the synagogue.

We gathered to remember my earth husband—the gentle dreamer, the careful craftsman, the obedient believer—a simple man who dared go against the grain, take the night road to Egypt, marry a teenage girl claiming to be pregnant by God; a man chosen to step-father the divine and be fathered by him; a dreamer who did things right while doing the right thing, down to the last detail.

The sun, halfway swallowed by the earth, turned the sky into a blood-red riot of color. The cemetery became a mix of darkness, almost darkness, and shimmering glimmers that hit my eye—spirits swooshing around us all. I imagined Heavenly Husband wandering the perimeter of our gathering, drifting among the lepers, gazing soberly over his collected creation.

He said to me, clear as a bell, *you alone, Mary, will be with our Son at his birth, here in the middle stretches of suffering, and at his death.*

I harbored his words and replied, You must be exhausted, perpetually standing at both cradle and grave. But at least, in this moment, at this grave, you linger around our Son. I see your wind flowing through his hair. Also, wrapping me in your arms.

I turned my eyes to the patch of ground where Joe lay. *Oh, my baby, why did you fall?*

44

LEAH

Rabbus and I led Mercy and Goodness. Laz had ridden Betsy for the last day, claiming a case of body ache and the runs. He'd stop, time to time, disappear back of a rock. A few minutes later, he'd catch up, looking pale and exhausted. We plodded into Nazareth, arriving at Jesus and Laz's family quad the day after Shabbat.

John was the first person to meet us. He sat on a bench outside the compound, scanning the street. Once he saw us, he ran to greet us. He stumbled around, "Uh, I want to talk to you first, Laz. Over there on that bench, the one I brought from Mary's garden. Then I want to talk to you, Leah." He flashed a fierce look at Rabbus.

We waited and watched while John sat with Laz on the bench. Laz looked puzzled at first, but then John leaned into the space between them and burst into a flood of guttural whispers. Laz's foot danced around and tears came to his eyes. A minute more, and Laz ran inside the gate, tears coursing down his face.

John approached us. When Rabbus wanted to speak, letting him know our news, John held up his hand, saying he wanted to talk to just me. Rabbus shut up and patted Mercy's nose.

John took me a few steps further down the street and asked me to sit on the same bench, the same spot where Laz sat. He wiped it off with a cloth first, got all the edges clean of something I couldn't see.

He lowered his voice and flattened it. "Sorry to be the bearer of bad news, Leah, but Joe fell from up high off the fortress, fell on some stones. He died."

He studied my face before he kept talking. "After Joe fell on those stones, some stones fell on your abba. He died. Happened after you left town. I feel bad, really bad, for you. Sorry."

I didn't know what to say, so I sat in silence.

Rabbus hovered at a distance, watching John like a falcon might eye a rabbit. If I'd started to weep, I had visions of him coming after John with a knife. I breathed deep and kept my face solemn. A frantic feeling clawed its way up my throat.

Oh, John was talking again.

He asked, "How did I do?"

I managed to say, "Do what?"

"Uh, telling you all this bad news on Jesus' bench."

"You did good to tell me." I glanced at Rabbus. "I'd say you're brave and kind, and a little awkward."

"Good. I'm practicing this whole sensitive, feeling thing." When he stood, his sandals moved a few pebbles. The sound felt jagged, like a crate of dinnerware splattering on the cobblestones.

Rabbus walked up. John bounced his eyes off my man. He said, quite loudly, "You shouldn't associate with a heathen man like him, Leah. Those Samaritans should *repent*."

Flash fantasy of Rabbus' throwing knife ending up in John's throat. I looked at Rabbus and barely shook my head. Rabbus' hands held peaceably onto each opposite elbow, as was the custom when greeting another that you might want to kill.

My man and I moved past John and went inside Joe and Mary's home. A bunch of grown-ups sat still as statuettes, arranged in circles of care around Mary and her children. She was dressed in widow white, rocking back and forth, face hollow, eyes brimming.

Jesus sat on her right side. She leaned on his shoulder, he on hers. He caught my eye, and the edge of his mouth quivered up and back down. A welcome smile? I nodded, and we sat by the door, past the outer circle of those sitting Shiva.

James, thirteen, was on Mary's left side. He held a scroll with both hands. He brushed a bit of dust off it, then held it to his lips and kissed it. He held it to his nose, inhaled deeply. *I'm sure it was his Abba's smell he breathed in.*

After Go and I had moved in with their family, James once told me his first memory. "I was three or four, living in Egypt. Abba and I had both come home from the *mikvah*. The Torah was on the table before us. Abba put me on a stool so I could see. His hand moved my hand, and together our hands moved the *yad*. We inched it right to left, pointing to one letter at a time, and then down the page, one line at a time. Abba read aloud God's *very own* words!"

Now words spilled softly off James' lips and into the air. His whole upper body rocked forward and then back to vertical, back and forth, again and again.

Justus, a pale ten-year-old, sat sandwiched between James and Jude. His eyes flitted around the room, then settled on the patch of ground between his crossed legs. He wiggled, looking like he was digging his butt into the ground. James passed him a thin scrap of a scroll. Soon this scroll went to his lips, his nose. He inhaled, sighed, and words began rocking into his body through his eyes.

Jude, age eight, sat on Justus' left side. He refused a scroll fragment when James offered him one. He hunched over, drawing the same picture over and over again on the dirt floor. He used a pointy little stick to draw a tall wall with individual bricks. Stick man with a big head sat on the wall, on edge. A triangle truss dangled from a hangman's rope in front of the man. Jude then drew a zippy swirl, whirling toward the wall. Stopped, glared, gained control of the quivering stick. Drew it again. *Hmm, not quite right. Again.* In each drawing, one thing was the same. The man on the wall refused to fall.

The little girls, Miriam, five, and Deborah, two, stole the show on this first day of sitting Shiva. Everyone silently watched Joe's girls do grief their way. Miriam and Deborah lay on their tummies by their Ma's feet. They fussed with two girl dolls, each doll clothed in severe white—also, a taller man doll, smudged ash on his chin.

Both girls got on their knees and marched their dolls away from Mama's feet toward a make-believe burial cave in the far corner of the room. The circles of adults opened a passage for them to pass.

Miriam softly sang a traditional Jewish dirge in a high child's soprano. Deborah elbow-and-kneed her way behind her sister, picking up the tune. Together, a slow *levayah* processional.

One of them dripped tears from a water cup behind the dolls on little flower stems they had stuck in the dirt. Their dance of the dolls was in perfect rhythm with the lament. They moved from mother to corner, womb to tomb, before they placed the man doll faceup in the corner grave. His arms angled above his head, praising God. The little ones bent dolls down to kiss Abba's forehead.

Once Abba was honored in this way, the baby dolls made their way back to Mama. Each child popped her head on Mama's lap. Deborah snuggled into the space between Jesus and Mama; Miriam, between James and Mama. Their two shining heads lapped up mama love. Mother Mary smoothed their hair, caressed their cheeks, insulating her babies from death's terror.

Once refueled, the girls repeated the ritual march. They traded who got to drip tears on the bare flowers, who led the dolls to the grave, and the song they sang.

I liked the girls' good grief better than big people's still grief. Too much wool-gathering with this silent, sit-on-your-butt sadness. Almost as bad as sitting in a room with another person talking about sad stuff. Left too long in a place like that, and I'd become a real nutter.

I whisked quietly over to the little girls. "Can I join you?"

"Oh, yes!" They made room for me. Miriam reached into the pocket of her dress and produced another doll. She smoothed the doll's hair and gave it to me. I trolled along behind them in the dirt and silently turned Joe's Shiva into my pa's.

I imagined him lying in his grave. I seemed to be more comfortable with the dead than the living. When pa was alive, he often riled my stomach, like a cake of bitter herbs. Now I could rest, wrapped in memories.

I was someone who heard music and felt stuff inside my skin. Like Mama, the musician. I could hear her, thrumming out a dirge on her lyre in King Eglon's palace. She was a hot spot of light within me, vibrating. *Blend the tones, Leah. Bless the sounds. Listen to layers in the song. Feel the sound touch your skin.*

Yes, Mama.

I listened longer, allowing her words to become events, with power. They did things in me, pushed me to my knees, kneeled me, moved me.

Not only did Mama's *words* move me, but her jubilant flute—a solitary soprano, trumpeted Pa's death. That, too, moved my spirit. *He's done his worst, child, and will hurt you no longer.*

Mama's lyre trilled when she plucked the strings. *Let my spirit lift your head, little Leah.*

Her drums were like the stones' percussive clatter that crushed her. *Under the clatter, hear my voice, child. I wait for you in this still space where spirit rules supreme. My spirit twines with God's Spirit, closer than your beating heart. I practiced breathing Yahweh's name in and out with each breath, "Ya"on the inhale, "Weh" on the exhale. Spirit shwoosh.*

Mama's silent music mingled with her words, providing a hidden Shiva for pa, and her. The music of her memory moved me across the hard pack of mother earth.

Stuff dribbled from my nose. I scrunched my eyes tighter, leaned into the dark, night music. Mama said, *give my song—our song—a name, little Leah.*

All right, Mama. Silence, then, "Bittersweet, in grave minor."

Taste of her honey mixed with wormwood and filled my mouth. *Very good,* she said. *And daughter, one more thing. Choose your own life, not my unlived, cut-short life. That's the stuff of tragedy.*

I stood and walked to Rabbus, carrying my inside calm like a glistening harp made of spider's strands, trembling, easily torn.

When I rejoined Rabbus, seated by the door, he whispered, "I've finally arrived at death's door, safe. And I don't know what to do."

I squeezed his hand and spoke, my mouth to his ear, with words way beyond my knowing. "Hold on. It's a wave. Ride it. This suffering has come to pass, come to pass—not to stay."

45

JESUS

Shiva had been sat, silence endured, "Joe" stories told. The week was done, the grief begun. On this day in creation, the third day of the week, God pronounced creation 'good,' twice. How would Father doubly bless *this* day?

Rabbus asked, "Will you run an errand with Leah and me?"

I caught some urgency in his voice. Didn't know why this was a big deal. Even so, my bones vibrated. *This is the right thing. Do it.*

Rabbus dragged a little cart behind him with a covered chunk of something heavy on it. I pitched in, and Leah walked alongside. We ended up at the edge of the town dump.

The dump was a pocket of land outside the city gates that held stink close. All was empty, except for trash, blowing ash, and Father and Windy. They walked the dump together, picking over, under, and through the trash for anything wanting redemption.

Father bent down, unearthed a shattered vessel, held it in his open hand. *Windy, come here! Look at this beauty!* She swooped around him, *You crack me up, Pa! What a wonderful wreck!*

Windy then circled me and my friends. She broke into a requiem mass, singing all four parts, harmonic within herself—gorgeous grief enveloping, soaring, thundering, and then whispering her threnody.

Father kept picking over the trash, dancing in rhythm to her melody. He kept moving toward the lower edge of the burning fires, where Ach was buried.

We all arrived graveside about the same time. Rabbus troweled out a rectangular indent in the ground above the grave, about six inches deep. He went back to the cart, motioned to me. We each took one end of a marble slab and side-crabbed this heavy piece to one end of the mound.

We lowered it into the indent, and I stepped back. Leah and Rabbus positioned the stone, smoothed the edges, filled the borders.

We three sat around the grave, Leah between Rabbus and me. Ash blew through our hair and the smell of fire filtered into our lungs. She leaned forward and fingered the etched letters Rabbus had chiseled during the night hours:

Achan the Amalekite
"Bittersweet"

"You never loved me," Leah murmured. She wept silently at first, then wuffled louder and louder, sobbing furiously, shaking with the felt force of her lonely legacy. Rabbus held her.

She gently pushed away from him and sat straighter. Between hiccups and sobs, "You didn't know how to love me, Papa. No one ever taught you how to love—only how to work, hate, and take."

"Go got your 'too-muchness.' Too much false praise, lust, rage, greed, grasping. It wasn't her fault she was so pretty."

She paused, hiccupped. "I got your too-littleness—too little praise, too little speaking good about me, too little holding, too little play. You couldn't see anything beautiful about me. I was so plain."

Her voice gained strength. "You whacked us all about the head and heart. You taught me I was ugly, unlovable, unworthy, not ever enough. Wasn't right. Wasn't real." Her little fist slammed the ground beside his headstone. "I have to punch a hole in those lies to get whole. Too late for Mama, too late for you. Oh, Papa, what a gruesome way to die, both you and Mama! All of us, lost sheep."

Windy edged closer, nestled between Leah and Rabbus, weeping now, no longer swooping. Father stood beside her, presiding. His arms stretched out, a vase in his right hand, Windy under his left arm.

Leah whimpered, "Oh, Papa! Before I go, two things. Go's found the man you found for her, Laz. She's even starting to like him. And, Papa, I've found the man who first found me. He's loving, lovely, loyal. You may have seen him at work. Quiet, like you. Good with his hands. He made your marker."

She finished. "I think he sees good in me, Papa. He tells me what you didn't. First time in my life a man thinks I'm pretty. I might believe him one day.

"Papa, I'm thirteen now. I'm of age, a woman, not a girl anymore. I'm permitting myself to marry him since you and Mama aren't here. We'll have and hold one another till death takes one or the other. We'll live the life you couldn't, wouldn't. Goodbye, Papa."

She fell silent. She'd said it all, said it well.

The rest of us heard her words, felt their weight.

The baking sun inched higher, blinding blaze mixed with smoke. Wild weeds grew around the grave, scrofulous patches. The air was so dry, so acrid, that it burned my nostrils when I breathed.

Windy wisped inside Leah's veil, circled her head, and cooled her scalp, hugged her heart, and she whispered in her ear, *You're so gorgeous, my child. Oh, so brave.*

Leah's eyes widened.

Yes, Windy, she felt your hold, heard your whisper!

Leah faithed her face around, searching for the woman who voiced her praise. No one to be seen—just a gilded, glimmer-whisper. Leah looked again, behind her, around her, carefully searching.

She saw you, Father! Silhouette of Your back in blazing fire, unburned but glowing, liquid light coming not from around You, but within You. She saw You take that pot, stick it in Your chest for firing. Oops. She's lost you now—her faith's wallowing. Okay now, once again, there she goes, seeing and hearing! Looking, still harder. Her trust-eyes are gaining practice, Father.

Windy spoke, *Leah's listening to my music and blending it with her mother's music.*

Oh, okay, Windy, got it. And there You are, Father, shielding Your face from her view with one hand, leaking love her way, sheer radiance. Your other hand holds that broken pot toward her.

I saw, understood, stood.

Rabbus helped Leah up. She turned to him. "I think we need to cover this stone with dirt. Someone might steal it."

Together we took handfuls of dust with tiny pebbles, wisps of ash swirling in circles. Trash, dust, and ash invisibled the grave. Dust to dust; ash to ash.

Rabbus and I pulled the empty cart back toward Ach's old house in Nazareth. Leah walked beside us. When we were half-way between dump's edge and town, Rabbus and Leah stopped.

Leah piped up. "Jesus, we're thinking of settling Rabbus' old homestead in the foothills of Gerizim, a farm of our own, crops, vineyard. You know about vineyards—vines, branches, seeds, roots, right?"

I smiled, nodded.

She continued, "This might seem silly to you, Jesus, even worthless, but we wanted you to bless that ground in Samaria. You're just a few years older than me, nine years younger than Rabbus. Why is your blessing so needful? I have no idea. But it *is* necessary, like you. Each time I'm with you, I feel less a piece of fog. You're so valuable to both of us, precious."

I hugged her.

Leah added a burst of vulnerable feeling, "And when you hug me, I feel less ugly."

She picked up strength in her voice. "Also, another thing, Jesus. Could you stay in Jericho for a while with Laz and Go? She and Laz also need you to bless them, even if they don't know it yet."

Rabbus added, "I spoke with Laz. Mary and Ehud, Martha and Mordi—they'll all be settling in Bethany. It's time for them to leave and cleave—under their own roofs."

We kept heading up the winding trail a few more steps till we stood under an arch of hibiscus, bougainvillea, and red roses below, on a thorny vine. It was a free-for-all profusion of grace, a color riot of purples and gold, with a blood-red foundation. I stopped to admire the beauty, then laid down the cart. I turned to face my two friends, a little higher on the trail than where they stood.

"Rabbus, Leah. Will you face each other?"

They did.

Invisible to the couple, Father and Windy joined hands on either side of them, arching arms toward one another, joining the arching flowers.

Together they all covered this Samaritan-Moabite-Jewish couple.

I saw Them, smiled, felt so peaceful in Their embrace. Leah shivered. Mysterious, pulsing energy all-round, wombing her and her man.

"Take off your shoes. We're on holy ground."

They did.

"Now, hold hands."

They did.

"Rabbus, do you take Leah as your loyal wedded wife?"

Rabbus, delighted by surprise, surprised by joy, "I do."

I turned to the slight woman at his side. "Leah, do you take Rabbus as your loyal wedded husband?"

"I do." She busted into tears again, this time happy tears.

She and Rabbus looked at We three and saw only me—they beamed with borrowed glory, Eternity in their eyes.

"You are now husband and wife, in the eyes of God, We who assemble with you today. We bless you and keep you. We make our faces shine upon you. We give you our peace. From this day forward, you will be called blessed, because you trusted in me."

Windy whispered to Father, *dispatched and matched, all in one walk to the dump and back. Our boy's picking up speed.*

Father laughed, and I felt their pleasure. Windy whooshed around Father and me, once again faster than sound's speed, entwining, caressing, singing—a wedding march in four-part harmony for our pleasure, her music piped on the four winds.

Rabbus and Leah heard something that sounded heavenly, but couldn't quite make it out. If pure joy had a sound, perhaps that would be what they almost heard. As it was, they couldn't contain their amazement. Such an impromptu wedding, but it could not have been grander. Leah held her head high, stuck out her small breasts, and brushed ash off her wedding gown.

46
WINDY

Jesus said his goodbyes in front of his home on the Via Maris. Rabbus and Leah walked back to Ach's old hovel, approaching from the back.

"Rabbus, my lovely *husband,* can we clean this field of yellow rapeseed flowers off the roof? I want it gone. We need to make this place ours *before* we go inside. Ours. Not his."

Together they climbed the sides of the mud shack, dug their heels in, and yanked out the roots of all those bright, yellow flowers. Piled them up for burning the next day.

They walked to the front of the house. When they arrived at the door, they found Our wedding present under the lintel. I'd filled Father's vase with fine wine and set it solidly on the threshold. This pitcher was newly fired from Father's chest, still smoking from a close fire, pulsing light from within.

We had glazed the pot with royal purple and streaks of blood red. Jagged cracks ran down both sides, top to bottom. Each crack was sealed with pure gold, giving the vessel more beauty and strength than before it was broken. Beaten, polished gold also shimmered all along the rim of the pitcher's bottom edges. For the second time that day, their lives were purpled and engoldened, not with plants but a pot, fired with purpose.

Leah gave the full pot to her groom. She lay down on the threshold and asked Rabbus to hold the polished, golden bottom of the pot directly over her eyes. This mirror was only useful to Leah because she grounded herself and looked up. The pure gold mirrored her face perfectly.

She thought, hmm, my face, so happy. Her eyes flash-flooded with tears for the third time on this day. But this time, tears of insight and belief, not sadness, or even joy.

The newlyweds set the vase on the table next to their bed, then closed and locked the door. Each took more than a sip straight from the pot. They gazed into each other's eyes, full of liquid adoration. Fired desires intertwined. An hour or so later, according to Jewish custom, they displayed a bed sheet, smeared with unashamed blood, for all to see.

47

JESUS

I wandered out the back gates to stand on the very spot I'd been when my abba fell. I looked up and strained to see him once again, but the wall was empty. I plopped down with my back to the fortress wall, pried a sharp pebble out of one butt cheek, and pulled my blue prayer shawl over my head. I became a covered man.

Footsteps crunched gravel beside me. I shifted my head sideways, looked up. Claudia stood to my right. "So, here you are! I finally found you. Sit with you a while?"

I motioned to a spot next to me. Both of us leaned back against the white blocks of limestone. Our backs gathered heat from the stone wall of the garrison.

"What were you thinking about, Jesus?"

"Doubt. I'm not sure of anything these days, including myself."

"Isn't doubt what Satan does, not you?"

"Doubt isn't darkness. Father tells me mystery and paradox always do him more justice than clarity."

"Well, at least you know what you don't know. And your Pop gives you more knowledge than the rest of us dream about." She paused. "What's the latest info dump to Planet Earth, God-man?"

"Nothing new. I was whining. Telling Father, I wanted to be a kid again. Those days were sweet. Abba was alive. Israel and Egypt blended."

"How'd that work?"

"My playmate, Prince Julius, was the son of the Roman prefect over all Egypt. We were both five years old. We met because I was chasing down a dream Abba had shared at breakfast. Julius and I played hide-and-seek in the river reeds along the Nile, pretended to look for baby Moses in a tarred basket. We played tag in the palace, explored hidey-holes in the dungeons beneath, and found a whole wing of apartments in ruins.

"The furniture was all under white Egyptian cotton. I remembered turning back a white, cotton sheet that lay over a bed. A lifelike doll lay there, curled up, naked. Alone. It looked like you, blue eyes and reddish-brown hair."

Claudia winced, closed her eyes.

"Turns out these apartments once belonged to Cleopatra and Mark Anthony. Julius had discovered them. He told me, 'Come with me, Jesus. Yesterday, I found a tailpipe into the palace! We can climb up its royal ass!"

Claudia shook her head. "Julius lives in Rome now. He still has that wonky sense of humor. Also, he likes my curves." She sashayed out a flirty smile.

I rolled my eyes. "Memory lane helps with sadness. But a good flirt isn't in sight."

"Sorry. Trying to cheer you up." She grinned. "Like to see your buddy again?"

"Maybe one day, if he comes to Israel."

She shielded her eyes, looked down. "Go on, finish your story."

"Julius, I remember, crashed into his father's office one day, towing me behind him. He announced, 'This is my best friend, Papa. He'll bless you.' The prefect stood in front of his ornate, lacquered desk. It looked as old and frail as he did. I watched the veins under his paper-thin temples pulse. I remember thinking, maybe he's an alien visiting Egypt from a skinnier world."

"You can remember all that?" She seemed incredulous.

I nodded absently. "The prefect asked me, 'You're in the blessing business, are you, young man?'

"I said something like, 'Great Prefect, Prince Julius and I have been playing all over your palace. Did you know Queen Cleopatra's apartments are in shambles?'

"The prefect looked hard at me and said, 'Your voice—it trills, braids tones. Astonishing. Are you a native speaker of Latin?'"

"He was right," Claudia said. "You have a way with words. They flow from you—like you were a warehouse designed to house words."

"Thanks. Father tells me I am the Word, made flesh. Anyway, the prefect turned back to his work. I grabbed his sleeve. 'Before you go back to your desk, would you like your blessing, your Prefectness?'

He said, 'With the way my day has gone this far, a good blessing would be just the thing.'

"'Your physicians told you, just this morning, sire, you would die soon. But God told me that you will live longer. If you believe in Yahweh, you will live forever, a blessed man.'"

Claudia was intrigued. "You've had practice with this prophecy gig since you were a pip, huh?"

"Who I am and what I do is a unique Father-Son operation. We're willing to talk truth to anyone willing to listen and obey."

She replied, "I'm working on listening right now and not getting passing marks most of the time. Maybe the obeying thing comes later. What happened with Julius' father?"

"He said, 'Your family will live in Cleopatra's apartments. You will go to school with Julius.' He flicked his finger. His factotum wrote down the order on a tablet and said, 'The Prefect has spoken. Let it be done.'"

Claudia leaned against my shoulders and gazed up at the sky. "Cool story. You wander into town and *ba-ba-boom*, you're in bed with their worst nightmares. Never known a guy like you."

She sat straighter, turned to face me directly, "How're you doing with your abba's death?"

"Horrible. Do you know Satan caused that windstorm?"

"Nope. How could I see Satan at the well, but not the day your father fell?"

"Father gives clear seeing to those who honestly inquire after him. People who don't co-opt him for their purposes. Scheming people are blind people."

Claudia's face flushed. "Not sure what you're talking about, Mr. Mystic." She moved her foot away from mine, hugged her knees, leaned forward.

I spoke plainly. "You're holding back something. I can feel it. I do better with the simple truth. Yes and no. Half-truths are whole lies."

"Thanks, I'll file that." She laid her hand on my arm. "Jesus, the whole truth is that I want you. I don't think I can live without you."

"What do you mean?"

"How did you know about Claudius and me having sex?"

"Not a fan of subtle shifts, huh?"

"Nope. Same topic, different take."

She scratched her eye with a painted pinkie finger. Left a smudge, like a bruise leaking out. "Claud started messing with me when we were eight. Showed up in my bed one night, and that never stopped. It was like holding a bittersweet candy in my hand. I thought, don't taste! Then I put it on my tongue and thought, don't swallow! Then a string of sour hardballs, one after another. Soured that child's life. You are the sweetener now I can't live without."

I slammed the ground with my fist, angry tears popping out my eyes and down my cheeks. "I'm so mad *and sad* for that child, the innocent one lying on clean, white sheets. I couldn't protect her."

She startled.

"Yes, her! Windy revealed your fantasy that day at the well. None of us, Father, Spirit, or me—none of us could protect you and Claud from your own choices."

Claudia's eyes misted briefly. She looked away as if cramming her feelings far below an altar too hot to handle.

I was on a roll. "I hate this! I hate this wretched world—so *not* normal at Home—a world where hurt people hurt people right *here*."

She said, "Thanks for letting me in on what *normal* people feel. Maybe later I'll get there."

She smiled, suddenly chipper. "I have something else now—Gramps. You fingered him with the bony finger of fate, the one you carry in your back pocket. Gramps wanted to know when he's going to croak."

I wiped some tears with my forefinger, tasted them. "Don't know about that. I know only what Father tells me."

"Can you tell when *I'm* going to pass into Hades?"

"Nope. I only pick up what Father sends down. You dash from one hot topic to another, never sticking on one for too long."

"Nope. Might burn," Claudia said. "I'll be returning to Rome with Mother and Claudius in a month or so. When I found out we were leaving, I dreamed you were coming with me. Fun! I could feel the thrust of the ocean, rhythmic, pounding. Then … something else happened."

"Your dreams always feel this, uh … sensual?"

"They're erratic. Some feel weird, like they belong to another person. Others feel so real I can taste them, touch them, feel them move inside me, feel the heat of them—like the dream with the deer on the altar. All my senses fired up, knocked me over."

Claudia looked up from where she'd been staring at the ground.

She saw me looking at her. "Do you pay attention like this all the time? It's unnerving."

"I'm still distractible."

"I swear, if you're distractible, I'm three sheets in a typhoon. Your focus is like a thousand stallions, saddled, ready to charge."

"I do love you."

She took my hand, and her fingernails bit into my palm. "I wrote to Grandpa. He authorized you and your family to travel with us to Rome. God only knows, they could use a good Oracle."

Following this thunderbolt, a casual afterthought. "Grandpa will arrange your quarters. You can be sure your whole family will be comfortable."

She turned her head west toward Rome. "And you can choose when you return home."

Warning breezes jacked up the fine hairs on the back of my neck. "Do I have a choice about this trip?"

She said, "I'd like to make it *seem* you have a choice. You know, take the edge off. But when Grandpa speaks, things happen. A courier will arrive at your house tomorrow. Orders for you to sail with us to Rome after your Passover, departing Caesarea."

My world's axis clipped and dipped. I acknowledged her power to draw me closer or push me away. "As you say, Claudia."

What's happening here, Father—your plan, or Claudia's jumped-up idea of a good time?

Windy said, *don't be scared. Fear shrinks you. Let your fear settle into the sort of sorrow that enriches.*

I settled into a rich mist of not knowing. The fog started a step or two outside my front door, and forced me to take Windy's hand. He guided me into all the truth I could handle in any one moment[29].

48

MARY

Jesus sidled up alongside me while I was pruning my olive trees. He had a scroll with a broken red seal in his right hand. He didn't waste time. "Ma, these are orders from Rome. We're all going there, orders of Caesar Augustus. The week after Passover, from Caesarea."

I swallowed hard. "Any other trivial bits of news, Son?"

Jesus smiled at my faint humor. "Do you think we could all go to Passover this year in Jerusalem? No telling when we'll be back in Israel." He paused. "Pray. Father will tell you, for sure."

"Come here, Son." I hugged him hard and breathed out a sigh. "You're the chosen one, my Messiah. Father has huge plans for you. A big, fat, juicy life. Plans that stretch way beyond this tiny country or even Rome's tiny empire.

"I have no idea what *any* of that means. I'm learning to live with little. Too much of anything freezes me."

"Abba is so proud of your courage, Ma. He can't come back to us, but we'll go to him. He's one of many who cheer us on.[30]"

A week passed. Everyday parenting exhausted me. One round of cleaning, confronting, and comforting after another. Justus needed help with schoolwork. Deborah was cranky with teething. Miriam was in meltdown mode with her playmate, complaining about Hannah to her doll.

Jesus returned home from work. I pulled my growing Messiah to one side. "Come with me. Let's get away from this madhouse."

We stepped outside. A bucketful of water landed on Jesus' head.

Messiah, drenched, didn't even look. "Thanks so much for the shower, Jude and James. You two must have known I was stinky from work."

Hysterical laughter, just above the doorway. Jesus shook his uncut mane like a Judah lion and gave himself to laughter. He hee-hawed out loud, hands on his knees.

Miriam came over, laughing with Jesus without knowing why. She made a face and pulled up to her full height.

At almost four feet tall, she looked quite officious. "Your presence is required at my tea party, Sir Brother. Besides, your hair needs plaiting."

I said, 'no' to Her Highness, for now, and kissed the pout off her face. Jesus and I walked in the garden among the old olive trees.

I said to him, "This morning, early, standing alone back of this grove, I prayed for guidance. I asked Father what to do. I imagined Jerusalem in my right hand and held it toward heaven. I imagined our little village in my left hand. I let both hands hang in the air. A beam of sun caught my hands and hugged them sideways. My right hand floated down, all by itself. Heavy fingers tingled with weight, warmth, glory. My Gideon's fleece."

Jesus looked at me, his face a mix of wonder and laughter. "How'd you figure out this new side door to Father?"

"Think I'm crazy, huh? Father talks to you directly, but I can't hear His voice most of the time. He has to use other paths with me. When I'm dense, he sends Gabriel."

"Father uses you to teach me, Ma."

I felt his praise and I knew he was truing me. Both.

Jesus said, "Thank you, Father, for answering Ma's prayer for unity. We'll go safely together only because you go before, behind, and all around us—first to Jerusalem, and then, Rome."

49
WINDY

Go graduated from grinding to potting. She took turns with Cornelia and three other women on the potter's wheel. She became a "noticing" sort of person, learning from Roy's example, doing what he did. Cooperation replaced competing—at least outside. Not *all* her me's grew new eyes of the heart, but some did... some of the time.

One day, her friend Bilia pulled a smoking, glazed beauty out of the kiln. Bilia's eyes and mouth rounded with wonder when she saw what she'd made. Go daubed white, gluey clay on her face like war paint, whooped around the kiln in a bob-weave, up and down, celebrating Bilia and her fired triumph. All the other women joined her and made proper fools of themselves—painted each other's faces, danced in circles, sang made-up victory songs—all for a once-trashed, ground-down, and now-remade pot.

Roy watched them act silly while he chatted with me. He made a safe place for these folks who'd been forced to be grown-ups before they were grown up. This gang of women became a chosen, "makeup" family for each other.

That was the day before Cynico found Go. His platoon had rotated to Hade's inner strip mall. The legionnaires hated it. Hated guarding highway workers on the "Ascent of Blood"—ten days on, two days off. On this particular day, he wandered alone into Rahab's courtyard, looking for a whore to do. His mates had finished there already and gone drinking.

Go was lugging an armful of pots from workshop to street shop when she saw him. Their eyes locked. Fragile cracked into jagged pieces of helplessness, like a shattered porcelain vase. Escape lifted off, drifting into thin air. Cutter looked for a jagged piece of Fragile, so she could gut Cyn. But Shame had the last word. She rolled her eyes at the bunch of them and hissed, *you're all worthless. Getting what you deserve. Shut up, and take it.*

Cyn yelled, "So, *here's* where you escaped to, whore!" Two lightning steps later, he was man-handling her toward the back wall. All her part-selves, including Cutter, flopped and froze.

Cyn grinned, eyes fired with lust. Impatient, he loosened his belt, dropped his leather girdle, bent over, ready to do her on the spot. He was so focused on getting what he wanted that he didn't see Go's pottery mates. They'd stalked up from behind. Cornelia led them. She jabbed a white-hot poker, fresh from the kiln, in his backside. It burned straight through his undertunic, disappeared between his cheeks. She shoved hard, twisting, found purchase in new real estate. Her face was a rictus of vengeance, mouth open so wide you could see her back teeth.

Two other potters, howling, sat on his shoulders. Two others poked thumbs dripping with clay into his eyes. His right eyeball popped out, a surprised grape. Another stomped the glaring gob, smearing it between the cobbles. Still another mashed his left eye in the socket between thumb and bone, felt a satisfying collapse of yolk into jelly.

Smothered furies crackled into the wild sky over Rahab's courtyard. Furiously used women raged between synagogue and sex-house, their lightning storm falling on Cyn. He screamed, blind-sobbing. Cornelia rode him like a mustang.

The smell of roasting flesh filled the courtyard, mixed with this banshee howl of women in full bloodlust. Cornelia finally pulled her poker out, with a twist and sideways yank. Cyn, in a flash, had become an oldened, bent-over man. He'd felt no pain like the savagery of a sisterhood bent on retribution.

Roy and Lydia arrived through the front gates at the moment when Cornelia had jerked out her poker. They took in the scene at a glance. Lydia barred Rahab's thick courtyard gates.

Roy rushed over to Cyn, bent over the beggared man, and murmured, "Justice, done. Soldiering, done. Life as you've known it, done."

Roy continued, not without mercy. "Maggots will crawl out of your butt and eye sockets. Pain will be your unwanted companion for a good long while."

He paused. "We'll show you more mercy than what you've given others—bind your eye sockets, salve your butt, put compresses on your head—and you *might* live."

Cyn ground out a grotesque wheeze. "Mercy-kill me. Have Go run me through with my sword. She'd like that."

Cutter overheard and spritely volunteered her services.

Roy shook his head. "No, let us handle this."

Lydia and Roy carried Cyn upstairs on a litter. Roy nudged open the door of a cleaning closet. The smell of impatience and spent semen leaked from used pig-gut condoms. Cyn's cot found a home in this dark room. Effluvial stink seeped from his backside.

Lydia said to Roy, "Get the dittany salve for his eye sockets. I'll circle his head with clean menstrual rags and tuck another one with wound-wart up his butt."

Roy called over his shoulder, "be back soon."

Cyn's hand fumbled around in the dark, found his short sword. The blade glittered with a strange fire in this dark place. The glint was bright enough even for blind Cyn to see the consequences of his lifetime.

Roy returned shortly with a pot of water and a clay toilet basin. The pots he brought were Go's first two projects off the potter's wheel. They even held water. Roy prodded open the door, moved inside.

Cyn had flipped his sword around, the point under his sternum, the haft resting on the cot. He'd steeled himself to slump straight down but hung in a moment of indecision. Roy side-kicked the sword out of his grasp to the other side of the closet, tipping over the condom basket. "Death's always available. So many exits. Let's focus on redemption for now."

Cyn got on his knees, arms flailing, searching for his sword—beyond words, unable to bear the judgment executed on him.

Roy picked up his sword. "I'd hoped for more courage from you, Cyn-ico. There are other ways to grow a moral backbone besides being pokered. But Pain *is* a thorough drill instructor."

He spoke quietly, matter-of-factly. Cyn flopped his head back and forth, raised his hands to cover his ears. Roy waited for Cyn to settle down.

He put the two pots in Cyn's hands. "Fevers and chills will start in soon. Drink what water you can hold. It'll run straight through you. Drink from your right, poop in the left. Your nose will guide you."

He stood up. "Now that life has broken you, let's not waste a good breaking, not stop halfway." Roy turned to leave with Cyn's sword in hand. The door snicked shut behind him. He would bury this sword next to an old hatchet and wait to see what would grow from those seeds.

Cyn's liquored-up buddies soon came calling on Rahab's back door. Irenus, Cyn's adjutant, grinned at Cornelia when she answered the door. He'd done business with her a few hours earlier.

"Hey there! Seen Sergeant Cyn around?"

Cornelia shrugged. "You be welcome ta look, 'Renus, or come for seconds if ya got de coin. Hain't seen no one lately that be proud 'n tall like you."

Irenus was sure of himself. "He's got to be here. Tell him we're at Bloody's Bar. If the sergeant misses us, keep him here. We'll send a few guys to fetch him tomorrow. Too dangerous to travel alone."

The nine reds rolled off in a cloud of blood-red Jericho dust.

Corn popped her head in the closet just as Cyn vomited over Go. She wiped puke off her smock and tried to catch the bloody dribble squirting out of his butt. The Harlot part of her muttered, *which hole do you plug first—dribbling eye sockets, spewing mouth, or poop-spraying butt?*

She looked at Corn. "Remind me again, why are we doing this?"

Corn gave her a shoulder shrug and poked more balm in Cyn's eye sockets. A second swipe rammed balm up the butt she'd pokered. Then a funny thing happened. A flash of pain came over Corn's face.

"Corn, you hurt?"

"Don' rightly know. Had de mem-ry jab, men pokin' up *my* butt on de auction block. I felt de scorch. But I be quick. Slammed it down. Said to m' own fine self, He not like me. He be de *other*. Got my hate back. Feelin' fine now; pain jus' a wink and a wrinkle. Just do 'n be done, pump de hate. Dat's what I say to myself."

Go looked at her friend and saw a mirror of the only person she'd ever known.

50

JESUS

Seventeen of us traveled down the King's Highway from Nazareth to Jerusalem. Rocks rumbled in the river's narrows, then swooshed along in the redolent open plains of the Jordan River Valley.

This was not Ma's first donkey ride south. Life had changed for her since she was pregnant with me—six children now, and no husband. She seemed breathy, fragile, like she was tethered by a thin kite string, and yearned to take flight.

I rested my hand on Betsy's saddle horn. Ma put hers over mine. Her grief dripped into my spirit. The felt memory of Abba traveled with us—golden-scarlet threads pulled into a shroud. Windy blew that grief tapestry in places far beyond where I could see. We lapsed into soul-scrape done with a blue rasp that cut bone-deep.

When we passed through Jericho's southern gates, the adults closed rank around our smaller children—a pride of lions circling its cubs. People trafficked in and out the front door of a crowded general store, Maltesa's Dry Goods. We rounded a corner and an outdoor market spilled over us, flooding everyone with a riot of colors and smells. Persimmons, peppers, onions, eggplants, and tomatoes piled high in the stalls. Juicy currants, golden raisins, sweet dates, dried figs—and the close pack of people pressed on all sides. More than once, I felt energy drain from me and wondered why I was exhausted.

Windy wandered through my wonderings. *The sick in this crowd are drawn to touch you without even knowing why. There, that guy in the brown robe who just passed by you? Healed of tuberculosis when he bumped up against you. The veiled woman walking alongside? A uterine fistula, fixed, when she tripped and touched the hem of your robe.*

Really, Windy? You gave me those gifts?

Yes. Don't focus on your gifts. Focus on the people I bring you to love. Some I place beside you, and all they need is a touch. Others, in front of you, will require you to ask about things they need to say, but don't know yet. I will breathe my love into all of them through your words or touch. The work I give you to do will not get easier, but you will get stronger.

Deborah interrupted Windy's instructions. She wiggled out of my arms and made a beeline to a brightly-colored sundry stall, Sweets & Bangles. I kept an eye on her from a butcher shop, next booth over. I examined a rack of lamb chops hanging from a hook. They were covered with a blanket of flies that threatened a rack attack—picking up the lamb chops and winging them to fly to heaven.

The proprietor's hair and beard, curly and snow-white, framed his jovial face, punched-in nose, and brown skin baked almost black. He looked so much like a sheep that I smiled to myself and looked to see if his feet were cloven. They weren't.

I asked if he led his pen of sheep to pasture every day. The butcher-shepherd nodded solemnly. "I know them all by name. When its time comes, I separate that one from the flock. I don't want fear in the flock. I sit and hold the sheep. I thank it for feeding me, and those I must feed. After some quiet time, the sheep drops to sleep from the leak I'd made in its neck. The bucket beneath fills with its blood."

I took my lesson and lamb chops. I looked for Deborah in the bangle shop. No one in the front. I scrambled to the back of that shop and found her. Gray Prayer Shawl sat on the ground beside a table of hard candies. He bounced Deborah up and down on his lap and fingered candy into her mouth. When he saw me coming around the corner, his smile ran my composure into the ground. I picked my sister up in one arm and knocked the table over on his head with my other arm. The table spilled bangles, sweets, and coins all over the floor around him.

I said, "Deborah, see this man? He is *not* safe. Stay clear of him, child." I'm sure she had never seen me so angry. I banged the dust off my sandals, picked up my rack of lamb from beside him, and left him under the table. He snickered, his hand moving low, under his tunic.

Father, I want to hate him. I'd like to beat the sin out of him. I breathed in Windy's calm, exhaled my anger. My heart quieted down, but it took a long time.

I knelt and comforted Deborah outside the bangle shop. Tears trickled down her face. Her eyes searched mine. I said, "I was mad, little sister, but I wasn't mad at *you*. You're not bad. You're beautiful, and I'm proud to be your older brother."

I held her in my arms, and she held the rack of lamb chops in hers. Her full weight melted into my chest and her feelings melded with mine, each comforting the other.

When we arrived at Rahab's on the northern end of the open-air market, both Leah and Go saw each other at the same time. Go launched toward Leah, who stood by my side. Each held her sib by the shoulders, seeming to sure herself in the other's presence.

Leah said, "Pa's dead, Go. Stoned."

A fast-moving storm flickered on Go's face. I couldn't tell if her tears were joy or grief, but probably both. She looked through her tears and saw Laz, standing next to me. He shifted one foot to the other as she took two steps his way, leaving Leah behind her. Beads of sweat ran down his forehead. He held my shoulder, hand trembling.

She stood before him and said, "I almost became Devil's food. All my me's had given up, but God used whores to protect me. And yes, Laz, the answer to the question in your eyes is 'yes.' If you still want me." He busted out crying and held her close. She cried too, but those tears were now married to a smile.

While these reunions were going on, I overheard Rabbus in conversation on my other side. He chatted with a tall man. This man's very presence freighted his words with authority. I had the sense we knew each other.

Windy intoned, *Son, isn't Father a hoot in this guise? You do know he shows himself to humans now and again. Once before, a long time back, if you recall, he went by the name Melchizedek.*[31] *Now he goes by Roy.*

Roy spoke low and clear to Rabbus. "Travelers told me yesterday—no exact body count. Bodies stripped of weapons, money, and clothes. Except for one red tunic. The bodies were all missing one ear and already mauled by critters, limbs strewn around."

Rabbus weighed into the conversation. "Those same bandits killed my gang. Taking that one ear is their way of raising their leg on every tree in the neighborhood. By this time, we're nine days out. Vermin will have picked the legionnaires' bones clean and scattered 'em. Cynico's the lucky one. Us too. He won't be missed, and we won't be found."

51

WINDY

I get a real kick out of Zacchaeus, the fat boy, the one shading himself under that sycamore across from Rahab's. Yes, it's the tree with the twisted trunk that curves around a knot in the middle—Zac and the tree, both chock-full of crooked heartwood. In years to come, Jesus will haul him down out of that same sycamore and straighten him out. But right now, he's bent and brooding.

Zac mused, I'm one of the righteous persecuted, the guy everyone loves to hate. Bah, what do they know? I use my fat like armor. Thin, muscular men have been picked off by the Romans. I waddle on. One false look, this way or that, and their money's in my strongbox.

Zac loved fishing the Jordan River on his off-hours, which were most of the time. His favorite dish? Cutthroat—quick and juicy trout, swimming in the shallows. Loved those trout. Rainbows were tougher to come by, far as trout went.

Zac loved Rahab's even more than trout fishing. Both sides of the courtyard were juicy and quick—tension relief on one side, conscience relief on the other.

Today, Zac had ditched Esmeralda at the front door of the synagogue for her Torah lesson with Lydia. This willowy one of the high cheekbones was an elegant acquisition for Zac—irises like emeralds, teeth like ivory, lips like rubies—a jewelry shop gliding through life on the silver slippers Zac had bought for her (the gold ones were *way* overpriced).

Zac admitted that he and Esmeralda were odd bedfellows. Esmeralda stood a foot taller. He topped out around her armpits but gave her added traction since he weighed time and a half what she did.

She was black, with surprised eyes, set deep in her long, angular skull.

He was white, with gimlet eyes encased in pink, porcine flesh.

She wafted; he waddled. She knew his addictions—sex and greed. He knew her history.

After all, he'd bought her off a trafficker's mule train heading north just three years ago. The trafficker hawked her on the auction block as a honeyed, exotic African fruit. He'd gotten a real deal—half off. The slaver was pressed for cash.

Zac often reminded his wife how he'd made her an aristocrat. *Can't let this woman get too proud 'n uppity. What would others think of me?*

Esmerelda admitted once to him that his Jewish God was interesting to her, in a mildly disinteresting way. "Dat Dog be a bully. Lightnin' strikes, plagues, stoning for dis and dat—six hundred thirteen do's and don'ts."

I like honesty in a gal. She'd go far in the kingdom, once she caught wind of Jesus' loving-kindness. Zac, however, was not impressed with her mouth. "Yahweh and I both appreciate a tidy measure of lickspittle obeisance. You never know when another mule train heading north might need fresh Jericho merchandise, dear heart."

Zac jingled a few gold coins in his pocket. *A little more of my conscientious training, and she might turn into a decent human being.*

On this particular spring day, Zac asked Madame Beulah for his favorite—Cleo, a pliable, pouty Egyptian with fuchsia lipstick and magenta-painted mooneyes.

Beulah didn't look up from her books. She pointed. "Next-to-last room, on the left. She's waiting."

Zac slouched into the room, made himself comfortable. A rasping, snorting bellow from the next room. Not a happy sound. The guy sounded like he was buried up to his neck in army ants.

He stopped Cleo, motioned with his hand. "What's that?"

"Just a guy, no worries."

This response was a downer. Less than compelling. He buttoned up, rattled the doorknob on the next room down the hall. Locked. A closet. No answer, no break in the wails.

Zac headed downstairs. "Who's dying up there?"

Beulah looked at her ledgers, kept to the party line. "Just a guy, that's all."

Zac did not suffer fools gladly. *I'll kick this one up the chain.*

He walked across the courtyard, looking for Lydia. A young Jew, dressed in a tan tunic, came out of the synagogue, Torah scroll in his hand.

Zac eyed him up and down. "Where's Lydia?" *This cretin's got really weird yellow-brown eyes. He probably cheats on his taxes.*

Our Son replied, "Zacchaeus, the man you want is closer to the kingdom than you are. He's been broken, and you haven't, yet."

Well, now. Zac reared up to his full height—four feet ten inches. Puffed out his saggy chest, sucked in his gut, toyed with his forehead phylactery. "You probably don't know, but I'm a man of importance in this town. You, on the other hand, sound like a hayseed from a Galilee mud hole."

"I've been appointed to preach good news to the poor. Some will hear and believe, but this doesn't include you, yet."

"You are perilously close to blasphemy. Shut your yap, or a public flogging might be in order." He hesitated. "Young man, your name?"

"I'm Jesus bar Joseph, of Nazareth. And we will meet again one day— a day your heart will do backflips to see and be seen by me." Son turned and walked back into the synagogue.

Zacchaeus shook his head. *Here's an abscessed tooth that needs a good yanking. I'll tend to him later. Right now, I need to find out about that wailer of a wanker upstairs. Might be useful info with Herod.*

Upstairs, Cyn finally lay silent, exhausted by his wailing.

He was delirious, dehydrated, still out of it—but increasingly conscious. Whenever he roused, pain surged through him like a roaring furnace.

Lydia and Beulah came to fetch him. They slid his litter into the back of a mule cart, strapped it down, and sat down on the buckboard in front, ready to haul him away to a more private spot on the other side of town.

Zac slithered around a corner. "What's up, Lydia?"

"What's it to you, Zac?"

"I was disturbed by an upstairs wailer today. Might this, er, specimen, be he?"

Zac squinted toward the writhing, shadowy man in the back of the wagon. His presbyopia dimmed his focus for anything not right in his face.

Amid his wonderment, Zac was shat upon by a passing raven. He pulled a hanky out of his pocket to wipe the mess off his face. At the same time, he caught a whiff of corruption. Cyn had ripped out a loud fart. Confused by converging stinks, and still mopping his brow, Zac repeated, "Who might he be, perchance?"

Lydia said. "Someone's paid for him already." She looked up and to the right, forefinger on her lips. "Zacchaeus, we need someone to work a night shift. Can't hold his bowels, you see. Here's a bowl to hold the poo, and another for the maggots crawling from his blown eye sockets."

Zac swallowed a heave. "You're to be commended, righteous Lydia, for living out the great commandment." He spoke in stentorian tones. "I have other priorities tonight … in my official capacities, you know."

Beulah and Lydia watched him flow into the foot traffic, a human ox-cart stuffed with self-importance. I soothed their worries. They mended their course, reversed their decision to move Cyn. Roy helped carry Cyn back to his room.

Zac, for his part, slid out of the alley's shadows into the disco district. He fingered the few gold coins in his pocket, then hefted himself down the street. He stopped at a corner under a smoking torch and used it to light a smoke of his own.

Smoke drifted heavenward. His eyes followed. There, two low-hanging jewels adorned the sky close together—glittering Venus and a gibbous moon. Both were so golden he was tempted to snatch them down and stash them in his strongbox.

52

JESUS

Our caravan headed out of Jericho, bound for Jerusalem. We trudged up the "Ascent of Blood," a barren stretch of road frequented by robbers and murderers. Bones, some human, were scattered here and there, picked clean. Dwarf junipers clawed into the desiccating, desert bake. A cloud of blackbirds exploded from the thin shade of silent sycamores, skittering into space.

I walked in the rut beside my brother, James. Dried weeds crackled and broke beneath my sandals.

He complained, "I should feel happy for Laz and Go. But I don't. I'm jealous. I couldn't even get runner-up prize with Leah. She got prettier, somehow, since I last saw her. How'd that happen? I'm a two-time loser."

"Um-hm. I too argue with Father about the girl I can't have. She floats in front of my eyes, up close, and sometimes I can't see past her. Very distracting. I have to repeat to myself all the time, *stay on the path, stay on the path*."

We stopped in a snatch of shade. Shade from this thorn tree blended with James' own thorny mood. I asked, "If Abba were here, what would he say to you?"

"Not sure. Maybe joke me up a notch or tell me a dream. You're different. You let me sit in my crap and join me in it. I like being rescued, but I still don't get the girl, do I?"

"Na, you didn't get Go. And I'm not going to get Claudia. But sometimes I too like to pick green fruit, before either it or me is ripened. That fruit's mostly bitter. Tastes like a verse that's not yet a psalm. An impulse not yet a thought."

"How do you think of things to say like that, Jeez? I'm jealous of your way with words, not just the girls I didn't get. And you were closer to

Abba. You're still closer to Ma. You had a super-duper birth—angels and shepherds. They didn't belt out songs when I was born. I plopped on some swaddling, most likely, and someone spanked me a good one, just to get me sucking air."

We started walking again, out from under the thorn tree. I looked down, then over at him—my feet, his face, back and forth. I didn't want to trip on either one.

"I love you, hate you, Jesus. I love seeing this burning in your eye, like you're Destiny's child and you know what you're doing and where you're going. I hate it that I don't have that grand knowing. Compared to you, I'm smart as a cow pie."

We walked a bit further in silence. He mumbled, "I love that you walk beside me, even when I hate you."

I reached my arm out to give him a hug. He brushed me off. "Couldn't you just swap out your life for mine? I'd like that better. I want to feel like a hunk with chunk who clunks when he walks. Right now, I feel like a cloud wisp, a breeze that forgot to blow, a lake that forgot to ripple after a rock hit it."

"James, some people look in a mirror and walk away. Two minutes later, they've forgotten who they are and what they look like. Not you. You'll chew this bitter cud and turn it into something good. All the good stuff pipes down from Father, you know."[32]

My words seemed to go nowhere. James turned even more sour. Sweat poured off his forehead. He took a chug of water from the goat bladder hanging off his belt, offered a slug to me. I glugged, swiped my mouth with my sleeve, and gave the bladder back. Then I gave him one other thought to chew on. "I'm not trying to talk you out of your envy. Chew on it. Let it chew on you. You're a meal fit for a king."

James' anger beat hurt to the punch. His rivalry smacked me on my biceps, a brotherly dead-arm that would leave a bruise. He turned and went to check on our sibs.

I rubbed my shoulder, then looked back to check on Ma. She was gazing off into the hills, nursing Deborah. Father, when my time comes, like one of the shepherd-butcher's lambs, how will Ma manage? I shook my head. Unripened fruit, not to be picked till another day.

We'd been gradually overtaking another pilgrim family, strangers in the land from the looks of them. They carried the look of exiles—uncertain of step, hungry eyes, threadbare clothing. The father's skin was burnt black by birth or sun. Crinkly laugh lines etched the skin around his black eyes. His lips were thick as two sausages and his head bald as a goose egg. His beard had almost grown up into his eyes. Eyebrows foraged across his forehead. The man looked like a black forest aimed for the crown of his head, missed, and fell on his face.

I asked, "Where are you folks from?"

His accent was hard to understand. "Our family has been traveling for over two months. Our first Passover. We're Jews from North Africa, place called Cyrene. We're hoping to settle—Jerusalem. No work where I came from. My family was starving."

I believed him. His shoes were held together by twine and desperation, soles so thin you could read a scroll through them.

"I was hoping for a carpentry job up there." He gestured up-trail toward Jerusalem. He got distracted by his two small sons scampering off-trail, chasing a mangy rabbit. "Rufus, you and Alexander get back here right now. Many snakes and scorpions up there. If you get bit, there's no money for medicine!"

The boys reeled themselves back toward their ma, who rode a skinny burro. Rufus was a stroppy little fellow. Looked like he might elect himself dictator of a small princedom if given the chance. His hair was bright red, a regular carrot top. Strawberry freckles covered his honeydew-colored cheeks and nose. Eyes were palest green, like a ripe cucumber. A garden under one roof.

Alexander, the younger brother, was a skinny drink of water. His chestnut hair grew wild, spilling all around his dubious chin. He seemed a willing subject in his brother's princedom.

The family stopped under the overhang of a red rock boulder. The man leaned against the rock, angled his head toward the woman on the burro. "Penelope, my wife. My name's Simon."

I nodded to her, shook his hand. "Pleased to meet you. Jesus bar Joseph, from Nazareth, north of here."

Penelope's hood shadowed her face. I was standing close enough to see her skin and hair were snow white, like a blizzard had blown into town and she'd been caught in perpetual winter. Her eyes were light green, like Rufus' eyes, with reddish highlights dancing behind the green. Both irises flicked back and forth—a hoppy twitch that didn't stop.

Simon asked, "Do you know where there's work for a carpenter in Jerusalem, Jesus bar Joseph? We have no money."

"I'll ask around, Simon. Stay with us in Bethany till you get your feet on the ground." Simon's face flushed bright red, but he accepted my offer. Maybe in Cyrene, a gift was more like an obligation. I had a mysterious sense that one day the scales would balance out.[33]

Passover dawned clear and hot. Our whole group joined a massive traffic jam. The faithful inched their way up and across the Kidron Valley toward the steps of Herod's Temple. A deep wadi rifted from temple to Hinnom, where the trash burned.

On this one day of the year, a river ran through it—a red river, flowing with lambs' blood. Knee-deep in places. On this day, over 250,000 lambs were executed, mainly between the sixth and ninth hour. Many people, little time, so the sacrifices were done chop-chop. Each lamb's blood shunted down from the bronze altars into a ditch that led through the Kidron.

The Courtyard of Sacrifice was a feast for senses and spirit—fired incense, blown shofars, the sweat of crowds, aproned priests with flashing knives, and terrified animals all bleating protest.

Rav Moshe and his wife led our group. We followed in ranks, creeping toward our destination. Ma carried Deborah, and Miriam hung onto my right hand. She led Pasco with her left hand dumbly to the slaughter. She patted his head, calmed his wild eyes and jumpy hind legs. I felt our lamb's pain like it was my own.

Miriam started bawling. "You can't kill Pasco. I raised him! He's mine!" I hugged her close, not trying to staunch her sadness as much as contain it with her. A tense minute passed. I handed her to James, who hid her face in his robes and cuddled her.

I approached the altar, put my left hand on Pasco's head and looked in his eyes, grateful. My right hand held the knife under the priest's right hand. Together, we cut Pasco's throat, side to side. Pasco's eyes misted over as his lifeblood flowed off the altar into the ditch.

The priest was supposed to say, your sins are forgiven you. Instead, he looked me directly in the eyes and whispered, "Please forgive my sins."

I was the only one present who heard him, other than Windy. I murmured in his ear, "Your sins are forgiven."

He silently mouthed the words that Windy had given him back to me, "*Thank you, Yeshua,* Messiah."

53

WINDY

Passover night was wrapped in a light mist, like the night We created dreams.

Penelope reclined at table with her family, across from Mary's family. She sat in shadows to protect her eyes from too much light. Her eyes twitched—they always had. She despised herself, doubted God's goodness. *Why won't God heal me?*

Jesus sat opposite her, holding Deborah. He made goo-goo eyes at Deborah and she at him, each one's eyes steady, mirroring the other. He looked up from their play after a while and gazed directly at Penelope. Son's eyes unhinged her, but also sparked courage. Her senses mingled in the moment with his and mine. I built on his Jericho awareness, matured him in mindfulness. I exhaled through his lungs. "I heard your prayer, Penelope. Done."

Her albino nystagmus became a thing of the past in this moment of belief. She said nothing aloud, but her eyes, now steady, spoke volumes. She sat on edge and leaned forward into whatever was next.

Another party was going down at Herod's place, a couple of miles away. A fatted sow sizzled over a spit, turning, crisping, an apple shoved in her mouth. Waiters and waitresses served food and drink on gold plates, in jeweled goblets.

The main ballroom's stone walls, covered with fox pelts, were pregnant with secrets untold. Black mold quietly fissured, hemorrhoid-like, on the backside of the performer's stage. Gold brocade masked moral excrement.

Herod Antipas reclined at the head of table. His robe of purple was stitched with jewels along the collar. Painted-on eyebrows rose in thick arches, giving him a look of perpetual amusement. He shifted his bottom, cheek to cheek, scratched his piles, and simmered in his own sauciness.

Tribune Gaius reclined next to the puppet king. Herod told ribald jokes and caressed his big toe, soothing the gout that was acting up again. Gaius' mind wandered absently through memory's scrim.

Claud, sitting in his father's shadow, laughed at Herod's punchlines. His excess accentuated Gaius' absence. Claud was a step behind the music. He didn't understand the realities at play.

His father leaned over and whispered, "Shut *up*. This party's about the economy, stupid, not making nice with this cretin. His tax payment is being counted under your butt crack in the basement right now. If he doesn't meet quota, we may have to kill him before the night's done." Claud hooded his eyes in a shame fit.

Claudia, on the other side of the ballroom, loitered on a balcony, away from the maddening crowd. She wore a golden lamé evening gown. When the torchlight illuminated her, she looked like she was on fire. The bodice, held by a silk cord on one shoulder only, shimmered.

My warm breeze swirled around the shadowy corner where she loitered. She looked over the temple complex, admired the tall phallic columns that thrust upward, silhouetted against the deepening night. Bethany's lights twinkled in the hills west of town.

The breeze wallowed with the odor of a quarter-million lambs roasting. A smile flickered across her face. *If I opened my mouth wide enough, a slab of grilled lamb would drop out of the vapors and smack me in the chops.*

The entertainment began. She leaned on the balcony railing, observing a coffee-and-cream couple sway on stage to a popular love song. Their arms were held high and linked, eyes fixed on one another. Their slinky, sinewy dance was orchestrated to strings, tambourines, and thumping drums. Light from the central fireplace played with surrounding torchlights, melding dark and light. The couple became a mobile offering to amusement's vacant pleasures.

Claudia licked her dry lips as a disturbing dream image flickered—a doe rising from the fire, tasting her own breast meat. Was she done cooking? She called for a server with champagne flutes on a silver tray. She wasn't yet ready to feel my promptings.

Michael and his crew of angels wafted through the roof. Together we watched, from a distant closeness, this celebration of sensuality and wealth. Michael whisked up next to me. *Want me to clean house, Windy?*

I gave my archangel a hug. *Go fight battles elsewhere for Father. I've got this one.* He took his hit squad of angels with him out the side door.

The couple, at last, finished their dance. On moment's spur, a tipsy Gaius called out, "Claudia, come over here! Show them how we *Romans* dance!"

The daughter of his desire silked her way across the floor. She whispered to the orchestra conductor and stood in the exact middle of the altar, in the center circle of torches as gongs slowly beat out twelve strokes, signaling midnight. She blazed in her own beauty. Her dress reflected the fire imperfectly—flames leapt from her figure now and again.

All eyes were on this Roman goddess, only daughter of the top dog in the land. He reclined below her feet, growling contentedly, chewing on pork tenderloin. He rolled his head over to his son, poked him in the ribs. "Get a load of your sister, boy." Claud's sunken eyes smoldered under reptilian lids. He'd like to get a load of her, all right.

The music started slow, with a syncopated backbeat. Claudia followed, arms lightly moving around her body, over her head. Slight hip thrust with the beat. Her fingers smoothed loose strands of hair away from her face. Her eyes riveted on Herod. The music picked up, as did she. Face of an angel whirred around a dimmer, darker core.

Herod erected himself off his one elbow, itching to see more. Claudia's dance escalated with her music. Frenzied, thumping rhythm and satin slippers took her to where the host reclined beneath her. The music climaxed. She perfected a breathtaking split, arms twined overhead, torso slanting forward, face-to-face with the king. He lifted his wet lips for a kiss. She pecked his cheek and left the altar, undone.

Herod's wife, Phasaelis, sat on the other side of the room with her Edomite bevy of women. She and her girlfriends observed the dance from the shadows and tucked in celery sticks loaded with cream cheese. When Claudia walked off the stage, the queen laughed behind her cupped hand. Her face looked like a clenched fist.

54

JESUS

The next day I walked up a switchback paver path to the temple complex. As I passed, I glanced at Herod's eagle fresco over the temple's gates, his Jewish imitation of Rome's military insignia. The place was an anthill of construction activity. A bunch of Roman bigwigs hovered in a circle around Herod. Guards surrounded the lot of them.

Herod gazed at a fallen stone through eyes overgrown with fret. He'd forgotten to paint on his arched eyebrows. The object of his gaze was a twenty-eight-ton block of dressed Jerusalem limestone. It had slipped off the cart's log rollers, sheered down a slope, and crushed the men responsible for its transport. Bloody smears and ragged bits of arm or leg marked the forgotten fallen.

The driver of the cart leered at me. I immediately recognized my ancient Enemy. He'd embodied as a tradesman oxcart driver, for the moment. He said, "Scripture says, 'Straight is the gate and narrow the path that leads to eternal life.' Right, little Messiah?" He motioned to the squashed bodies. "Their path was exceptionally narrow." He clucked at his mules and chuckled as he went, a meat box of malevolence wrapped around evil.

This cold, killer stone, released by a stone-cold killer, sat on edge halfway down the incline. Mishandled, the stone would be further marred and crush several new buildings just below it.

Gaius' sixteen-year-old twins loitered behind him. Claudius dressed like his father. Both men, young and older, were imperfect images of the Roman goddess of Pride, Hybris. Red woolen tunic, scarlet cock's plume over helmet, leather breastplate, and balteus adorned both men.

Claudia wore a violet silk gown with an empire waist. Her neckline plunged daringly—a careful, composed costume. She turned this way and that, taking in the scenery, allowing the scenery to take her in. All the men present studied two mechanical engineering issues—how to get twenty-eight tons of stuck stone back on its rollers and how to leverage her into their bed. Both were weighty, improbable.

I walked over to the group. No one seemed concerned about the expendable Jewish laborers. The overweening issue was averting further collateral damage to the royal treasury.

Claudia perked up. "Father, there's Joe-the-Jew's son. I bet he'd know what to do here."

Gaius turned to Antipas. "This man knows foundations. He might be able to help you out."

Antipas said, "What would he know that I don't?"

Gaius shrugged and called me over. "What would you do in this situation, Jew?"

I gestured to the bodies under the rocks. "Your engineers are much wiser than me regarding this small stone, King Herod. However, the stones beneath your own foundation are cracking. In God's economy, is it not true that all kings will be judged by how they treat widows, orphans, the poor, and foreigners in the land—not by how many blocks they stack together?"

A look of consternation quickly replaced Herod's disdain. His forehead bunched up over his wispy eyebrows. He squinched his eyes, perhaps considering how he might add me to the other Jews under that same stone.

I looked at the tribune and prophesied, "This temple will be destroyed within fifty years by you Romans. Not this or any other one of these stones will remain one on another."

I turned to the king. "Sir, I ask you, what is more important, this soon to be destroyed stone or the immortal people under it? Yahweh alone decides which living stones will form His temple and which will line hell's foundations."

Windy whispered in my ear, *Son, your timing was premature. Herod didn't expect anyone to grind his chops publicly. King and tribune are two bobcats, tails tied together, pretending they like each other. You lit one of them on fire.*

Claudia sidled up next to Herod at that moment, batted her eyes at him. "I'm sure Jesus meant no harm, great King. You see, we had a wager between us about what makes for a stable foundation. I lost. So sorry for needlessly drawing you into our argument."

The red-faced king sputtered, "But, what…"

Claudia grazed her breast against his arm, wafted Italian perfume up his nose, and whispered huskily in his ear, "Please accept my apologies."

Herod's belligerence dithered into lust.

She seized the moment. "But he must go now. We must go now. We have another of your most stunning parties this evening. Such an excellent *affair* in the making! Perhaps I could dance for you again, Lord Herod? Ta!"

Gold veneer over brass served her well. She swept me away on her arm, air-kissing her father and the king over her shoulder. A phalanx of Roman soldiers guarded our exodus.

After a hundred yards, I commented on her saucy smoothness. "Claudia, why did you rescue the king from my grip?"

She stopped in mid-stride, slack-jawed. "Jesus! Excuse me, exactly who got rescued? He was about to have you dragged off to jail."

I turned to study the light and shadow in her eyes. "He would have no power if Father hadn't given it to him. And I did admire your truthfulness about foundation stuff."

She flipped me a saucy grin. "I generally don't know when I'm lying or truthing. I wear so many faces. Never sure which is the real me. And that's the truth, mostly."

I walked for a while silently, not wanting to get suckered into a heady argument about truth. I listened to Father and said to her, "The truth is I am the truth, boiled down to a single person."

Claudia's golden sandals slid across the cobblestones, and she stared at them, harboring a growing edge within her, quietness.

"Satan has shown himself to you. Because of incest and promiscuity, your Achilles' heel will be sexual. Others, like your father, will be more easily seduced by hubris. And still others, like Herod, by greed."

Claudia startled at the word incest. She said, "I hadn't said that word out loud to myself."

"Satan gloated as you worshiped hima. You're a wonderful student in Satan's school of seduction."

She pouted, "So, I'm doomed to be Satan's spawn?"

"Your story evolves, but now tips on rollers, hanging in the balance."

The satin of Claudia's dress roiled down her body, highlighting her figure. Magenta and violet purled, a liquid volution over breasts and hips, cascading into valleys between. I'd never seen anything as lovely until we rounded a corner, and I spied a wildflower.

An airborne seed had slipped the wind and dropped into shadow between houses. It had drifted its way to ground in this alley between cobblestones, waited for a friendly breeze to give it a dust blanket, waited for the sky to shower, waited for courage in the dark to fall apart, then waited, waited to blossom. This tiny flower now braved its way into a narrow beam of gallery lighting that Father had provided. This snatch of afternoon sun would quickly pass. But now, at this moment, the flower was a perfect showstopper. The golden sun flowed through thin petals of sky blue, veined with purple. I sat on my haunches and admired the flower's Maker.

Claudia rested her hand on my shoulder. "Its beauty beggars my dress."

I nodded. "But not *your* beauty. You are more valuable to Father than continents of wildflowers."

We fell silent together, gazing at perfection between two cobblestones in an alleyway. One of the guards harrumphed, broke the mood.

We stood. Claudia bent over, snatched the flower from its crack. She pinned the blossom over her left breast, above her undone heart.

Claudia walked with me to a major thoroughfare. Herod's palace, left; Bethany, right. She hugged me. "See you tonight at the going-away party, God-man. I'm sure you'll have a new installment of truth for us all."

Antipas' going-away party was more like a funeral rite for the two tons of gold he was burying in Augustus' treasury. Tax revenue had been melted, purified, poured into bricks, stamped with Augustus' sphinx logo, and stacked into neat piles. Two centuries of legionnaires showed up one story down, in the palace's foundations, even as celebrities filtered into the king's ballroom above.

Everyone heard the commotion downstairs—clanking sounds of metal, complaining squeak of wagon wheels, heavy tromping of soldiers departing for the seaport. Tribune Gaius had timed it perfectly.

Meanwhile, I swapped stories upstairs with a group of perfect strangers. Windy kept prompting me. The group grew, everyone joking back and forth. This promised to be a ton of fun.

55

CLAUDIA

When I arrived at the party with Claud, Antipas was out strolling among his subjects. Several goons guarded his back. Phasaelis, his politically correct wife from Petra, daughter of the Arabian Edomite King, Aretas the Fourth, stalked his perimeter.

I'd heard about this loveless marriage. It was a fruitless effort to unite Jews to Arabs. Both husband and wife allowed their mutual contempt to bind them to each other, except at parties, where cheerful duplicity served the same function. They'd cut their losses and hopes of happiness in the same stroke of compromise. Tonight, the queen allowed herself to be the king's arm candy. She segued my way and waved me to her with a waggling, bent forefinger.

"My dear, I wanted to commend you. Such a lovely dance you did for my husband last night!"

I bowed my head marginally, leaned in.

"In this part of the world, my dear, women's voices and bodies are welcomed, as long as we know our place. Too soft, and we're ignored. Too strident, and we're shrill. My advice? Don't rock the boat. Stay covered. Wear mousy brown."

I mock-bowed to Predator Patrol, "Thank you for your survival tips, highness."

I went looking for Jesus. There he was, circled by guests in a far corner. Zoo Boy lurked at his side. How did John get in here, anyway? I'd checked the vetted guest list and he was not on it.

Claud and I wandered over, hung in the shadows. My armored brother hovered, annoying me. I felt like an unwilling, registered Claudian protectorate.

I got a different feeling when I watched Jesus work the crowd. His gestures were animated, but he didn't spill a drop of wine from the goblet in his hand. People around him were listening, mouths open.

We caught his story in midstream. "And so, this old fox was having trouble with the truth. He'd encountered an unusual bush while walking to worship at the temple he'd dedicated to himself. The bush burned and confronted greed in whomever it chanced upon—without ever burning up.

"Now you must understand, this was a fox who enjoyed predictability and comfort, and this talking, burning bush scored zero on both accounts."

Oh my god. Here he is droning on about truth again.

Jesus' face glowed, a drama-mobile. "This bush mildly interested the fox, in the same way a dancing rabbit might—perhaps it would be a novel sideshow, but it didn't spend enough time admiring him."

Watch out, Jesus. Here comes King Fox and the Queen of Good Advice. They're standing in the shadows behind you.

"This fox wore a polished gold mirror, a small circle attached by a silver wire to his jeweled tiara. He'd positioned it at an angle in front of his right eye. He used it to admire himself and guard against a surprise attack from behind."

Jesus whirled around and grinned at Herod. The shadowed puppet-king glared back at him. His jowls drooped in wavelets over the jeweled robe he wore.

Jesus turned back to the circle of people in front of him. "This fox squeezed his left eye shut and plugged his left ear with wax so he could hear only that portion of truth he wished to hear."

Jesus set his wine goblet down and paraded around the circle. He plugged his left ear with his left thumb and squeezed his left eye shut. With his right eye, he gazed at an imaginary mirror in his right hand.

The queen was the only royal who smiled, even if it was a wicked smear of a sneer. Jesus smiled back at her and sailed blithely into the teeth of her husband's storm. He strode up to the king and switched to a baritone voice, one that might emerge from golden flames. "You, old fox, desire only to celebrate yourself. You're like the legendary eagle that flew in smaller and smaller circles, until one day he grew so small that no one could remember his name."

Jesus snatched a guttering torch off the wall with his right hand. He whirled it in smaller spirals, extinguishing the flame behind him. A thread of smoke drifted up from the handle.

I covered my laughter with my hand. *This guy truly has the balls of an elephant.*

A servant handed the king another torch. Herod Antipas carried this torch into the circle of guests. "We meet again, my young friend from Galilee. Are you enjoying my food, my drink, my party, my guests, and my house with your unusual young friend there?" He pointed to John. Zoo Boy had dressed pungently in a wild skin assortment, hair spectacularly askew in all directions, and eyes wide with social overload.

Jesus parried, "What do you make of my story, King Herod?"

Herod jabbed back. "You clearly are given to ungrounded fantasy. In this way, you're like many boys unsuccessfully struggling to become real men, particularly boys with *dead* fathers."

Jesus' face remained placid. He watched Herod intently.

Herod gathered momentum. "Well fantasized, dream weaver. One day your fantasies will grow into realities." He spiraled his torch downward, dropped it, and ground out the fire under his right shoe.

"Country boys can be extinguished in mere moments, as they circle downward into smaller and smaller prison cells."

John pointed a bony finger directly at the royal couple and me as well, since I stood directly behind the king. "And you, sir and lady, would do well to mind your marriage and not be tricked by dancing seductresses. You do know what happens when a camel gets her foot in the front door of your tent, don't you, *sir*?" Abruptly, John jerked his eyes downwards.

I admit it—I resented being compared to a camel. He deserved what he got next.

Herod snapped his fingers, not even lifting them from his side. Bodyguards escorted both young men from the room. Herod then smoothly moved to speak with one of his revenue streams, a midget named Zacchaeus.

Dwarf Despicable had flowed over to observe the verbal fencing match. He now spun his brown-nosing self into high gear. Piglet curls pushed out of his head. He'd waxed them straight up, perhaps hoping to give the illusion of added height. Oil dripped from his axles like an olive press in harvest time. He listened to the king with a tilted head, nodding with a smile while the king prattled on. A willowy black woman, dressed elegantly, trailed behind the fat midget. She observed her meat box oinking drivel through his snout.

Guards force-marched Jesus and John past me on their way out. Jesus smiled, as if to say, *this was meant to be. Leave it alone.*

I moved toward him anyway. Claud squeezed my wrist hard with his thumb and middle finger.

Ow, that hurt!

Before I slapped the snot out of him, I took a lesson from Zacchaeus' Black Willow. I smiled at Claud blankly, keeping my vex inside. Mother's story was probably right—when we were born, I grabbed his foot and tried to pull myself out first. Then I gave up, slid back inside, and let the male come first. Some patterns begin early.

I shook Claud off. "I'm going for more champagne."

Claud became distracted by a passing skirt. I headed out to find Jesus.

56

WINDY

The guards lofted the two cousins through the back door on their hob-nailed boots. Jesus and John skidded to a stop in the gutter. The gate clanged shut behind them.

Jesus removed his face from the muddy cobblestones. "Good to have family join me in low places. But how did you get in there?"

John sat up, checked to see if all his appendages were still attached. He twisted his head to one side with both hands. Satisfying crunch. "Got down, Jeez. Needed a wilderness wander."

Son leaned in toward him, silent, receptive, sprout-assisting posture. *Good, Son, keep helping him feel felt.*

"I lose faith sometimes, Jeez. I get these stinking pictures of someone with a dead baby inside. Someone with a stillborn faith in the coming Messiah."

Jesus replied, "Trusting me in stillborn faith gutters? Hm. A remarkable thing. How'd you find me?"

"Ah, that part was easy. I saw you on your way here. God told me to join you. I think it was God—might have just been me hoping you're the One. I walked in when the guy at the front door stepped away for a moment."

"We both got practice back there, pointing out uncomfortable truth, each in our own way. Maybe our deliveries could use more practice, though."

John shrugged and changed the subject. "Hey, you okay after his shot at you in there—you know, about Uncle Joe's death?"

Jesus teared up, surprised that John would notice and inquire after him. "That did hurt. Father sent you for my help and healing."

John rearranged his shoulders a bit straighter, now that he was a provider of healing. Settled into his new wrapper, letting it sink a bit below his skin.

Rustle of silk, slide of slippers. Jesus' gaze shifted to shadows by the door.

Claudia saw she'd been discovered. She'd been standing there a while, watching. She took a half dozen steps toward the two cousins, balancing two trays over white cloths. She threw a crisp linen sheet to Jesus, and asked him to spread it out for them to sit on. He pushed off the muddy cobblestones with both hands and spread out the white sheet.

He asked John to sit with them. John shook his head, once, and moved a yard or so away, on the far side of Claudia, with Jesus between them.

Claudia arranged her silver party dress prettily over the sheet beneath her and put another as a tablecloth for their laps. "Voilà! I finally got you between the sheets, clever me. I stole this stuff from a closet for our *own* party. Herod's such an evil wheeze."

Jesus and Claudia sat on top of mud between white sheets, eating and laughing. John examined the celery and carrot sticks, olives, and squishy appetizer stuff carefully, up close, checking the angles on each bit. He arranged morsels of food in the mud by his thigh, spelling in Hebrew letters, the word 'whore.'

Such armored vigilance wrapped my desolate prophet in a sukkot of surliness. I silently kept soul-company with him as he complained, *here I am, a faith abortion, watching my failed Messiah flirt with the Whore of Babylon.*

Jesus leaned to his right and studied John's new mud graffiti. He turned to Claudia and whispered, "He's desperately lonely. He needs me. I gotta go."

Claudia flicked an envious gaze John's way. "He's not the only one who needs you." She fingered the once white, but now muddy, sheets. "As you well remember, I'd put my child-me under a white sheet inside a lockbox and thrown away the key. You came along, picked my lock, and dumped us in an alley. Now you leave us. *Not fair*, I'd say."

Jesus put his hand next to hers on the muddy sheet and fingered the only remaining white corner. "So hard to be your true you inside a false story. She's a precious part of you, even while you forget her. But she keeps showing up, entreating you to claim her." His eyes clouded up. Tears spilled down his cheeks.

"How *do* you do that, Jesus? I don't even want to *know my drama, or* another's, and you actually *feel* it with me, *for* me, till I'm able. You get between the sheets with me. That's the good of it.

"On the other hand," and she lifted her muddy right hand, "Do you know how unbearable it is, being a *fake* in the presence of a *real* person? You're the only one who sees the genuine me, instead of the envoy I send out to throw people off my scent."

She looked at John, rearranging two carrot sticks and a spring onion around some button mushrooms. "*And,* not only do you join my envoy-burning-doe-me, and forgotten-and-locked-up-kid-me, but you join *him* too, in all *his* crap."

She sighed and leaned in for a kiss. After, she inhaled deeply. "I don't want you to go. Truth is, I want you in me, one way or the other. I'd settle for gobbling you down or rooting myself in your rib cage, but all I get is a taste or smell."

She pushed herself up with both hands, slipped, and splashed down again on her bum in the mud. Jesus stood up, solid. He pulled her up, strong and straight, out of the mud. Claudia allowed herself to be pulled toward the only real person she'd ever known.

She took a few steps away from him. In a mere moment, she felt like she'd lost ground. She got dizzy with a sense of sloshing, turning, tossing.

She took a few more steps away from him and tried to shake off her imbalance. She grabbed the corner of Herod's palace. Its stone texture was cool and grainy beneath the pad of her fingertips, but felt tippy, like it might rock off its foundation.

Get a grip, girl.

At the same moment, Jesus looked toward her. He waved.

She waved back. Premonition flickered, roiling her stomach. Smashing waves dragging her down, down, after a sinking ship, to the ocean's floor.

She stood in an alley in Jerusalem—drowning. *Oh my god, what will become of me without him?*

57

GO

Today was my wedding day. The sky was streaky white in a bed of blue, the air crisp and clear here in Bethany. Laz's aunt and uncle had decorated their courtyard with ribbons all around the white lace chuppah. Servants washed people's feet when they entered the courtyard. Mary and Martha circulated among the guests, laden with trays of food and drink. It was the third day of the week, the double-blessing day.

I was gorgeous, so they all said. All decked out in my wedding gown and veil, borrowed from Laz's aunt. The severe neckline was high and the sleeves low, covering my scars. I was grateful for small things, including the tiny vase full of precious perfume Laz's mother had given me. She hung it over my head on a long cord made of beaten gold. It nestled between my breasts. I wasn't sure what to do with it. Once the ceramic stopper was broken, it had to be used that day, manna for the nose.

I saw Jesus standing behind Laz, and a thought flashed. *This is for him, one day.*

I shifted my weight, one foot to the other, dribbling off nervous energy. Escape and Cutter chased each other around my guts. Harlot postured for her public. Fragile started to splinter into helpless shards.

Shame sliced into my consciousness. *Your love for Laz won't live. Used people use people. Fractured people fake it. And you're all of that. You're not a gift for your beloved, you're a pile of Fragile splinters. I'll use Cutter to bleed you both to death.*

I shook off his voice and faced my groom. We stood under the chuppah in front of an antique table. Borrowed wedding vase, now loaded with orchids, set on this table. Mysterious light from this vase hit Roy full on the face. A little of it spilled onto me, along with Roy's bright, seeing smile.

What was it that held my parts together? Lit Spirit-vase, seeing-Roy, or kind-Jesus? Whatever it was, from this trinity of possibilities, light flooded into me. I gained the courage not to run away, at least for this second. I took comfort in the fact that I could kill myself anytime. I'd just stack all my fractured parts in a high tower, climb to the top, and jump.

I smiled behind my veil and found my eyes had filled with tears—no mother on the front row, no father to hand me off to my groom. Only orphaned-me's, all of them clamoring for attention.

Escape wanted nothing to do with this terminal script, the one Roy had us practice over and over, the one ending, "*'til death do us part.'*"

She screamed, *Run, run, run! We still have time.*

I stuffed a gag in her mouth and hog-tied her under the table, practicing my best parenting skills. Denied, she burrowed down, grew huge, and invited Shame to chaperone the others. Shame directed Cutter to use my left hand to pluck out an eyelash and blow it onto my veil, right where I could see it.

Leah nudged me into the present, once again. She stood behind me and whispered in my ear, *"Breathe. Don't miss your own wedding."*

I looked at Jesus looking at me. He stood back of Laz and radiated confidence.

Roy started the ball rolling by saying aloud our vows, words we were to repeat. I zoned out and looked off to my right. There, close to the bottom of the table, Cornelia and my other whore friends from Rahab's beamed. Corn mouthed the words, *Go, girl!*

My adult-self, the seventeen-year-old mature one, the one with all the makeup, the one wearing another person's clothes, repeated terminal vows. She spilled out sweetness, words that promised faithfulness and obedience. My heart was in so many pieces, I wasn't sure if I had a majority vote on *any* of those promises. Were they sweet somethings or deceptive nothings?

A moment of silence after the vows. Fragile re-grouped, pulled Escape down from the cloud hanging over us. Cutter joined. Together, they un-stoppered this vow—

As much as we know of us, Laz, we'll give to as much as we know of you. And that, partner, is precious little.

58
WINDY

The wedding rite finished. Laz stepped on the wine glass contained in the linen hanky—a satisfying crunch. Father and I circulated among those present, mainly unseen. We'd heard *all* of Go's vows from all of her various selves, public and private, and smiled to each other.

Father said, *I'm so proud of her, aren't you?*

I squeezed an *"of course"* into his hand.

I showed Leah glimmers of Ourselves, goldening odd places among olive trees in the courtyard's corners. She blinked and looked again. Her little face was puzzled. Who had she seen come and go?

Leah and Rabbus approached Jesus during the feast that followed the wedding. Both squatted next to where he reclined at table. Leah asked Jesus, voice tinged with subdued rivalry, "Will Go and Laz get a vase too?"

Son shook his head. "Each couple gets something unique, tailored to fit them. Have you caught a glimpse of God? Always around, you know."

Leah said, "Apart from you, maybe not. My vision is misty, even for the one in front of me."

Rabbus bull-dogged forward. "Will you stop by our home on your way back to Naz, Jesus?"

"We'll stop over at your place for a day or so. But after that, we're not going home to Nazareth. We're boarding a merchant ship bound for Rome, at Augustus' decree. Our return date is uncertain."

Leah looked happy and stricken, both at the same time. She quieted herself with a deep breath. "I've been given an image of you as a blazing ship, lit from within, made of jewels. You spray rainbows of color from a sun within you over stormy seas. Your colors are the sufferings of shattered Light. Weird, huh?"

Son replied, "These images are Windy-plantings. You've always thought of yourself as Leah-the-Lesser—less beautiful than your sister, less than life requires."

Leah looked down—her gaze, lesser. Jesus put his left hand on her shoulder. The other hand raised her chin. "From this day, you will become a prophetess, feeling Father's Spirit and speaking Her voice. This is the gift your vase foreshadows—Spirit glowing from a broken, but now melded-together you."

She looked dubious but tried on a strong, confident smile for size. The smile searched for the right shape before it wobbled into place between her nose and chin.

Simon and Penelope, from Cyrene, interrupted Project Smile. "Your sister's wedding was beautiful. But the word on the street is that your wedding was much more unusual."

Leah flicked a look toward Jesus and then back at Simon. "Yes, the wedding after the funeral, midway between garbage dump and village, under a bloody bougainvillea. That would be the one."

Simon turned to Jesus. "Thank you for walking with me to Herod's Temple and pointing out the construction foreman, that man from Bethlehem in charge of hiring. Your father's youngest brother, I believe? A place opened up for me after three workers got killed the other day. Thanks for making the road for us, Jesus."

Jesus said, "that's me, Simon. Walk me. I *am* the road to Father. Sometimes I'm cobbled, or a paved Roman road, or a faint path in a dark wood. I go by many names. One of those is Via Delarosa."

Simon didn't know what to make of this. Penelope saw with steady eyes and believed *into* Jesus."[34]

Rastus, Zacchaeus' brother, stood across the street and watched the wedding from the second story of an empty apartment building. After, during the banquet, he poked his head in the open door and saw the vase on the table, pulsing light from within.

Zac would pay for something like that, pay a lot. This is better than good. It's superb.

He posted watchers.

59

JESUS

Two days after Laz and Go's wedding, we stopped overnight at Rahab's. Once James and I settled in our room, we walked through the workshop areas. Go, the new bride, was back at work on the wheel. Sweat glistened on her forehead. Her focus and hands had married as she shaped tiny perfume vases into beautiful, reddish-purple patterns.

We brothers walked to the synagogue across the courtyard, and James settled into a sunny corner, unrolled a scroll to Ezekiel, then dived into some memory work on good and bad shepherds.[35] His head and shoulders shuckled words into memory, letter-perfect. He was so focused on being right he didn't get it right. He saw *what* was in front of him, not *who* was beside him.

I stayed with him for an hour or two 'till Laz motioned for me to join him and Go during their afternoon visit with Cyn. He'd been moved to a slightly larger room, one with a window that let in light.

Cyn called out, "Sounds to my ears like my minder brought two others with her."

Go told Cyn, "You've survived your injuries. Let's see if you can survive yourself."

"I'd like not to." Cyn's voice was gravelly, a bag of rocks with all the sharp edges worn off.

I said, "Cyn, there's still time for life before death."

Cyn turned his head sideways at the sound of my voice. He rubbed an empty, shriveled eye socket. "Whoever you are, it's plain I'm done." He ticked off on five fingers just how done he was, "I can't fight like a legionnaire, can't hold my crap, can't stand up straight, can't see, can't keep my weight—lost half of it. What's left?"

I said, "Lots of "can't" wrapped in your grumbling, warrior. But there is a lot left in life that you *can* do."

Cyn said, "I remember your voice. You're the kid outside Naz's gates. You released that skinny loser early. Do the same for me. I ain't got nutin' to live for—I got no family in Italy, no job, no future, no hope, no faith, no nothing. Let me die."

I paused and knelt, doodled in the dust on his floorboards. "Cyn, go ahead, feel hopeless, for now. Feel it all, but in the company of others. Loneliness and Shame live together. They crush giants into dwarfs. Father's left you with old memories and a new community. Both will wound and heal you. Choose them."

Cyn seemed to shrivel inside his skin, like a month-old apple.

"This is a new kind of warfare, legionnaire. Join old warrior skills with new visions. Live and die for a God bigger than you or your grumbling."

Cyn's crooked jaw ground sideways, chewing on despair the way a camel chews her cud. He suddenly lurched to the chamber pot. Bowels erupted through his ruined rectum. The effort exhausted him and the noses of everyone in the room.

Go bolted to the window and took deep gulps of air to stop from retching.

Cyn grinned, a grim gash in his brittle crust. "I know how you feel. I make me want to vomit." He added, "Hey, seer, you mentioned a god. Which one's on offer today?"

I went over to the man on the chamber pot, rested my hand on his shoulder. "I'm the person God became when God became a person."

Cyn turned his head a bit more toward me, reached his right hand across his heart toward my left hand on his left shoulder, hovered it there, trembling. Moved it away. Something steamed off him, contagious, toxic, like a decomposing body leaking from an open grave.

Go resisted the contagion. "If you can't believe Jesus' words, the least you can do is wipe your own butt. Do what you can do now, until you grow up and learn other stuff."

Cyn reached over and took a wet rag, wiped himself, and threw it on the floor—a little less filthy, but not yet clean.

We left him, closed the door, and walked down the stairs.

Halfway down the dim staircase, I looked up at the two of them, a step higher than where I stood. "Can I offer you two a wedding blessing, two days late?"

Both nodded. They stood on the landing midway between whorehouse and workshop.

Windy breathed this benediction out of my mouth. "Go, your new name will be 'Slow.' You'll teach all those shamed, scared, scared, and warring parts inside you to get along. You'll build bridges between love and its denial, suffering and its denial. You'll spread a sweet fragrance within and around you. Windy will teach your hands to potter wholeness from your broken pieces."

I paused. "And you, Laz, my dear friend? Love will rise from lust's grave. You will realize our work is not to make sick people well. We're here to make dead people *live*. You'll point people to me as resurrection and life."

Both stood silent, sober. Blessing sifted slowly from bones to beliefs.

We said goodbye to Go and Laz at the northern gates of Jericho. We moved north, each step laden with pain and possibility. Toward evening on that same day, our northbound group of ten people and three burros overnighted in the same place where Rabbus, Laz, Go, and Leah were attacked on their way south.

The sun had pulled back its orange cloak, revealing a gathering darkness. Venus winked on. The moon rose as our group prepared dinner with stories, laughter, jokes. I sat at fireside and passed fresh Jericho goat cheese around the campfire to everyone. I popped a chunk of cheese in my mouth. *Ah, wedges of moonlight, folded in cream. That's exactly what this taste is like.*

We all savored the food and each other's company. Galaxies wheeled on their axles overhead. Sparks flew into the night sky. Windy whispered in my ear, *eat nothing further, Son, till Father gives the okay. Tune to our voice. Sync more closely with our breath as you fast. A big test is coming up for you in Shechem.*

I was digesting my Partner's words when Rastus and his gang of a dozen men stepped into our small circle of light, each gang member armed with a sword in one hand and a dagger in the other. Necklaces crowded with dried, human ears dangled around their necks. Faces, painted black and red, rose from eyebrows to their hairlines. Miriam and Deborah started wailing.

Rastus had positioned himself immediately to my right side. He said, "All we want is that wedding vase. Give it up, and no one gets killed. You got ten seconds. Gimme the vase or this girl is the first to get her throat cut."

He casually yanked Deborah off the ground by her long, raven-black hair. She yelped, tears bubbling up, flooding her cheeks. Ma reached for her, but one of Rastus' men shoved her down on the ground. Rabbus' hand snaked up his sleeve to where he kept his throwing knife.

Leah looked her man in the eye and shook her head. She pushed off his leg and stood—Spirit powered. She walked to her tent and said, over her shoulder, "We'd love to bless you with God's blessing. Instead, you're choosing stuff. Shame, that."

"I don't believe in gods or demons," sneered the man who'd painted himself to look like a devil. "Gimme the goods, lady."

Leah carefully traded him the vase for Deborah, handed my sister to Ma. She eye-checked with me. I knelt, one knee on the ground, to get away from the smell of Rastus' breath. I looked up at her and nodded.

Leah stood her ground. Her felt faith extended reach beyond grasp with these words. "This vase was fired by God. Those who steal from His hand will reap from His hand. Your natural lives will be cut short, and soon."

Rastus paused, hesitating between fear and greed. Greed won. The bandits moved from the campsite into the darkness. Rastus tripped over one of two graves that were out there. He recovered, moved on. Shadows flickered across his painted face from the light within the vase. Rastus put his hand over the vase to stopper the light. Light moved through his hand and heart, leaving him in the dark.

60

WINDY

My small group of travelers moved north toward the place Rabbus and Leah would call home. As they came around the last bend, Rabbus was the first to see the old farmhouse. Rapeseed had grown into a sea of heavy-headed flowers, yellows and buffs that bowed low, bent under a dominating blow. One wild arm of pink bougainvillea wound out the blackened hull of a house, moved in the breeze.

Rabbus stared at the charred ruins. They spoke to him. *You'll always carry us, like a corpse on your back, bound, chains of vengeance.*

Leah whispered in her husband's ear another story, "Those pink bogies spoke just now, husband … I'm fresh, new. Choose me."

Rabbus was torn. What to believe—black or pink, past or present? He chewed on his choices. "Men, let's tear down those black beams, pile 'em up, and make a bonfire."

They took what had been burned, added more fuel, and burned it some more, burned it all down to smoking ash. Later, they would mix this ash with concrete powder and gravel. Pour a new foundation.

Toward noon on the second day, Jesus laid down his crowbar to explore the property's edges—the perimeters of the possible—with Rabbus and Leah. They walked past the outhouse toward the cliff where Rabbus' parents were buried. A gnarly crop of ancient citrus trees, tangerine and lemon, formed a spray over the cave grave.

A bubbling spring-fed pond incepted a stream. Mount Gerizim's peak poked into view, along with Mt. Ebal and its hanging valleys, to the north. The capital town of Samaria, Sebaste, rested peacefully below. Sun-'n-shadow dappled eastern ridges. They looked to Jesus' eye like crinkled curtains splotched with sprays of red wildflowers. Dots of blood, giving silent witness to what had soaked this ground.

Leah took off her sandals, raised her skirt, and moved to the middle of the pond where the spring bubbled from below. The water was bracing and only knee-deep. Her toes sunk into silt, kicking up mud, dead leaves, and a few crawdads that swam away to the edges of the pond.

The spring was a steady pulse flowing cool and dark from below her, within her. She let her skirt drop in the water and leaned forward, placed her hands on the surface, and felt its tension. Water spiders raced between her fingers, playing with a new friend.

Rabbus and Jesus leaned against two junipers, whose roots twined together, holding each other up from below. The men's two branches of thought wound together in easy conversation as they watched the young prophetess working My gift into her bones.

Leah said, over her shoulder, "I want to plant a vineyard around this pond, over there in the full sun. Yesterday your ma checked the soil. She told me that would be the very best place."

Leah walked back to them. Jesus stood between them and put one arm around each of their shoulders. He spoke Father's words, "Love will cover a bumper crop of sin on this land. Your faith will melt ice, scorch deserts, and warm hearts to faith. Be blessed, friends."[36]

Leah sat on her haunches, hands in the loamy soil, eyes closed. She felt a tremor of grapes being stomped beneath her bare toes. Olive oil dripped off her chin from olives just harvested.

Justus and Miriam ran over the crest of the hill. "Come quick, Jesus! Those robbers are back, and they look like dead men!"

We hurried back to the front of the property where the fires were burning. Ten lepers loitered there, at the edge of the woods. Ear necklaces dangled on snow-white necks mottled with raw red patches.

Rastus called out, "Unclean." He approached Leah, stopped at a distance, and set her vase on the ground, "Here, take it. Your curse is killing us."

Leah picked up the vase and returned to her husband's side. "Rastus, what happened?"

He looked down at his right hand, now missing two fingers. "*You* happened. We had a party that night we harvested your vase, filled it with booze, and passed it around. We all got drunk. Next morning, this is how we looked. The mirrored bottom showed us our own faces."

John commented, helpfully, "Your disease looks like you've had it for years. Probably die soon."

Rastus and his men looked pathetic without their face paint—just vicious middle-aged boys with paunches. Overgrown bullies who'd never grown up. Now their bodies were falling apart in a hurried, worried heart-beat.

Leah's face showed my own presence within her. We refused quick and narrow edges to our love.

She looked at Jesus, and he at her. My energy flowed, passing secret gifts through Jesus to Leah, gifts better caught than taught. I trickled cour-age into Leah's bones and made her gifting actionable. Leah stood still between her husband and Jesus.

"We have a pond on our property. Not much more than a mud hole."

She looked at Jesus. "If you believe in *this* man, go wash. Your faith will force your fate."

Leah surely didn't know what she was doing. Healing lepers was *way* beyond her. This fourteen-year-old Jewish-Moabitess, faced with ten Arab lepers in Samaritan hill country, responded to my will-o'-the-wisp injunc-tion. With each new step she took into her promised land, I whispered, *the only bit of me you will know is the bit of me where you stand.*

John came over to Jesus, cleared his throat. "Should they hope for heal-ing, like Naaman's dip in the Jordan, Master? Or is this the hopeless leprosy of Gahazi, Elisha's right-hand man?"

John spoke of stories from the prophets. He stood at Jesus' right hand, looked down at Son's hand and his own, making sure which was his. Then he snapped his fingers twitchy-like, gaze fluttering off Jesus' face, like a moth bouncing off a fired kiln.

Leah, suddenly off-kilter, looked to Jesus for guidance. Jesus shrugged, happy to be present.

He said to John, "The Spirit blesses whomever the Spirit chooses— whether Jew or Gentile, man or woman. What you're seeing now is the Spirit's gifting, lived out through Leah's faith. Watch and see Windy work through Leah. She's very good."

61

LEAH

I looked at Jesus, then at husband. Was Jesus talking about Windy or me with his "very good"? Maybe he was talking about both of us? Okay, let's go with both.

"All right, listen up," I said. I had the lepers' complete attention. One of them scratched his nose absentmindedly, and a chunk of it came off in his hand.

"Here's what you do. Walk into this pond and form a circle. Lie stomach down in the water, arms bent at the elbow, chins up, feet toward the edges of the pond. Put your left hand down on the silty bottom for balance. Stretch your right hands in front of you. Hold hands together in circle center. Keep your noses barely above water."

They started to move.

"Not done yet." They stopped.

"When Rastus gives the order, put your heads beneath the water. Push your faces down in the mud. Hold them there. Count to ten. Raise and lower your hands up and down as you each count to ten—arms up on the odd numbers, down on the even. When you reach ten, heads up—noses just out of the water. Breathe. Repeat. Dunk seven times."

I exhaled more words that blew from light inside me, passing through my mouth to what was left of their ears. "Choose what you believe carefully. If you think this is dumb, walk right now. If you believe *into* my words and Jesus' power to heal, stay. Whatever you choose, act on that belief."

Spirit's voice, *you've got their attention, Leah, even if it's only a raspy gasp. Remember Ezekiel's dry bone valley, Leah. Obey me, and see these lepers live!* [37]

I stood on the pond edge and responded to this fresh Wind, "After you do what I've said, come to Jesus."

I put our wedding vase on the ground at my feet. "Rastus, bring this vase, full of muddy water from the pond, with you. Hand the vase to Jesus."

The men flopped in the water, legs splayed out behind them in a daisy-chain circle, tunics billowing up around their legs.

Rastus yelled, "Down!"

James, Jude, Justus, and Miriam counted out loud to ten while lepers' arms slopped up and splatted down ten times. The men's heads bobbed up, gasping for air. Waited. Mother Mary, the Rav and his wife, Esther, prayed, lips moving.

After repeating their ups and downs, all seven times, each man struggled up the slippery slope of faith toward Jesus. He stood over them, but didn't look down on them. In fact, he reached down to help them up, one hand at a time, toward himself. The violent of the earth found they couldn't take the kingdom by force. Instead, something different was happening. God was on their side.

Rastus was last. He returned the vase he'd stolen, full of muddy water, and handed it to me. I handed it to Jesus. Jesus gave it to John. The men, without being told, had formed a standing circle around John and Jesus. These two cousins walked around the circle of drenched men.

Jesus looked each man in the eye and asked the same question, "Do you believe you can be cured of the incurable?"

And each man nodded—downcast eyes, fierce eyes, pleading eyes, confused eyes.

Jesus instructed John, "Pour water on each man's head. Give all you've got to each one."

John took the vase, full of brownish pond water. He tipped it over the first man's head. Crystal clear water flowed out.

John said, "Be baptized in Jesus' name."

Once each man was soaked with clean water, down to the last drop, John righted the jar. Took a step to the right. Lifted the jar. Tipped it again. More clean water came out of what had been an empty jar. They continued around the circle. I caught glimmers of misty swirls, golden. Light spilled out of the vase with the water, spilled over the men. Drenched all those who came to be baptized.

At the end of the ceremony, each man still looked leprous. Each man examined his neighbor's face. One grabbed the vase and looked at the mirrored bottom, hopeful. Same face.

Jesus walked around the circle of disappointed men. "Because I didn't answer your prayer *your* way doesn't mean Father didn't answer it *anyway*. I'm telling you, your sins are forgiven! You will receive your physical healing on the way, as you obey, not today."

He paused. "Tell people your experience—nothing more, nothing less. Stop lying, cheating, stealing, and murdering. Give better than you get, be lively, not deadly. In a word, *grow up*."[38]

Jesus' face was lit from within, spilling sunshine from his eyes. "Bless these people, whose faith has made them whole, Father. Cause their hearts to be thankful for the healing that has already happened but is yet to be revealed."

The Spirit leapt within me, did somersaults, giddy with the Glory I harbored.

Rastus looked over at Jesus. "We've been our own village. Most of us don't know a soul in our home villages. These men's villages are scattered over six countries up and down the Jordan River valley. But nonetheless, at your command, we will go and hope for healing."

Jesus looked at him and loved them. "Your gang will not heal you, your faith will. This blind trust in my word activates Father's power. And Rastus, did I hear you say that Zacchaeus is your brother?"

"Ten years apart," Rastus said. "Same father, different mother."

Jesus nodded. "On your way home, men, your bodies will show what only your faith can know. Believe, act, and know. That's how we spirit warriors roll—believe in faith, act into your belief, know new life."

Rastus sputtered, "But Jesus, this is too new. Doesn't make good sense, doesn't…"

Jesus held up his hand. "Rastus, stop. Believe. The other stuff comes later."

Rastus grumped but shut up.

"Go to your younger brother, Zacchaeus. Tell him what's happened to you and your gang. By *that* time, your physical healing will be accomplished. And Rastus, Zacchaeus won't believe. Not for years."

The band of lepers made departure moves. All of them leaned on his fellows. And now, for the first time, they hoped for a life beyond themselves.

62

JESUS

Our band of travelers approached the bustling crossroads town of Shechem. I walked alongside Rav and bounced Deborah on my shoulders. She played with my beard, plaited my uncut hair into braids.

Rav Moshe taught the younger ones, a living Torah school without walls. He told the ancient story of this town.[39] "Children, this is the place where Jacob bought a patch of ground for a hundred silver coins and built that altar right over there. Yes, that one, off to the right." He pointed to a pile of old rocks.

I picked up the story. "Moshe, is this where the man, Shechem, uh … abused Dinah?"

Rav agreed, and added, "She was Jacob's daughter by his first wife, Leah."

Leah's ears perked up at the mention of her namesake.

"Leah also was the mother of half of Jacob's twelve sons. Two of these sons, Simeon and Levi, were very cunning." Rav Moshe hunched up his shoulders, looked left and right, wiping his hands together, a pair of slippery eels.

"They publicly agreed that their sister, Dinah, could marry Shechem, but only if the men in this town agreed to be circumcised. Shechem, the town's poster child, spoke for all the men.

'Let's do it. I want that woman for my very own!'"

John asked, without preamble, "Is this where Simeon and Levi whacked them all?"

Moshe nodded. "Jacob appointed an experienced elder with a sharp blade to sit in their town square. All the men of Shechem lined up, dropped their drawers, and he went to work on their weenies. Zip-zop, watched 'em flop. Before long, he had a bag of bloody foreskins at his feet.

233

"A few days later, when all the men of the town were still sore from their town square surgeries, surprise, surprise! The two brothers arrived back in town, whipped out their swords, and killed all the men in this city."

Rabbus had listened to this story with great interest. "So, Yahweh approves of *vengeance*?"

Moshe said, "Yahweh allows us to choose. We inherit consequences, over many generations. This town had been a center for prostitution since Jacob's time. Let's see, that's about 2,000 years, 6,000 generations. Demonic roots are deep in this area."

I remembered Windy's words about a test coming to me in Shechem. Dread filled me.

I kept walking, one foot in front of the other, breathing in Windy's soothing, Father's strength. We all passed through Shechem's city gates into a tangled skein of sellers and buyers. The air was a thick mélange of sweat, spice, and avarice.

A hundred feet or so into the middle of the market, my test came around a corner. A curvy young woman, dressed in rags, ran toward us. She ran unerringly, despite milk-white eyes that rolled up and down, unseeing, in her eye sockets. Her strawberry blond hair was unruly as a thorn bush.

A legion of demons mingled their voices with hers, shrieking my name. "Jesus bar Joseph, Son of Man, have mercy on me."

I said to Father, *demons and foreigners recognize me even before I have fully claimed myself.*

Father replied, *ask her if she wants to be clean.* I asked His question.

A strangled squeal, "Yes, Lord."

Immediately, a different voice—a powerful, masculine voice—roared through her still quivering lips, "Get away from her, Messiah of the Jews. She's our property! We are many. We are Shechem. We rape when, where, and who we want." The voice deepened and sharpened, like a sheering blade. "And you too are in line for our services, precious Jesus. Wait for Rome."

I trembled, not knowing what of this devilish mix to believe. *What to do, Windy?*

A swarthy man with a bulbous nose stood a few steps behind the blind woman. His thick lips were so curled with contempt that his mouth looked like a poked oyster shell. He spat on the ground, then complained to a man next to him, a man covered by a gray prayer shawl. Crispus, again! Satan haunts me, hunts me, using him.

Thank you, Father, for help in my time of testing.

I breathed in, felt the cool wind whistle softly through my nose, filling my chest first, then my belly. Windy blew through my voice box on the exhale, strumming cords into sound, moving my tongue into speech. A calm, weightless vapor with the force of lightning came out my mouth. "Leave her, demons. Return to your home, Satan's hellhole."

The rasping voice cackled, "Your time will come, good-looking Jew. Believe me, butt-boy, we'll see a lot of you." A salacious stream of smut blasted out her mouth.

As soon as she'd stopped speaking, she threw herself down and writhed snake-like, as if her skeleton had gone missing. No sooner had she stopped writhing than she popped back up, strong-legged, pulled her dress up to her waist, and pooped a long stream of diarrhea down both legs. A bright yellow stream of urine also flowed, with the force of a broodmare. Once emptied, she spread her legs wide, arched her back like an upside-down cat, headfirst between her heels and then her head poked up between her knees, leering at me, cackling.

All in our band of travelers stood, open-mouthed, at this display of the demonic. Ragged talons invaded my head, clawed at the back of my brain, pulling my head backward like they had done with this woman. I thought, *hell has emptied its demons to break my neck.*

I dropped to my knees next to this woman and fought with devils.

John said, "Rav, quick, help Jesus! They're trying to kill him." The two men, one on either side of me, held the back of my head in their hands, pushing back, pushing back, trembling against the force that inched my neck to the breaking point. Rav and John together shouted out Yahweh's name.

I joined them, "Helllllp, Help, Father!"

Razored claws dissipated, vanished into thin air. I rose from my knees, in my right mind. Their property curled on her side around my right leg, clasping my calf, fingers white with the pressure.

John slapped me on the back. "Shazam, Jeez! We showed 'em, didn't we! A real Shechem showstopper!" He looked at the woman. She'd gone limp, arms splayed out to either side of her. "Uh, think you should check on that lady? She might need some burying."

Leah slipped inconspicuously over to the woman. Gently took her face in both hands. The woman roused marginally. Ma knelt behind the woman, shielding her, while Leah took a wet cloth and cleaned her bottom. Ma retrieved the soiled cloth and carefully wrapped it in another cloth for later washing.

Both Leah and Ma helped the woman try to stand. Her legs were floppy, like boiled pasta. They carried her to Moshe's burro. Rav helped hoist her on its back. Unease rippled through the crowd. Whispers skittered across the square like drops of water on a red-hot stove.

I motioned to Rabbus. "Let's leave. Now."

We booked for the city gates at a trot. We were about there, city gates in sight, when a bunch of armed men panted into the open area and planted themselves between us and the city gates. Swarthy led them. Crispus followed their pock-faced leader, shrugged off his grey prayer shawl, and revealed his gloating face. His one steady eye, if it were a tongue, would have licked the child who sat on my shoulders. A creepy sizzle of evil frissoned the air. He menaced himself into the crowd and faded from view.

Swarthy looked at the woman on Rav's mule. "Cyrena, down! You're ours." The woman went splat in a heap on the ground. She began to froth, as if desperate to lose consciousness.

Leah looked to Rabbus. He looked to me. I looked to Father. Courage, Father given, bunched in my chest. I launched words, each of them a divine act. "She's God's child, now clean. We're taking her with us."

John was the only one in my group that didn't look terrified. His chin was up and his chest out, fists balled. He was one step in front of me, not seeming to know or care that we were standing in a powder keg and throwing off sparks.

Swarthy faced us, shaking with rage. "Kill 'em, every one … including her." He pointed to his quivering piece of property on the ground.

The twenty men reached for their swords. Bloodlust rose in their faces. Muscles sprang into action. But then, in the act of pulling swords from scabbards, two obstacles presented themselves.

The first was a wall of fire. This wall contained angels led by my friend, Michael. The attackers immediately fell to the ground. Swarthy picked himself up first, refusing to look at the angels. He yelled, "Get up, pussies!"

His companions shakily stood, eyes down, or on each other. Then something else happened.

Windy said, *I'm shape-shifting these people. Each man's best friend now looks like his worst enemy. Wait. Watch.*

I relayed Windy's message to family and friends. "Stand still. We need do nothing."

Each man fought the other. Old rage, new stage. A riot of red flooded the ground.

I cradled Deborah's head in the crook of my arm, shielded her eyes, and rocked her. My other arm held Ma. She closed her eyes and massaged my sore neck. A circle of soothing.

Men dropped all around us, some missing body parts; others, spear shafted. Swarthy was the last man standing. He brayed a victory call, pumping his massive, muscled right arm overhead.

That was when he saw us standing unharmed. He stalked our way, left hand grasping his short sword in stabbing mode, blade tip down, knees bent, arm extended. His long sword he held straight out in his right hand.

He stepped over a corpse on the way. This friend swiped his arm upward in one final, mighty protest. His sword cleanly severed both of Swarthy's arms above the elbow. Plumes of crimson erupted. The man laughed, triumphant, and breathed his last.

Shechem's last fighting man dropped to his knees, lifeblood pumping into the sand from both arm stumps. He looked in shock at his alarmed arms, jumping about in the sand. I assisted him lower still, resting his head on his companion's chest. He bled out.

A hush of fear swept through the city crowds who had gathered. This was not the show they'd come to see. Not a man, woman, or child taunted or resisted us this time, as we moved to leave their town. We walked silent, stunned at the display of vicious demons and an even mightier God. A mile from the city gates, my muscles still trembled and my neck ached.

Windy whispered, *you would have asked for this, if you knew what will yet come. You need everything He sends—and all he withholds, you don't need.* I took her words under advisement.

We all stood at the intersection of Israel's main north-south and east-west highways. We kissed one another all around our circle and divided into two smaller groups. Rabbus, Leah, and Cyrena moved south on an upward, bending trail into the woods. The rest of us went west on the highway, toward Caesarea—and Rome.

63

WINDY

Tribune Gaius sat in his penthouse office suite on the third floor of the white limestone fortress. He overlooked Caesarea's Sebastos Harbor. The ocean glowed in five shades of blue when the sun hit it just so. Aquamarines and darker violets mingled over submerged reefs. Pelicans, formation-flying in chevrons, fished for dinner. Seagulls wheeled in the wind, cawing.

He studied a new message from Rome. The sealed scroll had just arrived by fast courier. It had taken the messenger only forty-six days to bring the message, changing horses every ten miles at Roman outposts—a sign of civilization's break-neck speed.

The writing was Caesar's own, a shaky script:

Gaius, my son-in-law, I am unwell, a palsied seventy-three-year-old.
I strive unsuccessfully to hide my shaking sticks from these yapping wolves.
Doctors here dither, obfuscate. No one tells me how long or well I will live—
with the possible exception of that young seer from Sepphoris.
Do not mention my sickness to anyone. Send the seer.
May Neptune be with your family, and him, on the sea.

Caesar Augustus

Jesus' family camped three days southeast of Caesarea. They'd set up their tents by the side of a stream, in a hollow ringed by a grove of birch, cypress, and eucalyptus. Mediterranean salt sea breezes swept over the hills and tangled with forest scents. The wind luffed, leaving the air thick as cream.

Jesus' family had passed through a village with a general store earlier that day. They'd roamed the aisles and stocked up on matzo bread, hard cheese, barley grain, black beans, clusters of grapes, and ripe figs. A leg of lamb roasted over the fire. The lamb sizzled as Rav Moshe tended it.

Mary sat next to Esther and kept an eye on the younger children. She sighed as she stirred the black bean stew, wafting the odors toward her nose with her left hand.

Everyone was tired and cranky. Deborah scrapped with Miriam. James, Justus, and Jude play-wrestled, too hard. Jude ended up with a black eye. John's emotions were mercurial. Even calm Moshe snapped at John, who had gone off on Herod, his wife, and infidels in general. "John, crusaders like you don't change. You finger point, shifting judgments to fit your moods." John retreated to the woods, licking his wounds.

Even Jesus was on a moody-blue caravan, missing home, wanting his abba, impatient to see Claudia once again. I exhaled a wee breeze around him, soothing his sore neck, penetrating his skull, and stretching neurons in his pre-frontal cortex into greater maturity.

Son's brain in this area was still half-baked, like all other young people his age, not becoming fully functional till his young twenties. He remained a bit impatient, not using the excellent timing and judgment that would become him as an older male, not yet thinking through consequences clearly before speaking or acting.

Father's tests were helping him grow up. Another one was just a day or so ahead of him. Father used me to lay out Son's next assignment. *Tell your mother you'll be gone for a few days. I'll tell you more later.*

Son moved to obey. Mary argued, "Jesus, I'd like a break too. Your abba's grave is still fresh. I need help with the younger ones."

Jesus leaned in, rubbed her back, said nothing.

Mary said, "This country girl is scared. Scared of what might happen here, what this sea voyage might hold, and whatever's on the other side of the sea there in Rome. I'm having nightmares."

"You've always said hard things grow us up, Ma."

Mary shook her head. "You listen too well."

"This dreamy son needs you too. Chunks of me feel like they're spinning off into space." He sat back on his haunches, cupped both hands into a bowl like he was blowing a wispy ball of comfort between his fingers—a ball solid as clouds and evening wind song.

Mary said, "you're so much like Joe. Dreamers. Joe was a dreamer, but he yanked his dreams to the ground and acted. The fortress where he fell was real, not built on clouds."

Jesus nodded.

Mary kept speaking over his nodding. "We often pillow-talked about you. When you were new, a babe in bed with us, in my arms, on my breast, eating me, I would smile into your eyes and say, 'Hello, stranger.' Joe would hug me, caress your cheek as you sucked away, and say, 'When I think of the task God has given me, fathering the Messiah, *I* feel that tiny!'"

A slight smile quivered at the corners of her mouth. "I remember coming around a corner when just the two of you were working in the carpentry shop. You were about ten. I remember you saying, 'What a good choice Father made in giving you to me, me to you.' I loved you even more for that."

She deliberated. "Oh, go, Jesus. Go with God."

Jesus trailed his fingers across her shoulder as he stood, looked around him, and spotted Miriam. She sat alone, chewing quietly and playing with a doll. Jesus sat down on the ground next to her, watched her play, arm around her shoulder. She nestled into him.

He said, "Remember that general store this morning?" She nodded, body tightening, swallowed.

"The candy you tucked in your pocket on the far aisle? You know, the stuff you swallowed just now? You don't need a sermon about right and wrong, do you, Sis?"

She shook her head. Tears sprang up in her eyes.

"Here are some more pieces of candy, Miriam. I paid for all of them, including what you stole. Our secret. Pay this forward, okay?"

"What do you mean?"

"Two things. No more shoplifting. Share what you have."

Son gathered a few things and then slipped away into the gathering dark, his backpack slung over his shoulder. A sling whirred in his hand. He took potshots at the trees, blowing off steam.

Another person lurked under a thorn tree at the eastern perimeter, just beyond the stream. He stood in a patch of thorns and poison ivy, waiting for his moment.

The boys played Romans and Zealots, but nicely now. Miriam shared candy with Deborah. Moshe, Mary, and Esther busied themselves around the campfire.

John studied Torah fragments, arranging them in cryptic patterns around him. Deborah sat just behind the tent she shared with Ma and Miriam and her brothers. She loved her sticky 'sister sweets.' Miriam hugged her and made a beeline to her brothers to share more, as Jesus had asked her to do. Paying it forward.

The boys crammed the sweets in their mouths and asked her to join their play.

Deborah got thirsty and wandered over to the creek, sat in the middle of the cool water after she had a drink. She played with small sticks and rocks, building a tiny dam in a side eddy.

Crispus made his move. He approached from behind, sapped Deborah on the back of her head with a sand-filled cloth. He picked up the unconscious child, slung her over his shoulders, and disappeared in the woods. He moved silent, fast. He headed toward Judgment Cliff, the crumbling limestone karst cliff just south of Caesarea.

64

JESUS

Slight movement on my ankle woke me up from my long sleep in the forest. Slippery coil sliding across my thigh, down to my foot. *Not good.*

I woke up enough to see a viper rising from between my legs. He'd been sleeping there, attracted by my warmth. His hood expanded into a cowl, grew into the form of a man, my mirror image. My tan singlet with a darker brown sash was matched by his darker brown tunic with a tan sash. Lucifer.

"Hi there, my precious, little Glory Hound. Our team's desperately been trying to help you along your path. We're tirelessly working, night and day to keep your *oh-sooo-special* feeling in place."

"I seek Father's glory, not mine."

"Of course, dear boy. Don't get discouraged. This isolation from family and friends, a minor cost in the service of such glory, for your father, of course. Like your little jaunt right now. Excellent social distancing. So essential to specialness. Remember, don't settle. Being a regular person would be *so* boring."

"Father's appointed me to this destiny."

"Why, certainly, Mas-ih. Remember our goal—the same for all the messiahs, Jew, Arab, or whatever, who bear your sense of destiny—suicide and murder. First, you fall off a cliff, or climb on a cross—doesn't matter. It's all the same. And after you become a martyr, thousands will follow. Leemings. Such fun. A foundational strategy, you might say."

I felt his poison leeching into me, looked to see if I'd been bit. As I looked down, I noticed his feet growing vaporous, shape-shifting.

"See you on the cliff, Master Messiah. We have a special surprise for you there." In a flash, he switched back into a viper.

In a surprise move, Windy whisked my hand around his viper's head, just behind his fangs, before he could slither away. I lurched up and back in one movement, slicing my heel to the bone on a sharp stone. No matter. The snake's body went inert, but I smashed its head on my stone pillow. Stoned him again and again, screaming, crushing his head.

After a long or short time, Windy whispered, *you can stop now. You killed it. He left before you started pounding his head.*

I threw the carcass to the ground beside the still-warm ashes of my campfire. Slumped down beside the brook and stuck my foot in the cold water, numbing the pain to a dull roar. I watched the trickle of blood thread downstream into nothing. I took a small pot from my backpack, something Ma had tucked in there before I left. I smeared a fingerful of her wound wart on the gash. A strip of Ma's all-purpose cloth bound the wound. I skinned the snake.

I blew yesterday's warm ashes into a quick flame, slowly adding moss and twigs. I heated water for tea and held some pita bread over the flame on a stick, also warming my hands. I worried the snakeskin into a heel wrapper and slid my sandal over this new binding.

Windy step-by-stepped me another few miles until I crested a loamy dune. The white-capped ocean lay beyond a deserted beach. This patch of sand, and a warm wind, became my home for the day. I was *so* tired. Tired of conflict, struggle, and the pain of putting one foot in front of the other.

I wiggled down into the warm sand, felt younger, like a boy. I napped. Ate Ma's homemade bread, a chunk of Rav's leg of lamb. Made a fortress in the sand, complete with turrets—like David's Jerusalem tower. I thought, *this is a castle to be proud of.* Right before the tide came in and waves pounded it flat. I soaked and soothed in the empty fullness of sand, sea, and sky; played in the waves, body surfed. After, I crawled out of the sea and laid naked on the beach, warmed by Father's sun.

Toward evening, I put my short tunic back on and dropped into the soft sand along the berm. The dune lily in front of me showed off her spikey white blossoms, bobbing up and down in the sea breeze. The day waned, evaporating in its own heat. Clouds arranged themselves in feathery bands of lilac, coral, and orange, deepening into mauves and scarlets.

The fine hairs rose on the back of my neck. Another was with me.

"Like how I painted the clouds just for you? How I bobbed the lilies' heads up and down in praise to Father?"

"Spectacular artistry, Windy. You do know how to make a grand entrance." I turned to look at her. She dazzled me with her demeanor—not a lioness or windstorm, but a sleek madonna today, with a wispy smile and eyes like jade polished by stardust. Bright, jet-black hair rippled behind her from the wind swirling within her.

"You're looking a little worse for wear." She looked at my heel. "How's this 'human body' experience working out?"

"Why ask me when you already know?"

"So, *you'll* know. I know already, but you don't. Speak it, 'get' it. Some think to speak, some speak to think. You're a mix."

"Okay, got it. I *hate* this body, at least today. I don't wear my zits. They wear me. Messy wet dreams, embarrassing erections, bad breath, flash-flood hormones—everyday companions.

"My body aches for Claudia. I see her face, remember shared jokes, and feel physical hunger for her. Also, I feel her hunger for me. But we can't have each other that way—not in Father's plan. Apart from all that, I'm magnificent."

She smiled at my diatribe. "All those struggles make you stronger." She ran her hand over my heel, making the pain tolerable. Barely.

I kept up my rant. "Surprise tests like that last one with Lucifer in the woods, and not seeing or feeling your presence, or Father's during the test."

Her eyes flooded with tears. She said, "Teachers are silent during tests, so you can grow your faith muscles. But I do give you a hand, time to time, when you need to catch a snake."

I fingered my viper skin. "Thanks, but Windy, I want to *belong*. I feel like odd-god out, living in this gap-riddled space so full of tests. Fully God and fully man feels fully neither."

She beamed her thoughts to me, *Father and I can trust you to speak truth, for sure.*

"The fully human me has this crummy gift of compassion—a God-sized gob of three-fold empathy. I discern other's thoughts, feel their feelings before they do, and do right on their behalf. On top of *this* ratty present, Father's guaranteed a ghastly future—abuse, and a perfectly horrible death. Lucifer nailed it back in the woods."

Windy said, "He is skilled at stirring a smidgen of truth into a pot of lies."

"The fully God-me gets to fight Lucifer and his demons. Almost get viper bit, almost get my neck broken. I get terrifying images of sufferings yet to come. And for my trouble, Father sends me to hell. Being God-man *severely* sucks. I hate it."

Windy nodded, kept soothing my heel. "If our roles were swapped out, I'd be mad too."

"I'd rather be in heaven. Can I leave now?"

"Son, you're getting life at ground zero in ways Father and I will never know. You've got skin in the game."

At the mention of his name, Father allowed himself to be seen. He plopped down in a heap on the other side of me, radiant in the glow of the setting star we circled, the sun He'd created. "All you said just now to Windy is true. We're truing your heart, our perfect Son."

He paused. "We have a full life for you, full to the brim with laughter and mourning. You're learning to be a master storyteller who wakes people up. But even if people here and now don't *get* you, or your parables, even if they don't love you, Windy and I do. A standing ovation!"

He and Windy pulled me to my feet. Sound of many waters, thunder, and sheets of lightning.

I was cheered by their applause, and still sulked. I gazed over the water to my right, where Caesarea glimmered—a smudge on the horizon.

"You wanna trade places with me, Windy?" I asked. "Snap your fingers, Father, and swap us out. I'm going to hate what's coming."

Father absorbed my grief and didn't leave me to myself. My eyes fixed on the night sea, inconsolable. The wind picked up, the smell of rain on the way.

Father took my mind off me. "This dust dot on the outer arm of this small galaxy is the smallest place we've populated, and with conflicted, choice-filled creatures more in need of love than any we've yet made."

You got that straight.

Father overheard my thought, nodded solemnly.

I smelled food cooking. Windy sat around a campfire, baking fresh bread and firing kabobs on skewers over coals.

How did she do this? Twitch her nose and fish flew on her skewers? Snap her fingers, and along came zucchini and onions?

I looked again. There she was, sitting with two other people, laughing, animated conversation. *Who in the world were these people?*

Father and I walked over to the campfire.

Windy got up and hugged me long and hard, strength flowing from her to me. "Talking with God only gets you so far. We thought you could use some human conversation too. Here's a couple of guys, Elijah and Moses."

Law and Prophets moved toward me. Both were solid in the grizzled sort of way that came to people who'd fallen down many times, been broken, and risen again.

I'd expected a blinding radiance to glow from Moses' head, a tablet of stone in either hand, still smoking from a fiery chisel. No, he was someone you'd pass in a crowd, not even notice. Bronzed skin stretched over a placid face, broad as Sinai's summit. Salt-and-pepper beard and snowy eyebrows shagged down over russet eyes. He had dirt under his fingernails, bunions on his hammertoes.

Moses fell to his knees. "I've waited for centuries to ask forgiveness. My rage hammered me when I struck that stone twice, when I killed that Egyptian. Forgive me, Messiah." He bent over, tears spilling on my bare feet. Briefly, blinded by his tears, he grabbed my wounded heel with his right hand and opened the scab. Blood flowed.

Father and Windy looked on—did nothing but feel our pain.

I put my arms around the kneeling man. "Moses, you are forgiven. My blood now covers your murderous right hand. The meekness that made you great does so now, once again."

Moses looked up at me and realized what he had done. He pointed to me with his bloody index finger. "Even my best repentance is clumsy. All those laws, sharp-edged, cutting."

"I've memorized all your words, Moses. And the good part of your anger was how you plowed it into justice. I could have never led all those complaining people in military ranks, precise, organized. Your laws, schoolmasters."

Moses risked a shy smile. We turned toward my Partners. Elijah stood between them, a horned owl on bandy legs. His sharp, black eyes flashed in the firelight. His widow's peak of jet-black hair dipped toward his nose. Raven-black eyebrows slanted up on either side. A dyed blue cloak of spun camel's hair, with gold stitched borders, hung on his shoulder.

I looked squarely at him, "You didn't quit, did you?"

Elijah replied, "I *felt* like quitting more times than I can remember."

I felt relieved, reminded that discouragement *was* normal, along with doubt.

Elijah continued, "Moses' rage beset him. Depression got me. I ricocheted between highs and lows. High on Mount Carmel, over there." He nodded to the north of us. "Then I plummeted into suicidal thinking beside Cherith brook down there."

He knelt. Gently rested his head beside my feet, careful not to repeat Moses' mistake. He smelled of earth and honest effort. "Forgive me for believing lies, those that led to depression."

"I'm a work in progress too, friend."

I loved the feel of his cloak beneath my fingers. The fire crackled, sea oats rustled in the evening breeze, and fish kabobs sizzled over the fire.

Windy called, "Enough for now—good grief, though it be. Dinner's ready!"

We all circled the fire with full plates of fresh sea tuna, zucchini, and slices of onion on skewers, hot bread, big mugs of good Judean wine. The food tasted heavenly.

Elijah and Moses shared stories of their time on earth, raising their voices so I could hear over the rising wind. Tendrils of fog blew around us, ragged clouds like herded sky-sheep flew over the full moon. I wondered aloud how Elijah had managed his low spots.

He said, "Angels fed me bread. Told me to sleep. I was expecting deep visions of the divine and I got whole-wheat toast."[40]

Moses vowed, "Things always seemed to get worse before I got better. Swear to God."

I looked at Father and Windy. Both nodded.

Windy chimed in, "Time to say good night, Elijah!" She took him down into a depression in the earth before she shape-shifted into a fiery chariot and lifted him up. Elijah was up and away like a comet, heading Home.

Something fluttered, landing on my feet. Elijah's cloak. I held it to my nose, inhaled a double portion of prophet strength. I whirled it around my shoulders and raised my hand in thanks.

The front edge of a thunder squall began spitting rain down. I looked around. Where had those other two gone?

I wandered through the rain down the beach. Father and Moses huddled together on the sand above the scalloped surf line. Intense, focused light flashed between them. I walked over to the glowing. Father's hands were over Moses' hands, and fire flashed from their joined fingers, etching a tablet in the sand. I read over their shoulders.

"Love the Lord your God with all your heart, mind, and spirit—
and your neighbor as yourself."

Moses wiped rain out of his eyes and grinned. "I'd gotten out of practice. Father helped me boil 'em down, all to one."

Father tendered a look my way. "I made this silicone implant to regulate your heart and steady your pace." He moved his hands together, tablet between his fingers, working it smaller and smaller—indiscernible to my eye. Flashing beams from his eye twinkled, nestling it into my chest. Something freshened within me, something between a click and a hug. Whatever it was, I don't know. But I felt like I didn't have to force anything any longer. Iron settled in my spine; my vision got keener.

I looked up from examining my thoughts to thank Moses and Father. They'd gone. One of them had drawn a heart in the sand with his finger. As I watched, the rain washed the drawing away.

I pulled my new cloak over my shoulders, curled up under two pieces of driftwood beyond the berm. Rain pounded all around me, dripped off the driftwood on my fingers, lulled me to sleep. The next morning, I would return to camp another way, north along the coast, up and over Judgment Cliff.

65
WINDY

*C*rispus was having himself a think. *My buddy, Luce, is so persuasive! Eyes like mine—penetrating, strong, wily. The more I hang with this guy, the more I look like him. Glad he whisked me and that brat away from the creek. Not a bad view, here on top of Judgment Cliff. I can almost see Pirate's Cove. My gang and ships are getting ready for that Roman treasure ship with all the tax money on board. How long till they sail, a week or so?*

Crispus fomented with Lucifer, who showed up now and again. Today he dressed in a flowing, jet-black thawb, just like the robe he'd given to Crispus.

Crispus complained, "Luce, this snot-nosed pip doesn't stop screaming. I'm gonna plug her gullet. She doesn't even like it when I touch her!"

Lucifer, the rebel, commiserated with Crispus' plight. He leaned over the crying child and instructed Crispus by example. "Deborah, your elder brother will come again soon, sweetheart. He'll be here before you know it." He then dropped her back on the blanket, none too gently, and drafted down, shrink-wrapped with scheming, through a steam vent in the cave's floor.

Deborah settled down, expecting Jesus anytime. Crispus played dice games with her, in between touching games. *Crispus mused, A regular romper-room attendant, me. Let's give this rug rat some more sugary porridge, laced with Luce's power-powder. Gets her all excited, bouncy for my attention.*

Crispus looked around, snuck some up his nose, and dreamed of greatness. When Luce came around the next time, Crispus asked, "Where do ya get that white powder?"

Lucifer grinned. "My research department is perfecting the formula. We're getting this stuff ready for a real crisis one day, along with a virus or two—the happy stuff of pandemics. Might take a while, but no worries. Humans aren't known around the galaxy as stalwarts of sanity."

He pointed to the chunk of limestone where Crispus sat. "There's more sanity in that one still stone than all you people put together."

Crispus didn't know what he was talking about, but he wondered, whose team is he playing on, anyway?

Lucifer whisked himself away. The hours passed slowly. In the moments when Deborah was awake, he let her walk the edge, balanced over jagged rocks and sounds of surf, far below. Only snatches of ocean could be seen through the swirling mist and rain. The time was almost at hand. They had an appointment together with Jesus, soon.

66

JESUS

Judgment Cliff was the highest spot along the northern Israeli coast-line—best view ever over Caesarea to the north and Nazareth to the east. I wanted to tie future and past together in my heart, fine-tune my judgment before we left this country for another. The wind was at my back, blowing me up trail, steep, slippy, zig and zag, up in this blasting, driving rain.

I wanted Elijah's chariot, but that ride had come and gone. Windy's cryptic words from long ago came back to me. *No heights by sudden flights. Character grows with fights, climbing up through nights.*

Her words mixed with viper Satan's words in the woods—*see ya on the mountain, messiah-wannabe.*

I wondered, *what am I doing here? Am I courting craziness or specialness? Should I wait for a sunny day and climbing companions?*

Shivers rippled through me. I kept moving under what my bones told me was Windy's impelling. Or was this something else, darker and danger-ous? I felt the world around me, more than saw it, as I pulled up, one step at a time—foot on rock, hand on tree trunk. Lightning strikes lit the sky up to my right.

I counseled myself, *step up, plant yourself solidly on rock, pull. Careful with your wounded heel. Repeat. How did these olive trees grow out of this harsh, karst limestone?*

Pygmy cypress and olive trees had somehow rooted here, slowly crum-bling the rock as they elbowed their way into the light. *I lifted myself to the next ledge with my elbows. Waves crashed far below me. My skin goose-bumped.*

Father, so many innocents have been pushed off this cliff. I'm scared. Are you sure this is my path?

Father's voice, wispy in the wind, came to me—*Tempests clarify calling. How else can you know who you are, till suffering has stripped all else off your frame?*

I had no answer, so I kept moving up in the fog—awkward, uneasy, scared. Moving up. I strained my sore neck back, searched the heavens through the festering, spitting clouds. It seemed about the sixth hour.

Craggy clifftop through mist, now and again, at the end of this goat trail to nowhere. Clouds parted and closed. Sheet lightning off to the north. What was that just now? I wiped rain out of my eyes and looked again. That looked like a *person* up there, like my little sister, Deborah! Thirty yards or so above me. Her little face peering down, searching.

The fog closed.

I was losing it, big time. Seeing things that aren't so doesn't make you a prophet. It shows you're a lunatic.

I picked up my pace, panicked. Rock-scrambled, leapt between boulders. The snakeskin on my trailing foot slipped on a wet boulder. I grabbed for a handhold on wet karst, missed. Both hands clutched crumbling scree.

As Satan had predicted, I fell off a cliff. Maybe ten feet into the void before a twisted olive tree caught me in its spreading arms. The mist cleared for a moment. I looked down. White foam pounded sharp rocks hundreds of feet below me. If I'd missed that tree, or it had missed me? I wouldn't think about that now.

A familiar voice called to me, echoing off the rocks. "Precious Debbie's waiting for you, sucker-savior. Giddy-up. No sleeping on the job for all you messiah wannabe's."

Lucifer leered at me from atop the cliff, a gash of glee on his face. He'd bundled Deborah in what looked like swaddling clothes. Handed her to… was that Crispus? What? Had he tied her onto the end of a stick?

The fog swallowed them.

Help, oh help, now, Windy, Father! Help sister!

Deborah's voice echoed my prayer. "Help me, Jesus! Help, I'm scared!"

I stopped, looked, listened. The fog parted. Crispus had indeed tied and bundled her to the end of a thin-cut branch. The wood was bent almost double with her weight. He jerked his fishing pole up and down, bouncing her over the void, hoping to catch my attention. His laughter filled the distance between us.

Lucifer merged with Crispus, as he had in the moments after slamming Abba from his wall. His voice roared from Crispus' mouth. "Watch careful now, wannabe-Messiah!" He flicked Debbie high out over the void. Let go of the pole.

Deborah's scream faded and fell, faded, fell.

Her scream met mine. Time passed, a few minutes or seconds. Nothing remained but the cutting wind, the mist, and the olive tree where I hung spread-eagled on its branches.

I made my way down the mountain and searched jagged boulders where sea met cliff. There, crumpled between two rocks, I found her body. She lay twisted like a broken rag doll, arms and legs bent at angles not fit for the living. I held her close to my chest, unable to get enough air in my lungs.

How could Windy and Father have allowed this? How could they have sat at the campfire with me hours before, telling jokes, laughing, when they knew this would happen now? I felt so tricked, betrayed. Both of us by both of Them. I wanted her alive, Crispus dead, Lucifer dead. I wanted to wake up and cash out this nightmare.

I moved Deborah's body to a higher, flatter rock. Once there, I adjusted Elijah's mantle below sister, stretched myself over her three times. Elijah had raised a child from the dead doing this.[41]

Windy, Father, I'm sorry. Rage got out of hand. You author life. Do it now— please, please, please.

I blew into her mouth, praying all the while. Raised her eyelid with my finger. Listened with my ear to her mouth. No sight from that eye, no breath from that mouth, no nothing. My bargaining met only whipping wind, inchoate, keening.

I kept at my whining, trying to make a deal with Father. I won't be mad if only You'll bring her back. Please, Father, make her new! I won't complain. I'll be a good Messiah. Promise.

Nothing but a lungful of emptiness met me.

I tried the Elijah lay-down thing once again. I stretched out far as I could over Deborah's cooling body. Just in case Miracle Center needed more *oomph*.

Again, nothing. The thought flashed. *They're leaving me alone, like Hezekiah, to know my own heart.*[42] Truth was here in these words, but with a razor's edge and no comfort, none at all.

I began my journey back, over Judgment's shoulder, Messiah-the-flop. This failure, this death, would crush not only Ma but me. No comeback would be possible, no, not from this.

Rocks cut into my heel. I welcomed the pain, all that day. No glittering insights on judgment. No finer shades of wisdom. No *nothing*, except death from that cliff.

That night, I made a fire in a clearing within the forest, stretched my sister out before the fire. Prayed, fasted, didn't sleep. I fed my little fire, walked the perimeter, sling in hand, guarding sister's body from predators.

Father, You could still bring life to her. You are the Master of life over death. How many earth years passed before You spoke the Word, and life appeared from nothing? Even Crispus—walking, stalking, living death—he could be brought to life with Your help.

The next morning, I wrapped dear, dead Debbie on my back. Her body stank, so I wrapped my face in a wet rag smeared with crushed eucalyptus leaves. I picked my way through the forest, tripped over fallen tree trunks, swatted mozzies and bottle-nosed flies. I stormed at Father, exhausted myself, fell silent. No stir from Windy either. Absolute quiet.

The silence of God.

Another pitch-black night with no food or water, the same dead and now stinkier sister, the same silence. The same sleeplessness, perimeter stalking, the same guttering campfire.

On the third morning, the weather continued its sheer wretchedness—squalling, spitting, complaining skies. Rain dripped off my Elijah cloak, ran down my face, little sips on lips that refused to drink.

I walked through the morning, despising the shame. Around three in the afternoon, the rain let up, and a tepid sun steamed the banyan and bald cypress trees. Humid heat clamped my lungs like a living thing. I felt it on my skin, sweltering, a reptile panting on a hot rock. Inhaling, holding a breath, being held by that breath, required immediate and absolute focus.

My legs trembled with fatigue. A leech latched on my leg and started to suck the life out of me. A snarl of swamp wrapped around my ankles, dragging me down, face-first in the mud. Something wormy crawled over my neck. I left my face in the mud.

Seductive voice—*Another messiah, finished. What'd I tell ya? Suicide and murder. We could even spin a double martyrdom out of this, Jew-boy. Get some glory mileage for your Pops. Up the leeming quota.*

I shut that voice down. *Father? Are You there? Windy, do You care? Where are You two?*

In that moment of no feeling and black thinking—even in their silence—my *bones* knew what my *mind* did not—they loved me, Debbie, even Crispus. We were their creation.

I said with Job, *Though You kill my family, and me, and I know You will—yet I will trust You. Father, there's no one else to trust, nowhere else to go. Only You.*

I pulled my face from the mud. Suction popped. Tiny clapping noise. I inhaled.

Windy sat next to Father in front of me on the roots of a bald cypress, under stringy moss. Tenderness wrapped their faces. Sadness streamed from their eyes.

Father ... Father crawled through the mud toward me on all fours. He lay down next to me, wrapped His arms around me, around Debbie. I wailed on his shoulder, in his arms, shaking, howling.

Windy hovered, brooded over me, over us. She unwrapped Deborah and laid her out naked before Father and me in the muck. Deborah sank down, more than half-buried in black mud. I couldn't tell where mud started, where sister stopped. A single beam of sun found its way through the forest canopy and landed on Deborah's face.

Windy placed my hand under hers; Father's hand over hers. Together we laid our hands on my littlest sister's head. A maggot crawled out of Debbie's mouth. Windy wiped it away, leaned over, and blew a tiny puff of air into Deborah's mouth.

Silence. The world held its breath.

Father had the last word.
"Daughter, rise."

End of Book One

ACKNOWLEDGMENTS

My thanks to all my editors—Jeff Gerke, Mick Silva, and Dianne Gi. Thanks to Karen, my good friend of over thirty years, who went over the manuscript with a fine-toothed comb. Dorine Deen's artwork invites further depth of imagination and association in her illustrations.

My wife, Bethyl Joy, was a continual source of encouragement and help. We spent ten weeks walking Israel north to south, 685 miles, to get a feel for where and how the 3-mph Messiah walked and worked.

Once home, we spent a lot of time in our fancy recording studio (walk-in closet with rugs and blankets on the walls). I'd narrate, and she'd follow along with the text, catching errors and suggesting a different tone and voice for the characters. There are worse ways to become more married than working cheek by jowl in a stuffy closet.

DISCUSSION QUESTIONS

1. The foundation for Jesus' fast-changing identity rests in his relationship to his abba and El Abba. There is no substitute for close, side-by-side contact with your father or someone who's aged into a sage. We all weave a "father" quilt. People put patches of fathering into our lives, cradle to grave, some more than others. Who instilled values and beliefs by word and deed, showing you how to protect and provide for those you love?

2. Another foundational idea is the border between visible and invisible, real and not real. Voices, dreams, visions, whispers in the Wind—all thin the border between what can and cannot be apprehended with the senses. How do you sense the world of spirit? What are your 'tells'? Do your fingers twitch, toes tap, images come unbidden to your mind's eye, a memory burns within you, a sense of being compelled to make an apology? A big part of growing up is waking up.

3. Jesus' adolescent identity, like all of ours, is fluid. He falls and fails, rises again. He doubts himself, then regains confidence. Back and forth, up and down. Thirteen to sixteen-year-olds have to figure out:

   how to shape your own thinking, values, and sense of reality from what your parents have given you,
   form close peer relationships,
   handle a changing body,
   channel sexual & aggressive energies in constructive ways, and
    gain a growing sense of their life work.

   How're you doing with these foundational tasks? If you flubbed and failed, no worries. You have a fresh chance now to take another shot at growing up your inside adolescent.

4. Like Jesus, you too have a very human part of you, and a very divine part of you. How do you recognize the "divine spark" speaking in you, to you? What moments do you recall in your experience when you felt God speaking through others, circumstances, sacred writings, or persistent thoughts?

5. Think of a recent experience where you weren't sure whether God was speaking or you? Write it down, or draw it out, or fiddle with clay. Spatialize your experience. Talk about that experience. Try to tease out the different parts of what makes you tick—the divine part of you, the younger selves within you, the villain, or the hero.

6. There is a little bit of us in each of the characters in this book. With whom do you feel most comfortable or most distant: Jesus, Go, Mary, Claudia, Leah, Laz, John, Rabbus, or Crispus? Speak for each, first-person, present tense: *"I'm the _____ part of (your name). Here's my tell. This is how you will recognize me. I (speak, act, feel) in these ways.*

7. In chapter 64, Jesus complained to Windy and Father about how hard life was as a human teenager. He persisted with his Partners, speaking out loud his lonely *feeling* of "odd-god out," neither fully human nor fully god, even though he was both. Recall a time when your feelings and your knowing were at odds. Write it out; talk it out.

ABOUT THE AUTHOR

Vance Shepperson is a third-generation Presbyterian preacher's son. He attended schools in England, Switzerland, Illinois, and Florida, earned a doctoral degree in clinical psychology, and worked in a general hospital as an Air Force neuropsychologist. He worked on faculty at an accredited psychology doctoral program in California and owned a group psychotherapy practice with his clinical psychologist wife, Bethyl Joy. Together they worked for an international charity in southwest China for five years. They both served as "boots on the ground" for Palo Alto University's international program in their Graduate School of Psychology. They have also lived in the Lake District of the UK, New Zealand, and now live on the Big Island of Hawaii, where they practice psychotherapy, but mainly write stuff.

To find out more about
Vance and his writing,
visit him online:

Website: www.vanceshepperson.com
Blog: www.vanceshepperson.com/blog
Email: vanceshepperson@gmail.com

Here's a peek at Volume Two
in this Four-Volume Series, *Parable*

Follow Jesus as he adventures away from Israel
into a much bigger world

1.

JESUS

Deborah's eyes popped open. She didn't even know she'd been dead for three days. She lay naked in the warm mud, sinking into it up to her chin. A leech had fastened onto her ear. I picked it off, careful to get the suckers out of her skin.

Did she remember Crispus tying her in a bundle on the end of his fishing pole, hoping to catch my attention?

Did she remember him dropping her off a cliff?

Did she remember screaming on the way down?

Did she remember hitting the rocks and crumbling like a broken rag doll?

Did she remember dying?

Thank you, Father, for all your selected not-rememberings. You keep an ark around my memory when I'm in danger of being flooded.

What I did remember was this. I wanted to go home with Debbie, be done with this stinking planet and its people. Maybe try another world, another galaxy. I was done with these Jews, this Messiah stuff. Finished, pure and simple.

A vine had snarled around my ankle. I'd face-planted in the mud. I'd left my face there in the mud for a long time. But then, in that bleak, no-hope place, a conscious breath raised my head out of the muck. Father and Windy, His Spirit, were there in front of me. Father had crawled through the mud to me, on all fours, and said words in that mucky place for all of time—words for her, me, and all who dared to believe in the resurrection from the dead, *Rise!*

I returned from that memory to this moment. Father and Windy were no longer visible. My baby sister smiled at me from the mud, teeth so white and bright I could have read the Torah by their light. She said, "Jesus, happy, happy!"

I picked up her two-year-old body. The mud burped its release. I said, "Deborah, Father was happy, happy to give you back to me." She babbled happy noises and held tight to my neck. I washed her in the creek, put her dress back on, and looked for Father and Windy. Their seen presence was gone, but they were not.

I felt the presence of evil as well. Hangry shadows lurked and, as usual, weirded me out. Weeping willow trees pointed twisty fingers at us. I could feel him. I stopped, scanned the forest. And there Satan sat, lounging in silk pantaloons under a huisache thorn bush. He rested on a plush, red-velvet cushion. No horns. No red tail. No pitchfork. Ordinary face. Maybe an angel of light, but with an attitude and a six-pack. His chest and stomach muscles rippled in the morning mix of light and shadow.

He looked up from what he was doing and sipped a steaming drink with some whipped cream on the top, shaped like a little heart. He put his drink down and continued braiding thorn branches in a circle, holding them this way and that in the slippy shade to better see his work. His eyes glittered, familiar to me from days gone by, days when we were friends. Now mischief was his mission—many spikes in his handiwork, but only one point.

He called me over, "Like me to pour you a Trinidad Scorpion? My barista skills are outta this world, if I do say so. Guaranteed to blow the back 'a yer throat right out yer butt."

He gave me his most fetching smile and offered me his drink. Tipped his head slightly toward the sun, "Do you think this is my best side, bro? I have so many of them."

A tiny flame escaped his eyes. He blinked; it disappeared. He reached up for Debbie on my shoulders. "Come to Uncle Luce, little one. As it is written, suffer the little ones to come to me." In the process of reaching, Satan spilled his drink, as if by accident. The viscous liquid ran all over his thorny handiwork.

I pulled Deborah off my shoulders and held her close to my heart. She'd begun to cry, sensing the presence of evil, perhaps remembering whatever had happened in that cave. I shushed her with a soft lullaby, my face inches from hers.

I softly sang, "Jesus loves you, this you know, for I'm here to tell you so. Little one, to me belong. You are weak, but I am strong. Yes, yes, I love you. Yes, yes, I love you. Yes, yes, I love you. Your brother tells you so."

Satan jibed, "Well, well now, ain't that precious? A regular crooner. But no drinkie-poo with your ol' bro, Luce, from back in the day—or should I say, before days began? I'll whip up a couple more, *Toots Sweet*." I declined.

He tsked, "My, my, *my*. Where's the walk in all this 'love your enemy' talk?"

I turned to leave. He drawled, "Somehow, your ol' buddy Luce ain't *feelin' the luuuv*, Jeez. Not even an itsy-bitsy, coochie-coo from precious Debbie?" I walked away three, maybe four steps. Swooshing sound. Searing pain. His woven crown of thorns, drenched in drink, had landed on my head and dug in deep. He must have looped it high. Stung like hell, little bleeds, all around my head. Debbie looked up and saw the blood. Her eyes grew wide, and her whimper grew into a wail.

Lucifer laughed. "Just getting a hat-size check for your Jerusalem finale. Perfecto! Little souvie from Luce. Preview of coming attractions, King of the Jews."

END NOTES

[1]The Holy Spirit will be mentioned throughout this series by the name, Windy. Sometimes male, sometimes female. *A new power is in operation. The Spirit of life in Christ, like a strong wind, has magnificently cleared the air, freeing you from a fated lifetime of brutal tyranny at the hands of sin and death*—Romans 8:2, MSG

[2]*If you open your eyes wide in wonder and belief, your body fills up with light. If you live squinty-eyed in greed and distrust, your body is a dank cellar*— Matthew 6:22–23, MSG

[3]Isaiah 58:12

[4]Genesis 19:26

[5]*Psalm 56:8*

[6]*Achan answered Joshua, "It's true. I sinned against God, the God of Israel. This is how I did it. In the plunder I spotted a beautiful Shinar robe, two hundred shekels of silver, and a fifty-shekel bar of gold, and I coveted and took them. They are buried in my tent with the silver at the bottom*—Joshua 7:20-26. Israel stoned Achan in the Valley of Achor.

[7]1 Samuel 15:7; Esther 3:1

[8]*Go, marry a promiscuous woman and have children with her… so, he married Gomer*— Hosea 1:2–3, NIV

[9]*The way to life—to God! —is vigorous and requires total attention*— Matthew 7:14, MSG

[10]*Mitzpah* is a Hebrew word referring to a ritual stake in the sand. A monument that seals a memory.

[11]*"If you loved me, you would be glad that I'm on my way to the Father because the Father is the goal and purpose of my life*—John 14:28, MSG

[12]Deuteronomy 22:22

[13]*You're blessed when you've worked up a good appetite for God. He's food and drink in the best meal you'll ever eat*—Matthew 5:6, MSG

[14]*Now Laban had two daughters; Leah had weak eyes, but Rachel had a lovely figure and was beautiful— Genesis 29:16–17, NIV*

[15]See this story of King Solomon—1 Kings 3:16–28

[16]*So, let God work his will in you. Yell a loud no to the Devil and watch him scamper. Say a quiet yes to God and he'll be there in no time—James 4:7, MSG*

[17]*Surely goodness and mercy shall follow me all the days of my life; and I will dwell in the house of the Lord forever—Psalm 23:6, NKJV*

[18]*Then she called the name of the Lord who spoke to her, You-Are-the-God-Who-Sees [El Roi]; for she said, Have I also here seen Him who sees me?—Genesis 16:13, NKJV*

[19]*So, I went down to the potter's house, and I saw him working at the wheel. But the pot he was shaping from the clay was marred in his hands; so, the potter formed it into another pot, shaping it as seemed best to him—Jeremiah 18:3–4, NIV*

[20]*Was not even Rahab the prostitute considered righteous for what she did?—James 2:25, NIV. See also Hebrews 11:31*

[21]*This kingdom is promised to anyone who loves God—James 2:6, MSG*

[22]*Then, leaving her water jar, the woman went back to the town and said to the people, "Come, see a man who told me everything I ever did—John 4:28–29, NIV*

[23]*Greater love has no one than this: to lay down one's life for one's friends—John 15:13, NIV*

[24]See Revelation 19: 6-9

[25]*Jesus answered, "Those who have had a bath need only to wash their feet; their whole body is clean—John 13:10, NIV*

[26]See 1 Samuel 28:7–21 for the story of the witch of Endor.

[27]*Love covers all offenses—Proverbs 10:12, NRSV*

[28]The Bible records many instances of rending the clothes after the news of death. Jacob saw Joseph's coat of many colors drenched in blood and rent his garments. David tore his clothes when he heard of the death of King Saul. Job rent his mantle. Rending allows grief-relief. Mourners give vent to pent-up anguish with a controlled, sanctioned act of destruction.

[29]*I still have many things to tell you, but you can't handle them now. But when the Friend comes, the Spirit of the Truth, he will take you by the hand and guide you into all the truth there is—John 16:12, 13, MSG*

[30]*Do you see what this means—all these pioneers who blazed the way, all these veterans cheering us on? It means we'd better get on with it. Strip down, start running—and never quit!—Hebrews 12:1-2, MSG*

[31]*Melchizedek* means "King of Righteousness." He towers out of the past—without record of family, no record of beginning or end. See Genesis 14:17-18; Hebrews 5:4-6

[32]*Every desirable and beneficial gift comes out of heaven. The gifts are rivers of light cascading down from the Father of Light—James 1:17–22, MSG*

[33]*They compelled a passer-by, who was coming in from the country, to carry his cross; it was Simon of Cyrene, the father of Alexander and Rufus—Mark 15:2, NRSV*

[34]A double prophecy, the first a foretelling of John 14:6; the second, a statement of their destined meeting on the Via Delarosa, the "Way of Sadness," where Simon's felt debt to Jesus would be paid by carrying his cross for him. The reference to believing "into Jesus" comes from the Greek word *eis*, denoting more than an intellectual exercise. Penelope, in this passage, mirrors Mary's believing *eis* at the tomb.

[35]See Ezekiel 34:1–24 for an interesting discussion of the difference between good and bad shepherds.

[36]*That's how God's Word vaults across the skies from sunrise to sunset, melting ice, scorching deserts, warming hearts to faith—Psalm 19:6, MSG*

[37]Ezekiel 37 tells the prophet's vision of the dead bones of an army becoming alive once again.

[38]*In a word, what I'm saying is,* Grow up. *You're kingdom subjects. Now live like it. Live out your God-created identity. Live generously and graciously toward others, the way God lives toward you—Matthew 5:48, MSG*

[39]See Genesis 34 for the story of Shechem, the rape of Leah's daughter, Dinah, and the resulting vengeance.

[40]*All at once an angel touched him and said, "Get up and eat." He looked around, and there by his head was some bread baked over hot coals, and a jar of water. He ate and drank and then lay down again. The angel of the Lord came*

back a second time and touched him and said, "Get up and eat, for the journey is too much for you" —1 Kings 19:6–7, MSG

[41]See 1 Kings 17:21–22

[42]*God withdrew from him, in order to test him, that He might know all that was in his heart—2 Chronicles 32:31, NKJV*